FIGHT TO THE DEATH

"The North Koreans and Chinese have hit Seoul with nerve agent." Quinn's voice came out of the speaker. "There're reports of hundreds of thousands, if not millions, dead."

Turcotte could see the brown sand of the Sinai Peninsula below. He wasn't far from Mount Sinai, where the Mission had hidden for so many years. "Seoul's just the beginning. Artad and Aspasia's Shadow don't care if they have to stand on corpses of billions of humans to win the war. We mean nothing to them."

"Why are you so certain of that?" Mualama asked from across the way.

"What do you mean?" Turcotte asked.

Mualama shrugged. "If humans meant so little to them, why didn't they destroy us long ago?"

"They tried," Turcotte said.

Mualama shook his head. "No. They controlled the balance of power with things like the Black Death and various wars. At any time in history they had the power to completely wipe us off the face of the planet as the Mission recently attempted with its plague. But they never did."

"Why are we important to them?" Turcotte felt the hair on the back of his neck stand up. There was something about the way Mualama was talking that disturbed him.

Mualama shrugged. "That is part of the great truth yet to be discovered." He spread his long arms. "There is much more to this universe than this planet." And with that he sank back into silence.

ROBERT DOHERTY

AREA 51
EXCALIBUR

A DELL BOOK

Published by
Dell Publishing
a division of
Random House, Inc.
1540 Broadway
New York, New York 10036

ISBN: 0-440-23705-X

Manufactured in the United States of America

Published simultaneously in Canada

April 2002

OPM   10   9   8   7   6   5   4   3   2   1

AREA 51: EXCALIBUR

CHAPTER 1: THE PAST

THE SOLAR SYSTEM
2528 B.C.

The starship used a slingshot maneuver around the star to decelerate from interstellar speed. It was a small ship, a scout, and as the craft slowed, its sensors aligned on the signal that had diverted it to this system from its centuries-long patrol. The nose of the ship turned toward the third planet out as the data was analyzed. The signal was strange—a passive one, a uniform reflection of light rays from the system's star off something on the planet's surface, but there was little doubt the unusual effect was contrived by intelligence.

Searching out, analyzing, and then eventually reporting back concerning any intelligent life was the ship's mission. The nature of the species that crewed it was to find, infiltrate, consume, and ultimately destroy any intelligent life not like it.

Having picked up no active scanning in the solar system or signs of advanced weaponry, the ship emitted an energy pulse as it sent a spectrum of scanning signals toward the third planet to determine the source of the crude signal.

Unknown to the crew, the pulse was noted by passive sensors as it penetrated the atmosphere and reached the surface of the planet. A sophisticated computer, operating on low-power mode, intercepted the pulse, analyzed it, and projected possible courses of action in a matter of moments. In low-power mode the options were limited and the course of action was quickly selected.

THE GIZA PLATEAU
2528 B.C.

The Great Sphinx glowered at the morning sun, while behind its left shoulder the smooth limestone sheathing covering the newly constructed Great Pyramid of Giza caught the
rays of light and uniformly reflected them into the sky. At
the very top of the five-hundred-foot-high pyramid, a blood-
red capstone, twenty feet tall, glistened, an alien crown to
the greatest structure ever built by human hands. The massive structure stood alone on the stone plateau, towering
over the surrounding countryside, the nearby Nile, and the
Sphinx complex.

The painted face of the Sphinx was sixty feet above the
ground. From the front paws to the rear, it was over two hundred feet in length. It was set low in a depression in the Giza
Plateau, stone walls surrounding it. To the east, in the direction of the Nile, were Khufu's Temple and the Temple of
the Sphinx, where both Pharaoh and stone creature could be
worshipped. A covered ramp led from the right rear of
the Sphinx to the Temple at the base of the pyramid. While
the pyramid was new, the surface of the Sphinx was scored
by weather, having been there since the beginning of Egypt
in the time when the Gods had ruled over seven thousand
years earlier.

Between the paws of the Great Sphinx stood the Pharaoh
Khufu, under whose leadership the Egyptians had labored
for over twenty years moving stone after stone to build the
Great Pyramid. The Pharaoh prostrated himself in front of a
statue set before the creature's stone chest. The statue was
three meters tall and roughly man-shaped with polished
white skin. The dimensions weren't quite right—the body
was too short and the limbs were too long. The ears had elongated lobes that reached to just above the shoulders and there

were two gleaming red stones in place of eyes. On top of the head, the stone representing hair was painted bright red. Even more strangely for the astute observer, each hand ended in six fingers. The statue's appearance was in great contrast to Khufu's dark skin and hair and human proportions.

The Sphinx had been squatting in its stone depression for ages, beyond the dawn of the time of Pharaohs. Only a handful of those alive knew why it had been built or what it marked. For all but a chosen few it was forbidden to come to the area between the paws in front of Isis's statue.

Khufu had succeeded his father when he was just out of his teens and he was now middle-aged. He had ruled for almost three decades and Egypt was at peace with those outside its borders and rich within its own boundaries. The peace and wealth had allowed Khufu to implement the building plan for Giza that had been passed from the Gods, to the Shadows, to the Pharaohs over the three ages.

The vast quantity of stone needed for the pyramid had been quarried upriver and brought down by barge. Thousands had labored seasonally on it, moving the stone from the barges and placing each block in its position under the careful eye of engineer priests who worked from the holy plans that had been handed down.

The red capstone had been brought up from the bowels of the Giza Plateau, from one of the duats (underground chambers) along the tunneled Roads of Rostau where only the Gods and their priests were allowed to walk. No one knew what exactly it was, but they had followed the drawings they had been given to the last detail, from the smooth limestone facing to placing the red object as the capstone at the very top.

In the Pharaoh's left hand as he prostrated himself was a scepter, a foot long and two inches in diameter with a lion's head on one end. The lion image had red eyes similar to that of the statue, but these glowed fiercely as if lit from within. Khufu had been awakened just minutes ago by his senior priest, Asim. The staff had been in the trembling man's hand, the lion eyes glowing. He had passed it to the Pharaoh.

Khufu had thrown on a robe and dashed from his palace to his place before the Sphinx, as he had been told by his father he must do if the staff ever came alive. He was now chanting the prayers he had been taught. The statue was of Horus, the son of Isis and Osiris, the Gods who had founded Egypt at the dawn of time and ruled during the First Age. According to what Khufu had been told by his father and the priests, in the First Age, the Gods had ruled for many years before passing leadership on to Shadows of themselves, the followers of Horus, during the Second Age. Then even the Shadows had passed the mantle on to men, and the first Pharaohs took command of the Middle Kingdom of the Third Age.

Asim was the only other person in the area. He was the senior priest of the Cult of Isis and garbed in a red robe. The priest's right arm was withered and deformed where muscles and tendons had been sliced when he was a child. Where his left eye had been, there was an empty socket, the skin around it charred and scarred from the red-hot poker that had taken out the eyeball. Both ankles and calves were carefully bound to allow the priest to move as the tendons in his legs had also been partially severed when he was a child. He could not run or even walk quickly. The priest had also been castrated before puberty.

The mutilation was what was required of the head priest of the Cult and Khufu and Asim knew there was a method to the madness. The idea was to make Asim's life so miserable that while he would be able to perform his duties, he would not desire to live a long life and thus not hunger for the source of immortality—the Grail—that was said to be located somewhere below them, beyond the statue before which Khufu bowed his head. The scepter that Asim had brought Khufu was the key to the Roads of Rostau, the underground passageways that ran beneath their feet, and Asim and his followers were the only ones who had ever walked those roads.

Around Asim's neck was a medallion with an eye carved in the middle, a symbol of his office. The priesthood he was part of traced its lineage back many, many years, to the time even before the First Age of Egypt when the people lived in the center of the Great Sea beyond the Middle Sea into which the Nile emptied, in the lands of the Gods, before they were cast out and that land destroyed. The priest stood five paces behind the Pharaoh, muttering his own prayers rapidly in the old tongue that only the priests still knew, his anxiety obvious.

The quick prayers done, Khufu stood and glanced at Asim. The priest nodded. Khufu placed the staff against an indentation in the pedestal on which the statue stood. The carving had the exact same shape as the staff.

The pedestal shimmered, then the scepter was absorbed into it. The surface of the stone slid down, revealing a six-foot-high opening. The passageway beyond was dimly lit from recesses in the ceiling, although the Pharaoh couldn't see the source of the strange light. Khufu hesitated, then reluctantly entered the tunnel, the priest following, moving quickly despite his crippled gait. The stone slid shut behind them.

Khufu hurried down the tunnel. The stone walls were cut smoothly, better than even his most skilled artisan could produce, but the Pharaoh, his heart beating furiously in his chest, had no time to admire the handiwork. He ruled supreme from the second cataracts of the Nile far to the south to the Middle Sea to the north, and many countries beyond those borders paid tribute, but here, on the Roads of Rostau, inside the

Giza Plateau, he knew he was just an errand boy to the Gods. His father had never been down there, nor had his father's father or anyone in his line. It had always been a possibility fraught with both danger and opportunity.

The priest had not said a word since handing Khufu the scepter, as was law in Egypt—no one spoke until the Pharaoh addressed them.

"Asim."

"Yes, lord?"

"What awaits us?" Khufu didn't stop as he spoke, heading deeper into the Earth, his slippers making a slight hissing noise as they passed over the smooth stone.

Asim's voice was harsh and low. "These are the Roads of Rostau, built by the Gods themselves in the First Age, before the rule of the Shadows of the Gods, and before the rule of Pharaoh. It is written there are six duats down here. I would say, lord, that we are going to one of those."

"You have not been in all these duats?"

"No, my lord. I have only gone where my duties have required me to."

Khufu suppressed the wave of irritation he felt with priests and their mysterious ways. "And in the duat we go to now?"

"That, my lord, is unknown, as I have not been to this one. The Hall of Records is said to be in one of the duats—the history of the time before the history we have recorded. This was the time when the Gods ruled beyond the horizon, before even the First Age of Egypt. The Old Kingdom of the Gods beyond the Great Sea."

Khufu wasn't interested in history or the Gods but the future. "It is said there is also a hall that holds the Grail, which contains the gift of eternal life."

Asim nodded. "That is so, my lord."

"But you don't think that is where we are headed?"

"It is possible, my lord. It has been passed down that we will be given the Grail when the Gods come again and we will join them. Perhaps by building the Great Pyramid and finally at long last completing the plan handed down from the First Age we have earned the honor of the Gods. However, I have not yet laid eyes upon the Hall of Records or the Grail."

"Maybe you haven't been looking closely enough," Khufu muttered. Building the pyramid had certainly been a feat worthy of some reward from the Gods, he mused. Even with the Gods' drawings, his engineer priests had been fearful they could not do it. Others had tried on a smaller scale in other places, testing the design, and none had succeeded, such as the one that had collapsed on itself at Saqqara. Using the practical knowledge learned from those attempts over the centuries and the Gods' plan, Khufu had felt confident he could succeed—and he had.

They reached a junction. The path to the right was level. To the other side, the path curved left and down. Khufu had been taught the directions even though, as far as he knew, no one in his line of Pharaohs had ever actually been down there. The Pharaohs ruled above, but the Gods ruled there.

He turned left. It was cool in the tunnel but Khufu was sweating. He who had watched ten thousand put to death in one day on his orders after a battle. He who held absolute rule over the lives of his people felt fear for the first time in his life. But burning through the fear was hope, for he kept reminding himself what his father had told him—that inside the Roads of Rostau, hidden under the Earth, there was indeed the key to immortality, the golden Grail of the Gods that had been promised. And that there would be a day when the Gods would grant that to the chosen. Despite Asim's pessimism, was today the day, and was he the chosen one? After all, as Asim had noted, he had completed the Great Pyramid that season after twenty years of labor, a marvel indeed, exactly according to the plans left behind by the Gods. And he had put the red capstone up there, a thing that had come out of one of the duats down here, dragged to the surface by Asim and his priests under the cover of darkness.

The tunnel ended at a stone wall. Asim used the medallion around his neck, placing it against a slight depression in the center of the stone. The outline of a door appeared, then the rock slid up. Asim stepped aside and motioned for the Pharaoh to enter. Khufu stepped through, into a small, circular cavern, about twenty feet wide. In the very center was a tall, narrow red crystal, three feet high and six inches in diameter, the multifaceted surface glinting. Set in the top of the crystal was the handle of a sword. Khufu walked forward, drawn irresistibly toward the crystal. Asim was at his side now. An ornate sheath could be seen buried deep inside the crystal. The Pharaoh had never seen such crystal or metal worked so finely.

"It is called Excalibur," Asim said. "Take hold of the sword, my Pharaoh. Remove it from the crystal."

Khufu reached down and grabbed the handle of the sword. The sword, still covered by the sheath, slid smoothly out of the crystal.

"Now free the blade, my lord."

Khufu hesitated. "Why?"

"My Pharaoh, it will free the red capstone we just put on top of the pyramid to act outside of itself."

"That makes no sense. What can the capstone do?"

"I am telling you only what I was instructed, my lord. It is important."

Khufu began to draw back the blade. A shock coursed out of the handle through his hand and into his body as he pulled it out of the sheath.

Khufu staggered back as a golden glow filled the entire

chamber. Khufu blinked as the smoothly cut walls flickered and came to life. A flurry of images flashed across them, so quickly he could barely note them: a massive golden palace that dwarfed the pyramid he had just built set on a hill above a beautiful city of white stone surrounded by seven moats of water; a wave-battered island with three volcanic mountains in each corner sitting alone in an endless ocean; a rocky uninhabited desert with mountains surrounding a dry lake bed; a desolate land swept by snow and ice; a strange land where the sand was red and a massive mountain dominated the horizon, and other images flashing by faster and faster so that he lost track. In some manner, he felt a connection to all those places.

Suddenly the walls went black, then a new image appeared, of a field of stars, so many Khufu could not even begin to count, and the stars were moving rapidly, wheeling across the walls.

Then blank again, before revealing a view of the surface above but from a perspective he didn't recognize at first. He could see the Sphinx and the Nile beyond as if from a great height and he then realized that in some manner, the walls in this deep cavern were reflecting the view from the top of the Great Pyramid. He was surprised to see that the red capstone was now glowing as if lit from within.

He started as a seven-foot-high red line appeared between him and the vision on the walls. The line wavered, then widened until a figure appeared, a twin to the statue above. Yet Khufu could see through the figure, to the display on the wall.

He was trying to take all this in when the figure began speaking. The speech was singsong, in a language the Pharaoh had never heard.

"Do you understand the words?" he asked Asim, his voice a whisper as if the image could hear.

"It is the language of the Gods, my lord. I was taught as much of the language as has been passed down and remembered among the high priests."

Khufu waited impatiently for the priest to translate.

"It was hoped the Great Pyramid would bring more of the Gods," Asim finally said, his head cocked to one side, his single eye closed as he listened closely and tried to understand. "That was the design." Asim's thin tongue snaked around his lips as he listened further. "It has not worked that way. Instead an enemy comes." Asim's good arm slowly raised until it pointed upward. "From the sky above."

Khufu looked at the ceiling of the chamber. He could see the sky displayed. It was clear, not a cloud or bird visible.

"What kind of enemy?" Khufu asked, but Asim was again listening and didn't respond right away.

"The Ancient Enemy of the Gods," Asim finally said. "The killer of all life. The enemy with the patience of"— Asim shook his head—"I know not the word, but something like the patience of a stone, infinite. And the specific word for the enemy, the closest I can come to is when the locusts gather—a Swarm."

Khufu had seen swarms of locusts so thick they made day into night passing overhead. When they alighted in a field, they stripped it bare within minutes. He tried to imagine a Swarm that could be a threat to the Gods but could not conceive of it. The vision continued speaking, the sound almost like that of a bird, Khufu thought.

"The capstone—what it calls the Master Guardian—will stop the Ancient Enemy," Asim finally said as the vision ceased speaking. "Excalibur controls the power to the Guardian. While the sword is inside the sheath the Master Guardian cannot work. You have freed it and thus the Master Guardian has power. The Master Guardian can now take action against the Ancient Enemy."

Khufu turned to the priest. "How will this Master Guardian do this? What Ancient Enemy?"

Asim was looking up. He pointed at the display on the roof of the cavern that showed the sky above the pyramid. "That enemy, my lord."

Khufu looked up and blinked. There was a dark spot high in the sky, rapidly growing larger. As it descended it began to take shape and Khufu felt his stomach knot and twist with fear. It was a large black flying spider—that was the only thing he could think. Eight legs, spread wide around a central, round body. And large—how big he had no idea, but its shadow was now covering the top of the pyramid.

"How will the Guardian fight this?" Khufu whispered.

"You have given it power by removing Excalibur from the sheath," Asim repeated. "Watch the power of the Gods, my lord."

Khufu wanted to strangle the priest. He could not tear his eyes from the rapidly approaching monster. Suddenly a golden orb of power streaked upward from the Master Guardian toward the object and hit it. The spider jerked sideways. Khufu kept his eyes on it and a second golden orb raced into the sky and struck the enemy. Bright red flames burst out of the side of the flying spider and it jerked once more, now going upward, trying to escape.

A third golden orb hit it and enveloped the entire object. It was still going higher and higher, edging toward the west. Khufu staggered back as there was a blinding explosion. When he looked up, the sky was clear.

The golden glow inside the chamber decreased and Khufu almost collapsed, feeling drained. The Pharaoh started as the image began speaking again.

"We are safe for now," Asim translated. "But"—he paused as he translated, eye closed—"it is not safe."

"What isn't safe?" Khufu demanded.

"The Great Pyramid. The Master Guardian. The pyramid did not work as intended. It summoned the Ancient Enemy and not the Gods of old. If the Ancient Enemy came once, it can come again. What drew it here must be destroyed."

The figure chimed on for a minute and Asim remained silent, until the figure stopped speaking, coalesced into a thin red line, then disappeared.

Asim opened his eye. "I have been told what is to be done. Put the blade back in the sheath, my Pharaoh."

Khufu slid the blade into the scabbard.

"Come, my lord." Asim was hobbling toward the tunnel. "There is much to do."

So stunned was the Pharaoh by the recent events that he didn't even question being ordered about by the priest. He simply followed him out of the chamber, the covered sword in his hands.

Wreckage from the scout ship tumbled toward the empty desert west of Giza. Among the debris was a black pod, approximately fifteen feet across, the metal surface unmarred by the explosion. As the pod approached the surface of the planet, its terminal velocity began to slow as some internal mechanism interacted with the planet's electromagnetic field. Still, it was moving so fast the outer surface gave off heat, glowing in the sky like a falling star. Despite slowing, the pod hit a dune with enough velocity to plow deep into the sand. It was completely covered when the pod came to rest, submerged twenty feet in the desert.

An hour after the crash, a camel rider approached. A Libyan who was heading toward Cairo to do some trading, he'd seen the falling star from his caravan ten miles to the south. Leaving his son in charge, he'd ridden in the direction the object had fallen, curiosity pulling him across the sand.

He'd already passed places where it was obvious objects

from the sky had impacted in the desert, but whatever had hit, they were deeply buried under the sand. He approached a sixty-foot-high sand dune and noted the disturbed surface near the top indicating another impact. The Libyan halted his camel at the base of the dune and dismounted. His robe flapped in a stiff breeze and all but his eyes was covered with cloth wrapped around his head.

The Libyan paused, his head swinging back and forth as he looked about. He had the sense of being followed, but his eyes detected no sign of another person. He'd had the feeling for a while, but there was no evidence to support the instinct.

He cocked his head as he heard a sound. A grinding noise. Then nothing but the wind for several moments. He took several steps closer to the dune where the sound had seemed to come from. Then he heard something different. Almost a slithering sound. He took half a step back, then paused. There was something inside the dune. Of that there was no doubt in his mind. He looked left and right but there was no movement. He could feel the heat of the sun on his shoulders but a cold chill passed through his body. The Libyan drew a curved sword from his belt. The noise was getting louder.

Mustering his courage, the Libyan took several steps forward until he was at the base of the dune. The sound was very close now. The Libyan jabbed the point of his sword into the dune, the blade easily spearing the sand. He did it again and then again.

He pulled the blade back and cocked his head. Nothing.

The tentacles came out of the sand underneath his feet, wrapping around his legs. He was pulled under, desperately trying to slash and stab with his sword at whatever was below him. His scream was cut off as he disappeared under the sand. His camel bolted off into the desert, desperate to get away.

Then all was still.

A quarter mile away, on the far side of a dune, two dark eyes had watched the encounter. The possessor of the eyes waited a few moments, staring at the spot where the Libyan had disappeared, then he slowly slid down the side of the dune to his waiting camel. He headed back the way he had come, toward Giza. The sun glinted off a large ring set on the man's right hand, highlighting the eye symbol etched on its surface. The hand the ring was on held the camel's halter, but it was shaking so badly from fright, that he had to let go and allow the camel to make its own way home.

It was the middle of the night and by order of the great Pharaoh Khufu no one was allowed outdoors in sight of the Giza Plateau except himself and his high priest Asim. Given the strange apparition the previous day of the flying "spider," no citizens tried to resist the command. Khufu and Asim stood on the roof of the temple at the base of the pyramid. The night sky was clear. The red capstone no longer glowed as if lit from within as Khufu had Excalibur inside the scabbard now strapped to his own sword belt.

Khufu could still see in his mind's eye the black spider that had come down from the sky. He did not understand what it was, but there was no doubt in him that it was a danger. Whatever entity controlled such a flying creature and was capable of fighting the Gods was indeed something to be feared.

"What are we waiting for?"

"When the sword is in the sheath, the"—Asim searched for the right words—"Chariots of the Gods cannot approach the capstone. You must take the blade out once more."

Khufu drew the weapon. He watched as the capstone glowed once more.

Asim continued. "Since you have removed the sword, the capstone can be approached."

"By who? What Chariot of the Gods?"

"There, lord." Asim was pointing to the north.

Something was approaching through the sky. Khufu started, and then realized it wasn't another air-spider. This object was shaped like an inverted dish and golden, reminding him of the glow that had surrounded him in the chamber far below during the day.

"The Chariot of the Gods," Asim whispered.

The object passed by overhead and hovered above the very top of the pyramid, five hundred feet above their heads. A glow extended down from the disk and surrounded the red Master Guardian. The Guardian was twenty feet high at the base and had been brought out of the Earth below by Asim and other priests, following instructions as handed down through the ages. It had been laboriously dragged to the top just the previous week to complete the pyramid by being dragged up the scaffolding that had been wrapped around the edifice. Although larger than blocks used in the structure, Khufu knew it was lighter because of the number of men needed to pull it, indicating that it was not solid. No one knew what it was made of, as the red surface had seemed to shimmer, and men feared to touch it.

Khufu started as the Master Guardian separated from the pyramid, lifting into the air as if by magic. The golden object, with the Guardian in tow, began withdrawing in the direction it had come from, to the north. Khufu watched until it disappeared into the night sky, then he turned to Asim.

"Where does it go?"

"To a secure place, my lord. Separate from the key."

"Why separate the two?"

"The Master Guardian will be more secure if the key is not with it." Asim absently rubbed his empty eye socket. "The sword you hold was once wielded by the greatest of the Gods. With it he controlled the Master Guardian, and in turn his entire domain."

Khufu looked at the smooth blade. He had never seen such fine metal. "It is a great weapon, then."

"It is," Asim said. "Especially as it controls the power for the Master Guardian. It allows whoever has the sword to be very powerful."

"And now?"

"Have your troops scoured the desert for the spider creature, my lord?"

"They have found no sign of the sky monster, but have apprehended all the people they found to the west."

Asim nodded. "The prisoners must be part of what we do in the morning."

"And?" Khufu pressed.

"My lord, tomorrow we must complete the undoing of what our people have worked so hard to do over the past twenty years." He pointed. "The facing of the pyramid must be removed."

"Why?"

"It sent out a signal, my lord, but it did not bring the Gods as hoped, but their enemy."

Khufu knew the pyramid could be seen far away, and he imagined that if one could be in the sky as the spider creature had been, it could be seen at a great distance indeed. He did not wish for a repeat of that.

"It will be done."

Hidden in the dark shadows of a refuse pile of cracked stone blocks the watcher from the desert had observed the same thing as Khufu and Asim. He'd noted the direction the golden disk flew off in, Master Guardian with it. Despite the darkness of his hide, he wrote all that he had seen down on a piece of reed parchment. As his hand moved, a large ring with an eye symbol reflected the scant starlight.

Then, keeping to ground he knew well, he made his way

off the Giza Plateau and to a small hut near the Nile. Inside, he checked the writing, making sure it reported accurately what he had seen, then rolled it and slid it into a tube. He poured wax from a candle on the end and then used the ring to seal it with an imprint—the imprint had the same design as that on the medallion worn around Asim's neck.

He slid the tube inside his robes and sat down cross-legged on the sand floor, waiting for the sun to rise. He'd managed to escape the Pharaoh's troops in the desert, sticking to the hidden ways. He'd noted that the members of the Libyan caravan had been brought to the plateau in chains, the man he'd seen disappear under the sand among them.

Tomorrow would be a most interesting day, he mused.

When dawn came, it was assembly-line murder.

The great Pharaoh Khufu, son of King Sneferu and Queen Hetpeheres, ruler of the Middle Kingdom, watched, his face impassive, as rivers of blood flowed down the smooth limestone facing of the Great Pyramid.

He was at the flat top where the Master Guardian had been, over 480 feet above the Giza Plateau, seated in a throne made of gold. Four sacrificial tables were spread out in the small space in front of him, manned by priests of the Cult of Isis.

Asim was working swiftly as there were many thousands of throats to be cut. A long line of stoop-shouldered men stood on the wooden scaffolding that led to the level platform at the top of the pyramid where Asim wielded Excalibur, the sword of the Gods, moving from table to table, sliding the razor-sharp blade across throats. Soldiers ensured that the line kept moving. Every worker who had spent even one minute inside the pyramid during its construction was in that line. When Asim's work was done, the only ones to have been inside the pyramid and live would be Khufu and Asim.

As each worker reached the top, two soldiers would lift him bodily, throw him onto a slab, pinning his shoulders down, and a priest would hold his head back, waiting for Asim to come by and draw Excalibur across the man's throat while quickly muttering the necessary prayer. Blood would spurt out of his carotid arteries, be caught by the lip of the slab, and be channeled into several holes to reed pipes at the bottom, which directed it to the edge of the platform and dispersed it onto the side of the pyramid. Three sides were drenched red and the reed pipes had just been redirected to the fourth side. As spectacular as the white limestone facing had been when pure, in an obscene way, the glistening red covering of blood made it even more awe-inspiring.

Dulled by years of labor, surrounded by troops, and conditioned to obey their Pharaoh and Gods without question, the men stood in line with little protest. Occasionally one would try to bolt, to be cut down by the guards immediately and the body hauled to the top.

Not only were priests and workers among the condemned, but so were all those who had been caught in the desert to the west the previous day. The Libyan who had approached the sand dune was dragged up with chains around his ankles and thrown onto an altar. He had his head up, looking around as if noting all. When his eyes fell upon Excalibur in Asim's hands, his calm demeanor suddenly changed and he struggled in the guards' grip. As Asim drew the sword of the Gods across the man's neck, the body convulsed, sitting straight up despite the blood pouring from the sliced arteries in his neck.

Asim stepped back in shock, Excalibur held up defensively. The two soldiers who'd brought the Libyan to the altar grabbed his shoulders.

The Libyan snatched the soldiers' necks and smashed their heads together, killing them. Asim used the opportunity to jab forward with the sword, the blade punching into the Libyan's stomach.

An unearthly scream roared out of the man's wide-open mouth. Khufu, behind a line of his imperial guards, was less than ten feet away, watching the bizarre spectacle. The Pharaoh gasped in horror as Asim struck once more before the Libyan's body was ripped apart from the inside. The tip of a tentacle punched out of the man's skin from his chest.

The tentacle was gray and tipped with three digits that bent and twisted as they grasped for a target. The body of the Libyan was bent in an extremely unnatural manner, as if the spine had been turned into a loose string. Asim swung the sword, severing the end of the tentacle. The end that fell to the stone shriveled as if baked, while the other slid back into the body. Then the priest stepped back, Excalibur at the ready.

"What was that?" Khufu demanded.

Asim jabbed the sword several more times into the body, but there was no movement. "Burn the body," Asim ordered several of the Imperial guard. "Scatter the ashes."

As they gingerly picked up the Libyan's body, Asim walked over to the Pharaoh, sweat staining his robes. "The Ancient Enemy, my lord. It came out of what we saw yesterday."

Khufu could only shake his head, the events of the past twenty-four hours threatening to overwhelm his sanity. "What kind of enemy is this?"

"It is the enemy of the Gods and our enemy."

"How did it get in that man?"

"I do not know, my lord. I was told to watch for this by the apparition yesterday."

"How did it survive? We saw the sky thing destroyed."

"I do not know that either, my lord, but the apparition

warned me it could. And it told me that the sword would kill it."

Khufu looked at the blade in Asim's hands. "That is indeed very powerful."

"It was designed so that whoever wielded it could rule supreme," Asim said.

Khufu understood that concept of consolidating power and ruling supreme. A thing that one person could carry and that held such power held both great opportunity and great danger.

Asim signaled for the soldiers to continue to bring prisoners forward and went back to his grim task. By the time the last worker was dead and the body unceremoniously tossed over the side to be burned, all four sides of the Great Pyramid were stained red. There was no repeat of what had happened with the Libyan.

Over five thousand had died in four hours. Asim came back to Khufu, his arm trembling with exhaustion. He handed the sword to Khufu, who slid the bloodstained blade into the scabbard.

"I have done as the Gods ordered me," Asim said. "Now you must have your men finish what must be done to the pyramid."

Khufu gave the orders. Soldiers hammered spikes into joints all along the edge of the platform, between the white limestone blocks on the facing and the more coarse building stones underneath. What had been so carefully placed and fitted onto the pyramid, was ripped off, the stone tumbling down to the ground, revealing the unfinished stone underneath.

The destruction of the facing begun, Khufu took his leave before the ramp was destroyed, Asim close at his side. When they reached the ground, they went to the Great Sphinx. The Horus statue between the paws had been removed, replaced by a stone one. The original had been taken by Asim and his priests into the Roads of Rostau in the early morning, to what destination, only the high priest knew. The men who had helped drag it underground were among those killed. Khufu and Asim stood between the massive stone paws, out of earshot of anyone else.

"You must decree that no one will write of this day's events, my lord," Asim said.

Khufu said nothing. He had begun the day with hopes of immortality, and as night fell, he was seeing his greatest achievement defaced. He had hoped that building the Great Pyramid would bring him the favor of the Gods. Instead, all was crumbling around him. It would not be hard to issue an order to ensure that no one wrote of this. He could sense the fear among his people—the flying spider thing, the killings, the creature coming out of the Libyan, and the desecration of the pyramid's facing. A cloud passed by, blocking the sun, and Khufu shivered.

"What should I do with the sword?" Khufu asked. "Perhaps I should keep it in case we are attacked again."

"It was the Master Guardian that stopped the Ancient Enemy craft," Asim said, "not the sword. Without the facing, the pyramid will not be found by the Ancient Enemy." Asim pointed at Excalibur. "Without the sword, the Master Guardian is powerless."

"How can that be?"

"I do not know but it is what I was told. And what people may desire in the duats along the Roads of Rostau are secure in one form or another."

"Why did you have to use Excalibur and not your ceremonial dagger?" Khufu asked.

"The sword has another special power," Asim said. "As you saw, it is the only thing that can kill the undead and the immortal."

"The undead?"

"The Ancient Enemy."

"The immortal?" Khufu stepped closer to the priest. "Someone has partaken of the Grail?"

"I very much doubt it," Asim said, "but all who could have had access to the duats had to die."

"I do not understand," Khufu said.

"I do not either, my lord," Asim said. "I only do what the Gods command. The sword is the key that must be hidden away again."

"Why did the gods have us build that"—Khufu jerked a thumb over his shoulder at the pyramid—"if it would only bring enemies?"

"The Gods hoped it would bring their kindred Gods from the sky," Asim said. It was the same answer he had given before, but Khufu felt despair.

"And now?" Khufu spread his hands wide. "Now what do I do?"

"You rule, my lord," Asim said.

"What will I do with Excalibur?" Khufu asked once more.

"We will leave it in the sheath and return it to its place in the duats so that the Gods may have access to it when it is needed. When the Master Guardian is returned or needed again."

On one hand, Khufu was reluctant to pass the sword back to the high priest. It was, after all, the sword of the Gods and obviously very powerful. But that same thought frightened him with the potential responsibility for having such a thing. He unbuckled it from his belt and handed it over to Asim, who tucked it under his cloak.

Asim left Khufu watching the desecration of the greatest achievement of his realm, indeed in the entire history of mankind, and headed toward the Sphinx. He used his scepter and the stone door slid open. He entered, the door sliding shut behind him.

He made his way down the stone corridor, scepter in one hand, Excalibur in the other. He paused, cocking his head, as if he sensed something was wrong. He waited several moments, then continued. When he reached the intersection, he turned right and came to a complete halt as a man stepped forward to confront him.

Asim held the sword in his good hand, across the front of his body, still covered by the sheath. "Kaji. I knew you would be about. Scurrying around like the rat you are."

"Even a rat is better than being a slave," Kaji said.

Asim spit at the other man's feet. "You Watchers. You have betrayed our ancient priesthood."

Kaji shook his head. "We betrayed? Whom did we betray? The 'gods' who left us to fend for ourselves? Who allowed our homes to be destroyed, our people killed? What did you perform today? How many people died today because of the 'gods'? How many more will have to die?"

"You are a Watcher," Asim said. "You can do nothing according to the laws of your order. Get out of my way."

Kaji's jaw was set. "My three brothers, my six nephews. Two of my three sons. They died today on the pyramid."

Asim took an involuntary step backward. "You took an oath to only watch."

"I am done with being a Watcher. My surviving son will be the next Kaji. The next Watcher of Giza, of the Roads of Rostau."

"Still, you took an oath." Asim took another step back.

"You know there are those beyond the Watchers," Kaji said. "Those who act." Kaji held up his hands, his fingers lacking the ring that was the symbol of the first rank of his order. "After opening a door to the Roads of Rostau I left my ring for my son to find."

That struck Asim as hard as a blade. The priest held up the

sword, but had not drawn the blade. "What good will it do to kill me?"

Kaji barked a laugh. "You're not that important."

"Then what—"

"Excalibur," Kaji said. "It is theirs. And it is the key. I will take it."

"You cannot. It is only for the Gods."

Kaji indicated Asim's wounds. "Have you ever looked at yourself? What has been done to you?"

"It is the price of service."

"To what end?" Kaji's voice shook. "To what end does your service go?"

"To get eternal life," Asim said. "To partake of the Grail."

"The Grail has been around since the dawn of time and we have never been allowed to partake!"

Asim's voice fell to a whisper. "It will happen someday. If not to me, then to those who follow. But only to the true believers."

Kaji took another step closer to the priest. He was in range of the blade, but Asim did not draw it. "Has it ever occurred to you that perhaps partaking of the Grail might not be a good thing?"

Asim's eyes widened. He blinked as if he had just heard that the sky was red, his head shaking in disbelief.

"Excalibur," Kaji said.

Asim shook his head more firmly. "It must be kept safe."

"You think this place is safe?" Kaji didn't wait for an answer. "The 'gods' fight among themselves. Both sides know of the Roads of Rostau. It must be hidden from them or else we will have repeats of today's disaster."

"But the Ancient Enemy—" Khufu began.

"Yes, the Ancient Enemy." Kaji nodded. "Excalibur must be protected from the Ancient Enemy also. I saw what happened on the top of the pyramid. What makes you think that was the only enemy that survived?"

"The enemy was destroyed."

"You don't know that for sure," Kaji said. "I saw the Libyan taken by the Ancient Enemy in the desert to the west of here. More danger could be close by. The sword must be removed from here."

Asim frowned. "What do you know of the Ancient Enemy?"

A strange look crossed Kaji's face. "The legends—" His voice trailed off.

"How did you know to go out into the desert?" Asim pressed. "Why did—" Asim continued but he didn't complete the sentence as Kaji slammed his dagger into the priest's chest.

Asim lay on the tunnel floor, dead. Kaji reached down and took the priest's cloak, wrapping it around his own slender body, pulling the hood up over his head. He picked up Excalibur and the scepter. Then he headed toward the surface.

Khufu was alone on the roof of the pyramid temple. The removal of the covering stones was complete about a third of the way down. People from all around were at the base, taking the limestone with them, as the Pharaoh had allowed it. They could build homes with the stone. It might as well serve some positive purpose. Several large rough blocks had been emplaced on top to keep the semblance of a pyramid and also hide the fact that something else had once been up there.

He heard his guards snap to attention below and turned. A slight figure came up the ladder onto the roof, moving with difficulty. He recognized Asim from the high priest's cloak and the sword in the man's hand.

"I thought you were taking that back underground," Khufu said. "Have you had second thoughts?"

The figure came closer. Khufu gasped as the sword was drawn and the blade came across his neck. He could feel the coolness of the metal against his skin.

"Are you insane, Asim?"

The man pulled his hood down, revealing his features.

"Who are you?"

"A man. Like you. My name is Kaji."

Khufu stared into the man's eyes. "Are you going to kill me?"

"Asim is dead. I killed him."

Khufu looked back up at the defaced pyramid. The sword pressed tighter against his throat. He waited to feel it slice his skin. Now, for the first time in his life, Khufu felt his mortality, and knew that he was not the favored of the Gods, that he was just a man.

"He lied to you because he was lied to," Kaji said.

"Lied about what?" Khufu asked, hoping to avoid this dark fate as long as possible, thinking that perhaps one of his guards might check on them, also knowing that hope was futile, as no one would dare interrupt the Pharaoh while he was consulting with his high priest.

"The gods. The empty promises." The sword was removed from Khufu's throat and Kaji sheathed it, before hiding it under his cloak. "My Pharaoh—" Kaji pointed toward the pyramid. "That is what has been done to your people in the name of the gods. Perhaps it is best if these gods are not part of our lives. I will let you live if you give me your word as Pharaoh to rule as a man and not as a puppet to the gods."

Khufu swallowed and nodded, his confidence shattered by recent events. "Yes. Yes. I can do that. I will do that."

"I do not believe you," Kaji said simply. "Still, killing you will solve nothing and in reality, you have little choice now but to rule as a man. And there is doubt in your mind now. Perhaps that is all I can do here. Doubt is the seed from which one day may grow independence. The ability to think for ourselves. We have been lied to many times, by the gods, by the priests. We must make our own truth."

With that, Kaji turned and disappeared down the ladder. He made his way along the processional path, the guards keeping their distance, recognizing the cloak of Asim, the high priest, second only to the Pharaoh himself. Kaji maintained the strange gait of the priest until he reached the Lower Temple. Then he went by the priest's path to the nearby Nile where a small boat waited, manned by a young man who wore the medallion of the Watchers.

Set in the boat was a wooden box, three and a half feet long. The young man swung the top of the box open. Kaji placed the sheathed sword into the box, then closed the lid. He then handed the tube holding his report to the man. The boat slipped away into the darkness to make its long journey to deliver the report and sword.

CHAPTER 2: THE PRESENT

AREA 51, NEVADA

Lisa Duncan looked down her blood-spattered robe, fingers reaching into the hole in the cloth where the bullet that had killed her had gone through. The skin below was unblemished with no sign of the fatal wound. She touched the spot herself, as if not believing her own eyes.

"Who are you?" Mike Turcotte was in front of her and he placed his hands on her shoulders, fingers digging in a little too tightly. "I saw you die." Turcotte said the words in a whisper, as if not believing them. "I held you in my arms and watched you die. I felt you die."

A deep, accented voice caused Turcotte to look over his shoulder. "She partook of the Grail," Yakov said, as if that explained everything. "The legends are true. She is immortal."

Given that Yakov was the one who had shot her, Turcotte wasn't feeling too kindly toward the Russian, even though Yakov had done it in a vain attempt to prevent the Grail from being stolen. The Russian was a huge man, standing almost a foot taller than Turcotte. He was a former agent of Section IV, the Russian equivalent of America's Majestic-12, set up to monitor alien activity on the planet. Both Section IV and Majestic no longer existed, victims of the events of the past year.

Turcotte wore camouflage fatigues that fit loosely on his solid body. On both shoulders was the same subdued military patch: an arrowhead shape, with a dagger insignia crossed by three lightning bolts: the patch for the US Army Special Forces. He was of average height and stocky, with short dark hair sprinkled with gray. The stubble on his chin indicated it had been a while since he had enjoyed the comforts of a warm shower and a sharp razor.

"I'm cold," Duncan muttered.

Turcotte let go of her shoulders and blinked, looking about, taking in their surroundings, as if realizing for the first time that he was standing in a morgue and Duncan was sitting on a stainless-steel autopsy table. She looked small and vulnerable inside the bloody robe. Her short dark hair was plastered against her skull and her face was pale and drawn.

Turcotte scooped Duncan up in his arms and headed for the door. Yakov, Professor Mualama, Che Lu, and Major Quinn followed, the core of the group that was leading the fight against the alien presence on Earth. By default they were the ones who now ran Area 51.

Turcotte carried Duncan to a parked Humvee and slid her into the passenger seat before going around and getting behind the wheel. The others piled in, Quinn just managing to get inside before Turcotte stomped on the accelerator. He drove toward the large hangar cut into the side of Groom Mountain. To one side a long runway stretched out of sight along the dry bed of Groom Lake. Various hangars and support buildings were clustered around the end of the runway, between it and the mountain.

Area 51 was about ninety miles northwest of Las Vegas, in the middle of nowhere on the way to nowhere, established on land that held no value other than its isolation. Numerous mountains surrounded the dry lake bed, land that the US government had gobbled up to make the location secure. The spot had gained its name from the training area

designation number it received on the military map for the
Nellis Air Force Base range of which it was ostensibly a
part.

Most had thought Area 51 was placed in the location
because of its remoteness. The truth, however, was that it
had been placed where it was because of the shocking discovery during the early days of World War II of a massive
alien spaceship in a cavern underneath Groom Mountain—
the mothership. Over a mile long and a quarter mile in width
at its center, the craft had both stunned and intrigued the scientists sent to investigate it. Images on plaques found in the
cavern led the Americans to discover smaller atmospheric
craft, called bouncers and shaped like golden flying saucers,
in Antarctica. They had been brought to Earth in one of the
holds of the mothership.

The entire discovery was classified at a higher level than
anything had ever been in the United States. A committee—
Majestic-12—was established to oversee the alien artifacts.
For over fifty years Majestic kept the truth secret from not
only other countries but Americans also.

But even Majestic hadn't known the real truth about the
aliens: that Earth had been visited by aliens over ten thousand years earlier and they had headquartered themselves on
a large island in the middle of the Atlantic Ocean—the legendary Atlantis. And that when other aliens of the same
species, the Airlia, had arrived thousands of years later,
there was civil war between them.

One side was led by an alien named Aspasia, the other by
Artad. The initial battling resulted in the destruction of
Atlantis and a tenuous truce. Aspasia was banished to
an Airlia base underneath the surface of Mars at Cydonia,
where human astronomers had long been intrigued by
anomalies on the surface. Artad and his followers, the
Kortad, went to China, underneath the massive tomb of

Qian-Ling, and like Aspasia and his people, went into suspended animation.

But each side continued a subversive war throughout the millennia on Earth. Aspasia's side was represented by the Mission, led by a continually regenerated human, Aspasia's Shadow, who passed Aspasia's memories and personality through succeeding generations via the *ka,* a memory device that could be updated much like a computer hard drive. Artad's side was represented by the Ones Who Wait, Airlia-Human clones, and Shadows of Artad, such as King Arthur and ShiHuangdi, the first emperor of China.

Throughout human history both groups fought covertly, using humans as pawns in their battles. Turcotte and the others had discovered much, but they still didn't know the full extent of this interference in human history. They knew about the clash between Arthur (Artad's Shadow) and Mordred (Aspasia's Shadow) in early Britain; the development and spread of the Black Death in the Middle Ages; the rise of the SS in Nazi Germany; the invention of the atomic bomb from studying an Airlia weapon discovered underneath the Great Pyramid, also in the early days of World War II. Many other events throughout history were the result of efforts by one side or the other to gain the upper hand.

Turcotte and the others had also learned that the human survivors of Atlantis had formed a group called the Watchers to monitor the aliens. The Watchers were former priests who had worshipped the Airlia as gods, and who tried to monitor their conflict.

The lid blew off all those covert actions when Majestic-12 was corrupted after discovering a guardian computer in South America. The guardians were golden pyramids secreted around the world by the Airlia, as part of their ancient outposts. Contact with one by a human resulted in a direct mind interface, with the guardian taking control and turning the person into a Guide. The members of Majestic were corrupted in this manner and Mike Turcotte was sent by Lisa Duncan to infiltrate Area 51 and discover what was going on.

Turcotte had learned that Majestic was preparing to fly the mothership on orders from the guardian, most likely to go to Mars and pick up Aspasia and his followers. He also found information that initiating the mothership's interstellar engine would attract the attention of the Airlia's ancient enemy, known only as the Swarm, and bring destruction to Earth. Turcotte foiled that plan and all-out civil war had erupted between the two Airlia sides, the human race caught between them.

As it stood now, Turcotte had killed Aspasia and destroyed his fleet coming from Mars, but Aspasia's Shadow was now secreted on Easter Island with the Grail in his possession and a burgeoning military force. And in China, Artad had been awoken by the Ones Who Wait.

It was this precarious world situation plastered all over the situation board at the front of the CUBE—command, control & communications C3—deep under Groom Mountain, that the small group saw as they got off the elevator from the hangar above.

Turcotte ignored the sit-board and helped Duncan to the conference room. The others trooped in and the door was shut as an uneasy silence pervaded. Turcotte sat Duncan in the chair at the head of the table and slumped into the seat next to her.

Yakov was next to Turcotte. Mualama, an African archaeologist who had followed in the footsteps of Sir Richard Francis Burton and uncovered that explorer's secret account of all he had learned of the Airlia and their influence on Earth, was next to him. Mualama had also uncovered the scepter that had allowed Duncan and him access to the Black Sphinx, deep under the Great Sphinx, which had contained the Ark of the Covenant and the Grail. They had also discovered that Mualama was a former Watcher.

Then there was the elderly Chinese professor, Che Lu. She had opened the upper levels of the ancient tomb at Qian-Ling. She had recently been trying to figure out an alien grid system that highlighted many of their ancient bases. She had cracked the code and was still working on fixing the various locations, which included Qian-Ling, Easter Island, and Mount Sinai, where the Mission had hidden itself for a long time.

At the other end of the table was Major Quinn, a leftover from the days of Majestic, the man who knew the inner workings of Area 51 and was able to get what was needed from the US government. Or had been able, as it now appeared that Area 51 was being cut out of the chain of operations. He was a small man, with thick-lensed glasses perched on a thin nose.

"My friends," Yakov began.

Turcotte didn't particularly want to hear whatever it was the Russian had to say. He was watching Duncan, who seemed to be slowly coming to her senses.

"My friends," Yakov repeated as he turned to the others at the table. "We must look at the larger threats."

"And what can we do about them?" Turcotte snapped. He was bone-tired. Since uncovering the secret of Area 51 he had been fighting the aliens and their minions almost nonstop. For every step forward, every victory gained, there seemed to be two steps back and more secrets uncovered and more defeats. They had learned much but Turcotte felt there was a level of all of this that they had yet to penetrate. They didn't know why the civil war among the Airlia had started millennia before, nor what each side's true agenda

was, although there was little doubt neither side cared how
many humans died in the course of their battles. Beyond
that, they didn't even know why the Airlia had come to
Earth so many years earlier or what the civil war had been
about.

Mualama steepled his fingers. "We have been approaching this incorrectly. This is a war. And war is all about
power."

Turcotte, who had been practicing the art of war his entire adult life, stared at the archaeologist. "And?"

"We must search for the source of our enemies' power,"
Mualama said.

"And that is?" Turcotte prompted.

"We must find and control the Master Guardian,"
Mualama said. "If we do that, we can control the Easter
Island—and most likely the Qian-Ling—guardians. Maybe
even the guardian at Cydonia on Mars."

Turcotte rubbed his eyes for a second. "Now you say we
need the Master Guardian but yesterday you said we needed
the Grail."

"We did need the Grail," Mualama said. "But we don't
have it. Aspasia's Shadow has it and it is now under the
shield at Easter Island. The Grail is indeed powerful, as it
holds the secret of eternal life. However, most of Aspasia's
Shadow's power comes out of the Easter Island guardian.
The guardian controls the shield wall and the nanovirus he
has infected his forces with. It is also the way he communi-
cates with his forces. It is the key to his power."

"We don't have the Master Guardian either," Turcotte
said. "We don't even know where it is."

"Burton's manuscript described Watcher records saying
it was removed from the top of the Great Pyramid thousands
of years ago," Mualama said.

"And taken where?" Turcotte asked.

"The Watchers—" Mualama began, then paused.

"Go on," Yakov urged him.

"Yes," Turcotte said, spinning in his seat toward the African archaeologist. "Tell us what else you've been lying to us about."

"Not lying," Mualama said. "It just did not come up."

"So we have to ask you specific questions to get you to help us?" Turcotte asked. He slowly got to his feet and approached the archaeologist. He leaned close to Mualama. "Where is the Master Guardian?"

"It is with the mothership," Mualama said.

"The mothership was destroyed," Turcotte said, turning back to his chair and dismissing Mualama. "It's floating dead in orbit."

"Aspasia's mothership is floating dead in orbit. How do you think Artad came to this planet?" Mualama asked in a level tone.

That caused Turcotte to pause for a moment. "There's another mothership?"

Lisa Duncan spoke up. "It makes sense. Remember we found the power sphere for an interstellar drive hidden in a cavern in Ethiopia, yet the mothership here had one already in place."

Turcotte slowly sat down and nodded. "The sphere we found came from China."

"And Artad is in China," Duncan said.

"But we didn't see a mothership in Qian-Ling," Che Lu said.

"It might be in the lowest level," Turcotte said, but he doubted it even as he spoke. The mothership was simply too large to be hidden there, even given how big the mountain tomb of Qian-Ling was.

Quinn spoke up. "The Nazi records you recovered from the Soviet archives indicated that they were searching for an ark—not the Ark of the Covenant, but Noah's Ark. It would make sense that a mothership would be called such a thing. Perhaps survivors from Atlantis were put aboard it? That would explain the legend of the Ark."

"But the Nazis didn't find it," Turcotte noted.

"We haven't gone through all the records," Quinn said.

"Do it," Turcotte ordered.

"Nor have I translated all of Sir Richard Francis Burton's manuscript," Mualama added. "He also was interested in the legend of Noah's Ark."

"And I haven't pinpointed all the locations that Professor Nabinger translated," Che Lu said.

Turcotte rubbed his forehead. Despite all they had learned, they were still far behind the information curve. The truth of the present hinged on knowing the truth about the past and that was still largely unknown. But they did have more than they had started with. Did they have the time to process it all? he wondered.

"And if we don't find and gain control of the Master Guardian?" he threw out.

Quinn spoke up. "The military is marshaling a fleet in Hawaii. It's our last line of defense in the Pacific. They are considering attacking Easter Island."

"They won't be able to break the shield wall," Turcotte said.

"Unless we can access the Master Guardian and shut down the Easter Island guardian," Yakov pointed out.

Quinn frowned. "There was something in that archive material you recovered underneath Moscow about a weapon and a shield."

"What something?" Turcotte demanded, leaning forward.

"I'll have to look at it again," Quinn said.

A sergeant came into the room and handed Quinn a file folder and just as quietly left the room.

Turcotte finally considered the strategic situation. "Without a miracle—or us finding and controlling the Master Guardian—that fleet is not going to be able to get through the alien shield with any degree of effectiveness," he said. "And according to the status board, the ships the aliens have captured are heading toward Pearl. We'll be lucky if they don't seize Hawaii and our ships that we'd need to attack Easter Island. Major Quinn, send a message to the admiral in charge there and warn him of that."

"Yes, sir."

Turcotte's eyes were on Duncan, who seemed to be following the conversation. He turned to her, going back to the more immediate issue, or at least what he considered more immediate. "What happened to you?"

Duncan blinked. "I—" She held her hand up, looking at it as if it were an alien object. "I put one of the stones in the Grail. Then I put my hand in the Grail. One end of the Grail," she added. "It burned. Up my arm. My entire body."

"We need to get her to a doctor," Quinn suggested.

Turcotte ignored the major. "So the legend is true—it grants immortality?"

"It must be," Duncan acknowledged. She touched her torso, where the bullet had torn through her, still not believing the unmarred skin. "I'm here." She said it almost as a question. "And you say you saw me die."

"How does it work?" Turcotte asked.

She slowly shook her head. "I don't know."

"It must do more than give immortality," Yakov said. "It brought her back to life."

Turcotte thought for a few seconds, then rattled out more orders. "Major Quinn, you check the Nazi records we brought back from Moscow to see if you can learn any more about the location of the ark/mothership. Also, I want you to go back through Majestic's records and see if there is anything on this shield wall—how it works, and if there is any way we can get through it on our own. Because if we can't, we're defenseless against Aspasia's Shadow and his forces.

"Professor Mualama, you go through Burton's manuscript again and see if we missed anything regarding the location of the Master Guardian. Professor Che Lu, I think you need to get with Larry Kincaid and check all the locations that Nabinger recorded. Perhaps one of those is the second mothership. I'm going to try to send a message to Kelly to see if she can tap into the Easter Island guardian and give us a better idea where those objects are. Any questions?"

"And me?" Duncan asked.

"We need to find out what happened to you," Turcotte said. "How the Grail affected you."

Turcotte looked around the room. They were the experts, the ones who knew the most about the Airlia and their technology, yet he felt grave misgivings about their loyalties: Yakov, the Russian, who had shot Duncan; Che Lu, the Chinese, who had delved into Qian-Ling at such an opportune time; Mualama, the African, who had lied to them about being a Watcher and only told them things when it seemed to be convenient to some agenda of his own. And most of all Lisa Duncan, the woman he had thought he loved—what had happened to her?

Quinn had a headset on and he pulled the small mouthpiece away from his lips. "A doctor is coming down on the elevator. We need to get her looked at." He was staring at Turcotte. Surprisingly, the tiny officer got up and went to the head of the table, where he extended his hand to Duncan, indicating she should get up.

As Turcotte started to protest, Quinn put his other hand in the Green Beret's chest. "A doctor can tell us more right now than anyone else. We need to get her looked at."

Turcotte was so surprised by Quinn's action that he allowed him to escort Duncan out the door, where a man in a white coat waited. Quinn returned, shutting the door behind him.

"What the hell—" Turcotte began, but Quinn picked up the folder that he'd been given and tossed it in front of Turcotte.

"I don't know who that woman is," Quinn said, "but there is no Lisa Duncan. I had the Agency do a check on her. Everything in her background is a lie."

CHAPTER 3: THE PAST

GLASTONBURY TOR, BRITAIN
A.D. 529

Surrounded by water, the Tor jutted five hundred feet above the countryside, crowned by a ruined stone abbey. It was a sacred place, one where few dared travel, yet on this dreary morning, a small boat, oars pulled by a single man dressed in a long black robe fringed with silver, slowly made its way across the placid water. It was a place of legend, rumored by many to be the legendary site of Avalon, home to strange folk with even stranger powers. Those who lived nearby dared not set foot on the island.

The bottom of the boat grated onto a pebbled beach. The man stowed the oars, tied the boat off to a stunted tree, then made his way up the track that wound its way up the hill. He walked as if carrying a great burden, stoop-shouldered and with stiff legs, but all he had in his hands was a long staff of polished wood that he leaned on to aid his climb. His face was hidden in the shadow of an overhanging hood, but a white beard poked out at the bottom.

When he reached the top, he paused, taking in the shattered stone of the abbey. Then he looked all about, at the country that surrounded the lake. Nothing moved under an overcast sky. It was as if the land had been swept clear of man and beast. A gust of cold wind caused the man to pull his robe tighter around his body. Ever since the great battle of

Camlann—the showdown between Arthur and Mordred—
the land had appeared bleak and cold.

He walked to the abbey and through a doorway. The interior was open to the sky, the floor littered with stone blocks
from the collapsed roof. With a gnarled hand the man
reached into the neck of his robe and retrieved a medallion.
On the surface of the metal was the image of an eye. He
placed it against the front of the small altar where there was
an indentation of similar shape. He held the medallion there
for several moments, then removed it, sliding it back inside
his robe.

He rubbed his hands together as he waited. He started as a
door swung open in the wall of the abbey. A figure stepped
into the abbey, cloaked in brown. He too wore a hood, which
he pulled back, revealing a lined face and silver hair. His eyes
widened as he recognized the man by the altar.

"Myrddin!"

The old man wearily smiled. "I have not been called that
in a long time, Brynn. At the court of Arthur the King they
called me Merlin."

"So I have heard," Brynn said.

Merlin looked about. "They would have brought Arthur
here."

"He died right there." Brynn pointed toward the nearest
stone wall of the abbey.

"And Excalibur?"

"No sorrow?" Brynn folded his arms across his chest. "No
sign of grief for the death of your king?"

"I knew he was dead," Merlin said. "I have grieved in
private."

"I doubt it."

Merlin straightened, drawing himself up, and despite his
worn condition, Brynn took a step backward.

"I did what I did for the land, for the people."

"It did not work," Brynn noted.

"It was better than hiding in a cave with old papers," Merlin snapped.

"Was it?" Brynn didn't wait for an answer. "The land is worse off than it was. Many have died. The Grail was almost lost. The sword too."

"I know about the Grail. One of your fellow Watchers has it."

"It is good that you don't consider yourself one of us any longer," Brynn said. "You betrayed our order."

"I went beyond our order as must be done at times," Merlin said. "You will return the Grail to Egypt?"

"That I cannot tell you."

Merlin shook his head. "Returning to the status quo. That would be fine, except what is the status quo?"

Brynn frowned. "What do you mean?

Merlin stamped his foot on the Tor impatiently. "Our order has watched since the time of Atlantis. We once worshipped the 'gods.' And when they fought among themselves, many of our people died and Atlantis was destroyed, the survivors scattered.

"I talked with Arthur many times—he was a Shadow of one of these creatures. He knew much of the great truth."

" 'The great truth'?"

"What do we know?" Merlin asked Brynn. "Do we know where the 'gods' came from? Why they are here?"

The look on Brynn's face indicated he didn't even understand the questions, never mind wonder about the answers.

Merlin sighed and dropped that line of thought. "Excalibur is more than just a sword. It does others things. And the war will come again. And both sides will want it. And men like me"—Merlin nodded, acknowledging his role in recent events—"will try to use Excalibur also as a symbol. But it is more than a symbol. It has a purpose, a very critical purpose. It is a critical piece, one of several, in a very ancient puzzle."

Brynn waited, listening.

"I am here to make amends," Merlin said.

"And how will you do that?"

"Excalibur must be hidden better than this place."

"I do not—" Brynn began, but Merlin slammed the butt of his staff onto the stone floor.

"Listen to me, Brynn. The sword must be hidden. Since it was brought out, those whom you watch now know where it is. We—I—awakened those better left sleeping and they sent forth their Shadows to do war to try to gain the sword and the Grail. Both were hidden for many generations but now this place is no longer safe. You know that or else you would not have sent away the Grail."

"How do you know this?"

"Watchers are so ignorant. I was ignorant, but I have traveled far and seen much. Have you even read some of the papers you guard so closely below? That is what I spent my time doing while I was here."

"I have read those scrolls I can," Brynn argued.

"And the ones you can't read? The ones written in the ancient runes?"

"None can read them."

"I could and can."

"And what do they say?" Brynn asked, interested in spite of himself.

"The decision that demanded that our sole function be merely to watch what transpired was made by a vote at the first Gathering of Watchers. And it was not unanimous. There were those who thought watching wasn't enough and action needed to be taken. That man would be best off if we continued to fight for freedom from the Gods and their minions."

"But the vote was to watch," Brynn said simply. "It is the rule of our order."

Merlin sighed in frustration. "But it was a decision made by men. And we are men. We get to change it."

Brynn shook his head. "The order would never change that. And there has not been a Gathering in memory."

"You are ignorant," Merlin said.

"What will you do with the sword?" Brynn turned the subject from things he knew nothing of.

"Take it—and the sheath that contains it—far from here. And hide it well in a place where men—and those who pretend to be men—cannot easily get to it."

"There is no reason for me to believe you," Brynn said as he turned back toward the doorway.

"I was wrong."

Brynn paused.

Merlin continued. "We should not get involved with these creatures and their war among themselves. We do not have the power for that."

"And?" Brynn demanded. "That is the Watcher's credo. To watch. Not to act. Which you violated."

"And that is wrong also," Merlin said. "We must not just watch. We must act. But not in the way I did, trying to imitate these creatures, allying with one side or the other. I thought Arthur—" He shook his head. "I was misled, as the priests of old were. We must keep ourselves separate. Completely separate. And fight them when we have to and when we can do so with a chance of victory."

"What does that have to do with the sword?" Brynn asked.

"It is a thing each side needs in order to win the civil war,"

Merlin said. "And now they know of this place and it is easily accessible. That is why Excalibur must be removed. It can not be found by Aspasia's Shadow or Artad's followers or others, even more evil, who would seek to destroy it."

Brynn's face paled. "The Ancient Enemy?"

Merlin nodded.

"I thought that was just a myth made up by the priests. Like the Christians have their Satan opposing their God."

"There is always some truth in every myth," Merlin said.

Brynn ran a hand through his beard, obviously shaken.

"You say it is the rule of the Watchers only to watch," Merlin said. "Then how did Excalibur and the Grail come here in the first place?"

"They have traveled far over the ages. Joseph of Arimathea brought them here for safekeeping from Jerusalem."

"And did he not violate the rules of your order by doing so?"

Brynn reluctantly nodded.

"Then let me right that wrong and remove them from here. Then you can go back to watching."

"Excalibur is safe now," Brynn said with little remaining conviction. "I know that—"

Merlin cut him off. "The Grail has been sent away. The sword must be sent away also. *They* came here to retrieve Arthur's *ka,* didn't they?"

Brynn slowly nodded. "Yes. The Ones Who Wait."

"Then they know this place. They will be back."

"It is what I fear," Brynn admitted.

"They can always find the sword here," Merlin said, "but I can put it in a place that will be difficult, if not impossible, for them or any others to find and bring back."

Brynn frowned. "Where?"

"On the roof of the world where someone might be able to reach it, but never survive long enough to be able to bring it back down."

"Where is this roof?"

"Do not concern yourself with that." Merlin smiled. "You have nothing to fear if the sword isn't here."

This last bit of logic finally came home to rest with the Watcher. "Come." Brynn indicated for Merlin to follow him.

CHAPTER 4: THE PRESENT

AREA 51, NEVADA

Turcotte opened the door to the med lab and jerked his thumb toward the hallway. "Leave," he ordered the doctor.

"I don't think you have the—"

Turcotte had his 9mm pistol out of the holster and pointed at the man in the white coat before he could finish the sentence.

"Leave," Turcotte repeated, pulling the hammer back with his thumb as punctuation.

The doctor scuttled out of the room, the door swinging shut behind him.

Turcotte threw the file folder he'd been given by Major Quinn onto the examining table on which Lisa Duncan was sitting. "Read."

She picked up the folder and opened it. She had barely begun to peruse it when she started shaking her head.

"What?" Turcotte demanded.

"This can't be right."

"Why would someone make it up?" Turcotte asked.

She looked at him. "Why have you been checking on me?"

"I haven't. Quinn has. And apparently he was right to."

Duncan frowned. "But this"—she shook the folder—"isn't correct. I am who I am."

"When was the last time you saw your son?" Turcotte asked.

The frown deepened as she tried to remember.

Turcotte didn't give her much time to think. "Was it before you ordered me to go to Area 51? Before all this started?"

She slowly nodded. "Yes. We've been so busy since the discovery that—"

"You had time to see him if you had made the time," Turcotte said. "When we were together at your house in the Rockies. I should have known something was strange. I was there but he wasn't. You told me he was with his father, your ex-husband. But there is no father—and no son."

Duncan's pale face flushed red with anger. "I have a son."

"No, you don't."

"That can't—"

Turcotte cut her off. "Why did you order me to go to Area 51?"

"There were reports of irregularities at Area 51," Duncan said. "My son—" she began, but he cut her off once more.

"Quinn hasn't found any of those reports. And he was part of Majestic's support team. He knows how tight security was. And he knows there were no leaks." Turcotte reached over and took the file from her hands. "And you were appointed as scientific adviser via paperwork—no one ever interviewed you. Hell, your entire background is a fraud. No one cared who the hell the national science adviser was. No one checked. In fact, it appears that someone used Majestic's clearance to get you the slot, yet Quinn has found no record of Majestic doing that. What better way to get someone after Majestic than by using their own security clearance?"

"No." Duncan was shaking her head. "No. I—" She fell silent, overwhelmed.

"Who are you?" Turcotte asked. The strain of the past several weeks, of combat, of seeing men die, of winning battles against the aliens and their minions but always seeming to be behind in the war, was too much for him. He stepped up next to the table, his face close to Duncan's, his voice rising. "Who are you? Why have you done all this?" His hands were on her shoulders, shaking her. "Why?"

"I don't know. I don't. I don't!"

Turcotte blinked, let go of her, and stepped back. Tears were streaming down Duncan's face. He went backward until his legs hit a chair and he collapsed into it. He put his head in his hands, his elbows on his knees. His body began shaking. Abruptly he stood, sending the chair flying. He grabbed the door and stormed out of the room, slamming the door behind him.

Yakov, Che Lu, and Mualama were in the hallway. The Russian stepped in front of him. "My friend—"

"I am not your friend," Turcotte snapped. He poked a finger in the Russian's chest when the man refused to move. "Your 'friend' Katyenka betrayed us in Moscow. You came back here with a bug on you. You shot her—" He jerked a thumb at the door behind him. "What do *you* know that you haven't told me?" He spun toward Che Lu. "And you? Why did you suddenly decide to go into Qian-Ling? Convenient timing there. Right after Majestic was compromised." Then he turned on Mualama. "And following Burton? Lying to us about being a Watcher. Telling us about his manuscript in bits and pieces and only the parts you want to." He shoved Yakov out of the way. "I'm done with all of you."

Turcotte made a beeline for the outer door and walked into the bright Nevada sunshine. He blinked, his eyes smarting. At first he thought it was the light, but when he put his sunglasses on they still hurt. He realized he was crying. Turcotte walked away from Area 51 toward the desert.

QIAN-LING, CHINA

The Silk Road was the first connection between East and West in the ancient world. It stretched over four thousand miles from Xian in the northwest of China, across the north China Plain, through the Pamirs and the Karakoram Range to the walled city of Samarkand, across the great desert to Damascus and on to the Mediterranean ports of Alexandria and Antioch. From there ships could sail on to Greece and Rome and traders could travel the land routes inside those kingdoms.

It was the route that Marco Polo traveled for three years to become the first Westerner to see the Inner Kingdom of China, but that was long after the road had been established. The Silk Road was also the path that the Black Death had taken in the opposite direction hundreds of years later in the fourteenth century. Historians had traced the deadly track of the bubonic plague from China, along the Silk Road, to Mediterranean ports and on to the rest of Europe. In five years it killed over twenty-five million people, reducing the human population of the planet by one-third. Percentage-wise it was the most devastating event ever to strike mankind, far eclipsing the devastation of the world wars centuries later.

And it had started right there in Qian-Ling—an attempt by Artad's followers to strike at the Mission's growing power in Europe and the Middle East and level the playing field. And the Mission had just recently tried the same thing in South America in an attempt to wipe out mankind and pave the way for Aspasia's arrival from Mars—an attempt that was stopped at the last minute by Mike Turcotte.

When China was young, the balance of power was in the West, and Xian was the capital city. The first true ruler of

China, the Yellow Emperor ShiHuangdi, held sway there during his reign. In reality, ShiHuangdi had been a Shadow of Artad. According to legend, when he died, he was buried in a massive tomb, larger than even the Great Pyramid of Giza. This tomb was called Qian-Ling. A man-made mountain, over three thousand feet high, Qian-Ling, like Area 51 and the Great Pyramid, was more than it appeared to be. In reality the Shadow had simply returned to the place where he had been "born," and his memories absorbed.

Deep inside was an Airlia base, complete with a guardian computer. It was also the site where Artad, leader of one side of the Airlia, had gone into hibernation along with his followers. The outside of the mountain was now blackened soil, the foliage stripped bare by the Chinese government's detonation of a nuclear weapon in a vain attempt to destroy the alien base. However, the same type of shield wall that protected Easter Island had limited the effect of the blast to the charring of the surface around the shield.

Inside the alien base, Lexina, the leader of the Ones Who Wait, had managed to gain entry to the lowest level of Qian-Ling and resurrect Artad and his followers. Now they were ignored as Artad accessed the guardian, assessing the situation in the outside world.

Artad was Airlia, standing almost seven feet tall and looking almost exactly like the Horus statue that had once guarded the entrance between the paws of the Great Sphinx. Red hair, red elongated eyes, six fingers, disproportional body—all indicated his alien heritage.

Artad rapidly processed information concerning the ten thousand years since he had gone into deep sleep, until he was current on the present situation: Aspasia's Shadow was moving, using the power of the humans. He cloaked his forces with a shield that rendered them practically impervious to the weapons of the humans. Infecting those humans his forces contacted with a nanovirus to control them.

Artad did a search of the guardian's database and frowned when he didn't get the answer he was looking for. He stepped away from the guardian and went out of the chamber. His Kortad, Airlia who had come to Earth with him so long ago, were lined up, awaiting his orders.

"Excalibur?" he asked Ts'ang Chieh, the human court adviser from the days when his Shadow ruled as the Emperor ShiHuangdi, commander of all the known world. While he had been working the guardian, Ts'ang Chieh had been outside the chamber questioning Lexina.

"The key to the Master Guardian?"

"Yes."

"The humans—the Watchers, or those who had been Watchers—hid it long ago. So long ago that it is only a myth now."

A strange look crossed Artad's face, what in a human might have been considered a smile. "Foolish." He crossed the chamber to a control panel. He waved his hands over it and a series of hexagons were backlit with runes written on them.

Artad tapped out a code on the hexagons.

MOUNT EVEREST

Near the top of the highest point on the planet three dead bodies lay on a narrow ledge in front of a frozen chamber that was little more than a four-foot-deep indentation at the top of an almost sheer cliff face. They were suddenly bathed in a red light as the sheath in which Excalibur's blade was encased powered up. The glow was refracted by the ice around the crystal and pulsed out into the atmosphere.

QIAN-LING

A red hexagon in the upper right-hand corner of the panel came alive. Artad nodded ever so slightly, then tapped in a new code. The wall in front of him shimmered and went white. A circular image appeared, coming into focus until it was obvious it was the planet as if seen from space. Artad tapped the red hexagon and the planet quickly rotated, then froze in position with a red flashing dot on the surface. He tapped the red hexagon again and the image grew larger. The location was on the border between Nepal and Tibet, in the midst of the Himalayas.

Artad nodded—it made sense they would hide it there. While Excalibur was in the sheath no mechanical transportation could come within several miles of it, a safeguard built into the system so that he—or anyone else—couldn't send a craft to swoop in and pick it up. The Watchers had placed it in the most inaccessible location on the face of the planet. There was only one way to retrieve the key.

Artad turned to Ts'ang Chieh. "Where are the Ones Who Wait?"

"They are outside, my lord."

"Bring them in."

Lexina led her companions Elek and Coridan into the guardian chamber, bowing low, fearing to look up and meet the red eyes of the one they had waited to serve for millennia.

"Is there a way to communicate with those who now rule this land?" Artad asked.

Lexina nodded, still keeping her head down. "Yes, my lord. We have radios. And their forces surround this area."

"Good. I have a message I wish to send them." His red eyes looked over the three Airlia-Human clones. "And I have a mission for you. Look up."

They raised their heads. Artad pointed at the screen. "That is where you must go." He reached to his side and drew out a sword. "And something like this is what you must recover. It is most important. I will prepare you as well as I can."

EASTER ISLAND

Aspasia's Shadow's right arm ended abruptly at the wrist. Raw flesh and white bone marked where Turcotte's shot had ripped the hand off. A tourniquet was tied around the middle of the forearm, cutting deep into the skin, but it had stopped the bleeding. His skin, pale to begin with, was ghostly white.

The bouncer he was aboard had just descended through the lake in the center of Rano Kao crater on Easter Island. The bouncer was a gold-colored disk about thirty feet in diameter. It moved through a tunnel at the bottom of the lake as easily as it passed through the air.

A half minute later it surfaced in a pool in a large cavern, went up into the air, and settled down on the dry rock, which made up the other half of the area. A half dozen US Marines awaited Aspasia's Shadow. Their eyes were glazed over, as they were controlled by the guardian computer via a nanovirus coursing through their brains. The nanovirus could send electrical impulses through the infected persons' brains, controlling their actions, essentially making them part of the Easter Island guardian network. The chilling thing about persons infected by the nanovirus was that while it controlled and directed their nervous systems, a part of their minds was aware of this and unable to change it.

Three of the Marines, part of Task Force Seventy-nine, which had been captured by Aspasia's Shadow's forces, climbed onto the bouncer and opened the hatch. While two of them grabbed Aspasia's Shadow and helped him out, the third picked up the Grail, which was covered by a thick white wrap.

Aspasia's Shadow staggered as his feet touched the ground and the Marines held him up. He had lost more blood than he'd thought. The Marines helped him into a tunnel lit by lines in the ceiling. The tunnel sloped upward, then leveled and turned to the right. Aspasia's Shadow and his escorts entered a cave. In the very center was a twenty-foot-high glowing, golden pyramid—the Easter Island guardian.

Aspasia's Shadow frowned as he noted that plastered on one side of the pyramid was a shriveled mummy with various metal leads connecting the guardian to the body. Aspasia's Shadow forgot about the figure as a Marine placed the shroud-covered Grail on a table to the right of the pyramid.

In his many reincarnations, Aspasia's Shadow had known much pain. It felt as if his missing right hand were still attached but on fire. He forced himself to ignore the feeling and went to the Grail. He removed the shroud, revealing an hourglass-shaped golden object. The end that was up appeared solid.

Aspasia's Shadow pulled a small wooden box from a deep pocket inside his cloak and opened it. Two stones were set inside—the thummin and urim of biblical note. They glowed as if from an inner fire. With difficulty, Aspasia's Shadow took one of the stones. He held it over the edge of the Grail. The flat end irised open, revealing a small depression inside, the same size as the stone.

Aspasia's Shadow paused. He knew his forces were moving and that much was happening around the world. He forced himself to put the stone back in the wooden box for the moment and go to the guardian. He leaned against the side, placing his only hand flat against the metal. A golden glow encompassed him as he connected with the alien device.

Acting with just a few commands from him when he had been headquartered at the Mission underneath Mount Sinai, the guardian had done an excellent job of preparing and initiating his plans. He was updated on his fleet moving toward Pearl Harbor; on what was going on above him on the surface of the island; he grinned when he saw the unanswered messages from the stranded Airlia on Mars spooled up and waiting for him—they could rot for all he cared, in retribution for the millennia he had suffered and fought here on Earth while they slept; his guides were growing in power all over the world—all was going quite well.

Centuries of battling, of maneuvering from the shadows in the halls of power, of seeing kingdoms and countries crumble, had made him suspicious of good news. There was always a weak link, a blind spot where disaster could strike from. Artad? Qian-Ling was shielded, the guardian informed him. While that might be an automatic defense reaction by the Qian-Ling guardian, it was just as likely that his ancient enemy had awakened. He knew the Ones Who Wait had been searching for the Qian-Ling lower level key.

He had to assume Artad was finally awake, or at the very least another Shadow of him had been imprinted. And if he were Artad or his Shadow? Aspasia's Shadow had learned early in his many incarnations to think like his enemy in order to outmaneuver his nemesis.

The Master Guardian. It was the tool Artad needed to destroy him and rule supreme on Earth. Aspasia's Shadow accessed the truncated line that had once been the link between that guardian and the Master Guardian. Nothing, which meant the Master was still powered down. He knew what was needed to free it, so he accessed the search program for Excalibur, the sword that was much more than a sword.

In the course of their long war against the Swarm the Airlia had had ships captured and worlds overrun. In the course of that, guardian computers, including system masters, had been lost to the Swarm. Because of bitter experience, the Airlia had learned to safeguard their computer systems with devices like Excalibur. While it did several things, it was primarily a microtransmitter that was on all the time. What it transmitted was the authorization code for the Master Guardian, which allowed it to power up and link and control its subordinate guardian computers. But the transmitter only worked when the sword was removed from the specially designed sheath, which was made of a material that blocked the transmission. Having such a device in such a compact form allowed one person to control all of the guardian computers. There was a destruct built into Excalibur that could be triggered, wiping out the memories of all the guardians and shutting them down in an instant. The way to initiate the destruct was something only the Airlia commander who wielded Excalibur knew. That way was one thing that had *not* been passed to Aspasia's Shadow when he was first given Aspasia's memories.

He knew the Watchers had hidden Excalibur long ago. The damn Watchers—Aspasia's Shadow had killed many members of the meddlesome human cult over the centuries. And there had been times when some of them had not simply watched but tried to search him out and kill him—a most foolish endeavor, as many had learned just before they died.

He had tried to gain Excalibur during his incarnation as Mordred, only to be joined in mutual defeat by Artad's

Shadow masquerading as Arthur. And Merlin the Watcher? What had he done with the sword?

The guardian accessed scanners built into the slope of the volcano above and even reached out to Mars and the base at Cydonia where the few surviving Airlia who had followed Aspasia huddled in their underground caves.

They had picked up a signal from Earth's surface. Aspasia's Shadow knew immediately what it meant—the homing device on Excalibur had been activated. Since he hadn't done it, there was no doubt who had. Artad was awake. And also looking for the sword.

And the location? When he saw the spot, Aspasia's Shadow cursed. Damn Merlin.

On the other side of the guardian, the withered body twitched, indicating there was life somewhere deep inside. The eyes were crusted shut, the muscles atrophied and consumed as the body tried to keep its core alive, the skin dried and leathery.

Deep inside the mind, the essence of Kelly Reynolds felt the contact of Aspasia's Shadow and the guardian like an electric shock, bringing her out of her almost-coma. She'd been there for weeks, ever since trying to link to the guardian when the island was occupied by the United Nations. She'd wanted to discover the truth about the aliens, to learn the advanced knowledge she had believed could be gained from the computer. Instead she had become trapped by the guardian, her mind scoured by the alien computer for information and then forgotten about.

During the intervening time she had slowly managed to regain some control of her mind although her body remained melded to the golden pyramid like an insect to flypaper. She'd even managed to tap into the massive flow of data that poured through the guardian. She'd slipped in the command for the nanovirus to leave her body and even managed to get a message out to her friends at Area 51.

She'd also learned some things about the Airlia. She'd "seen" the destruction of Atlantis—Aspasia's initial base on Earth— as a historical record inside the guardian. She'd "seen" one of the Airlia mothership float over the island and pulse down rays of golden power into the island, smashing it into the sea.

She'd also learned that the various guardians had once been linked together under a Master Guardian computer, allowing all the Airlia outposts on Earth, and even on Mars, to be coordinated and controlled. But during the civil war among the Airlia, the network had been shut down and the Master Guardian taken off-line.

As she sensed Aspasia's Shadow "work" the Easter Island guardian she saw that her minor efforts, which had taken so much of her willpower to do, were just drops of water on an ocean compared to the power that Aspasia's Shadow could exert as he became one with the guardian. She "saw" him absorbing data at a phenomenal speed. Kelly kept her psyche still, afraid to attract his attention. As quickly as information was going into Aspasia's Shadow's essence, orders were being issued by him.

Kelly tried to keep track of what he was doing but it was like watching Niagara Falls and trying to discern each drop of water going over the edge. Still she did glean a few things. And then she waited, crouching, hiding inside the computer, until Aspasia's Shadow broke free and his essence was gone. She had an idea of his plans, but more importantly, she had an idea of his priorities.

Then she began to work on the message she would try to send.

Aspasia's Shadow felt more confident as he disconnected from the guardian and went back to the Grail. Things were progressing well and he had a good idea what Artad had planned. He had instructed the guardian to implement a strategy to counter Artad's efforts to acquire Excalibur, and to recover the Master Guardian itself. The latter was something he had begun planning many years ago. Aspasia's Shadow had many potential plans in place.

He retrieved the stone and held it over the end of the Grail. The flat surface opened. Aspasia's Shadow slid his hand inside, placing the stone into the slight depression. He gasped as the opening irised shut against his wrist, trapping his hand.

A tingling sensation began to tickle the skin of the hand. The tingling grew stronger, becoming pain. His hand felt as if it were on fire, yet Aspasia's Shadow remained perfectly still. Rivulets of sweat coursed down his pale skin. Then the pain began to move up his arm toward his shoulder and, strangely, Aspasia's Shadow smiled.

All of Easter Island was enclosed in a hemispheric shield, impervious to most forms of attack. Inside the shield, on the surface of Easter Island, Aspasia's Shadow's orders only confirmed what had begun days ago. Thousands of humans went about the tasks the nanovirus inside of them directed them to do. At the same time, nanotechs went about their business.

Nanotechnology was a science that human scientists had just begun to explore while the guardian had perfected it. The concept was basic. All things are made from atoms. The properties of those things are determined by the way those atoms are arranged. If atoms could be rearranged at the molecular level then the possibilities of what could be constructed was limitless. Not only that, but the normal waste produced in most manufacturing processes would be eliminated.

The other thing the guardian had perfected with nanotechnology was self-replication. Its nanotechs could manufacture more of themselves, just as the nanovirus it had invented to control humans could replicate and spread, much like a regular virus. The Guides and the followers who had come to Easter Island, along with all the military personnel who had come into contact with the nanovirus, were now all under the thrall of the guardian.

Two men who had once been Navy SEALs, "Popeye" McGraw and Frank Olivetti, were summoned by the guardian. The two had recently infiltrated the island to try to discover what was happening, but they had been captured and infected with the nanovirus, absorbed into the forces on the island. Under the influence of the nanovirus they walked down the tunnel from the surface to the guardian chamber.

Aspasia's Shadow was lying on the floor to one side of the golden triangle, a smile on his face, eyes closed. The two ignored him and Kelly Reynolds's withered figure as they approached the guardian. The nanovirus was enough to control a person's body, but for what these two would be tasked to do, more control and adaptation was needed.

They both leaned against the side of the pyramid, bodies touching the metal. They were encompassed in the golden glow, the alien computer working on their minds, transforming them into Guides who would do what they were programmed to without needing constant activity and updating by the nanovirus. In addition to the mission they were given, the skills necessary to accomplish this were also implanted in their minds.

Since they would be traveling far from Easter Island into a harsh environment, a few special measures were taken. While they were still in the thrall of the guardian, several micromachines skittered across the floor of the cavern, metallic spiders with various appendages poking from their frames. They crawled up the men's bodies and performed several modifications to them in conjunction with specific nano-viruses for parts of their bodies.

A miniature satellite transmitter and receiver was inserted just behind their right ears, attached to the skull with bone screws. Skin was grafted over the device. The wire antenna for the satcom was slipped under the skin and looped around the skull. Variations of the nanovirus immediately went to work on healing the incisions. Also, a special form of nanovirus that the guardian had just designed was injected into each man's lungs and went to work on those organs.

When the guardian was done with them, the golden glow faded. Marines scooped up the unconscious and recuperating bodies and carried them out of the chamber to the surface. Other Marines picked up equipment they had been instructed to bring from a supply depot. The SEALs and equipment were carried to an F-14 Tomcat. The Marines stowed the rucksacks full of gear inside the cramped cockpit, before sliding the two unconscious SEALs into the seats and strapping them in. The Marines stepped back and the canopy descended, locking in place. The engine started up and the plane taxied to the end of the runway under the control of its flight computer. A second plane was right behind it, an S-3 Lockheed Viking.

The F-14 roared down the runway and into the air, turning hard as soon as it was airborne to stay inside the shield. The Viking was right behind it and with both airborne, the island shield was dropped for a moment and the two aircraft flew off to the west. The shield snapped back into place as soon as they were clear.

McGraw and Olivetti were unconscious inside the F-14 as the flight plan programmed by the guardian flew the craft. Somewhere deep inside their infected and transformed minds their essences as independent human beings still existed. That their bodies and skills were to be used in the service of the aliens was a horror of which they were aware but powerless to fight. It was the worst possible thing that could be done to a Navy SEAL, a fate far worse than death.

PACIFIC OCEAN

Six hundred and ninety-five nautical miles northwest of Easter Island Captain Porter, commander of the Los Angeles class attack submarine USS *Norfolk* was looking into the eyepiece of his periscope at the largest ship in the world, the *Jahre Viking*. It was cruising between two of the largest warships in the world, the supercarriers *Washington* and *Stennis*. Surrounding those three massive ships, each longer than the Empire State Building was tall, were the escort ships that had once been part of the US Navy's Task Forces seventy-eight and seventy-nine. Porter had been briefed that the human hands that now ran those shops were directed by minds infected with an alien nanovirus and were not to be considered friendlies. Since departing Pearl Harbor he had been operating under radio silence, cut off from updates.

That was easier said than done, Porter knew as he zoomed in on the *Washington,* the closer of the Nimitz class carriers. He'd been on that ship for six months as part of his career training and knew quite a few officers assigned to it.

His submarine was sitting still in the water, all systems reduced to bare minimum functioning. His sonarman had already informed him that the escort ships were actively searching the water for intruders—surface, subsurface, and air. His boat was one of six subs rapidly dispatched from

Pearl Harbor and set up in a loose semicircle between Hawaii and Easter Island to intercept the fleet.

Satellite imagery had tracked the fleet and Porter knew that the other five subs were closing on this location, much like the German wolf packs had gathered in the North Atlantic during World War II.

Porter turned the scope slightly, back to what appeared to be the flagship of the fleet. He knew from his recognition handbooks that the *Viking* was the largest man-made moving object on the planet. Even the supercarriers were dwarfed by the former oil tanker as it pounded its way through the waves.

Porter's mission was to slow the convoy down to allow the other five submarines time to get in place. With three major targets coming into range, there was no question which one he would fire on. Despite the orders and explanations from higher headquarters, he was loath to fire on a Navy ship.

The problem, as his executive officer/weapons specialist had pointed out to him, was that the *Jahre Viking,* besides being huge, was constructed in a manner that almost defied attack. Like all modern supertankers it was double-hulled to prevent oil spills, a feature that would also help defeat attack by torpedo. Additionally, its interior was composed of oiltight—which also meant watertight—holds. Even if he managed to breach the double hull, he would only be able to flood one compartment.

Porter had passed the problem on to his crew, letting them war-game possible courses of action as they steamed to their present location. His executive officer had come with a suggestion that Porter felt was worth the attempt.

There was the additional issue of a report that the ships might have the same sort of shield generator that surrounded and protected Easter Island. Porter clicked on a small button on the periscope handle, zooming in on the large tanker. He'd seen photos of the opaque shield that surrounded Easter Island—obviously, if there was one here, it was clear. If there was one, Porter thought once more to himself.

"XO, are we ready?"

"Yes, sir."

"Sending targeting information," Porter told him as he clicked another button and the top of the scope "lased" the *Jahre Viking* with a quick series of laser pulses that would give the targeting computer range, speed, and direction of the massive target. Porter knew missing was out of the question but the plan called for precise shooting.

"We've got it," the XO reported. "Ready when you are, sir."

Porter did a quick scan from side to side. To remain undetected, he had turned off sonar and the surface radar on the periscope. He wondered briefly how effectively the escort ships would react—he had conducted war game missions against his own Navy many times but had never thought he would be doing it for real. He knew the escort's anti-submarine capability and it was enough to cause a small trickle of sweat to go down his back.

"Fire at will."

Unlike the submarines of World War II, the tubes on the *Norfolk* were amidships and vertical. The reason—the MK-48 torpedoes they fired weren't line of sight, but guided either by wire or preprogrammed targeting. In this case, the XO had preprogrammed every MK-48 on board, all twenty-four.

Four torpedoes rushed out of the tubes. As soon as they were gone, crewmen rushed to reload. As the MK-48s rushed toward the *Jahre Viking,* they moved on two tracks, two torpedoes each. The trail torpedo was two seconds behind the lead missile. The XO's idea had been to blow a hole in the outer hull with the first one, then follow it two seconds later with another warhead to breach the inner hull. Right at a junction between two cells, flooding both. And subsequent volleys would do the same from stern to stern.

"Tracking," the XO reported. "Twenty seconds."

Porter looked through the periscope. He noted that the closest escort, a destroyer, was already turning toward their location. Through his shoes, Porter felt the deckplates shudder every so slightly as the next volley of torpedoes was fired.

"We're being pinged," the sonarman reported.

"Keep firing," Porter ordered. He could see the destroyer closing. He turned the handles, putting the *Jahre Viking* dead center in the crosshairs.

"Ten seconds."

Even without headphones he could hear the oncoming destroyer's sonar fixing their location.

"Five seconds."

Two geysers exploded out of the ocean. "Too soon," Porter muttered. Another two geysers as the sound of the first explosions reached the sub. As the geysers settled back, he could see the *Jahre Viking* unscathed, continuing on course.

Porter spun about to face his bridge crew. "Helm. Hard right rudder, flank speed. Crash dive." As the Klaxon announcing the dive sounded, he took a couple of steps toward his communications officer. "Radio Pearl. Tell them the ships do have a shield. Warn off the other subs. There's nothing we can do."

Checking the instruments, Porter noted that they were descending quickly while accelerating away from the fleet.

"Range to destroyer?" he asked.

"One thousand meters and closing."

"Prepare countermeasures," Porter ordered.

The captain had known when he committed to the firing

that they wouldn't be able to get clear without the escort attacking them. In simulations his crew had managed to beat an escort 50 percent of the time. Now he was going to find out how realistic those simulations were.

"MKs are in water," his sonarman announced. "Tracking two. Range one thousand."

The best weapon against a submarine was the same weapon Porter had just tried using—MK-48 ADCAP torpedoes.

"Launch decoy," he ordered.

A small, but very "loud" submersible was fired out of one of the torpedo tubes and raced away, in the hope of drawing off the two incoming torpedoes. Porter realized he was gripping the edge of his command chair, his knuckles white, and he forced the muscles in his arm to relax.

"Range five hundred. Still closing."

"Prepare for impact," Porter ordered.

"Three hundred." The sonarman's voice rose. "One is breaking off. Tracking the decoy!"

Fifty percent, Porter thought.

"One hundred."

Porter braced himself, his mind flashing to every submariner's horror of implosion. He, along with everyone else on board, flinched as there was a loud thud from the direction of the bow. Porter blinked. But no explosion.

"A dud!" His executive officer was the first to say it.

"Helm, keep us moving out of here," Porter ordered. "Damage control?"

The XO hit the intercom, contacting the forward compartments. "Any damage?"

Porter recognized the voice of one of his chief petty officers. "Nothing we can see. It hit"—there was a burst of static—"bulkhead. There's some"—another burst of static—"wrong with—" The intercom went dead.

"You have the conn," Porter yelled at his XO as he dashed toward the forward hatch. He raced down the passageway, his movement slowed by having to open every hatch. As he reached the hatch just before the compartment they had been talking to, he stopped in shock as he noted a ripple effect in the metal. As he grabbed the round handle, he felt a sharp pain in his hands as if the metal were hot.

He pulled his hands away and stared at them. No burn marks. But the pain was still there. Moving up his arms. His eyes widened as he saw the veins bulging in his arms—and they were black.

Captain Porter screamed as the nanovirus reached his brain. A scream that was echoed along the length of the ship as the microscopic metallic virus invaded every crew member.

IRAN

General Kashir commanded an army division headquartered in Tabriz in northwest Iran. It was a precarious post given the locale. To the north were Armenia and Azerbaijan. To the west Turkey, and below it Iraq. While the rest of the world had forgotten, no Iranian who had lived and fought through it could forget the brutal eleven-year war Iran and Iraq had waged against each other from 1979 through 1990. Almost two million had died during the fighting and neither side had gained more than a few kilometers of worthless desert despite countless offensives.

The illegal use of chemical weapons, children being forced to charge across minefields to "clear" them, and execution of prisoners were all practices engaged in by both sides. A cease-fire was agreed to in 1990 but no peace treaty had been signed. Add in the unrest in the former Soviet provinces to the north and east, and the ever-present revolt of the Kurdish people throughout the area, and the region was as unstable as it had always been. With the recent assassination of Hussein in Iraq, all the militaries in the region were on high alert. There were those preaching—as ever—for a *jihad* against Israel, but Kashir knew that blood spite between Arabs would always rate higher than enmity for the Jews.

There had been numerous "cleansings" of the officer ranks by the religious government and Kashir had not only survived them all over the years, he'd been promoted up the ranks to his present position. He owed everything to a secret alliance he had made early in his career.

His office was located on the top floor of the tallest building in the city, with a commanding view not only of the town, but the surrounding countryside. As he had done daily for the past several years, he turned on his computer and accessed a secure e-mail server.

Unlike every one of those days, today there was a message waiting from his secret benefactor.

At first Kashir simply stared at the screen in shock for several moments. The subject line was the proper code word: scimitar.

And there was only one person who had this address. Known for years as Al-Iblis to intelligence agencies around the world, he was now known as Aspasia's Shadow. Kashir owed his rank and this position to Al-Iblis's machinations over the years and now he knew that the marker was being called in.

Kashir clicked the mouse and the message appeared. When he was done reading it, his eyes were drawn to the wide windows on the northern side of his office. It was a clear day and far in the distance he could make out a white-covered peak on the horizon. The mountain was over 120 miles away, but high enough to be visible. It was also over the border in Turkey.

"Agri Dagi," Kashir muttered as he stood and walked over to the window. It was the name the locals called the peak. To the rest of the world, it was better known as Mount Ararat. And his orders from Aspasia's Shadow were to secure the mountain, even if it meant invading Turkey and causing a war.

General Kashir picked up his phone and ordered his aide-de-camp to assemble his staff.

MARS

From the base, the summit of Mons Olympus, despite being three times taller than Mount Everest, wasn't visible, as it was far enough away to be over the horizon of Mars. It was the largest volcano in the Tharsis Bulge, a ring of high mountains around Mars that were so massive they had caused the axis of Mars to shift over the eons.

The dimensions of Mons Olympus were staggering. Over fifteen miles high. Over 340 miles in width at the base. The volcano was surrounded by an escarpment over four miles high. It was the highest and largest mountain in the solar system.

And on the southeast edge of the escarpment, the greatest engineering feat in the solar system was under way by an army of robots. Eight-legged mech-diggers were tearing into the escarpment, cutting a path through it, using the rubble to build up a ramp that extended over one hundred miles into the surrounding plain.

Mech-scouts were ahead of the diggers, near the peak, scuttling about on six legs, setting beacons into the rocky soil in a grid pattern. The machines were being controlled by a guardian computer located underground at Cydonia, a location that had long stirred controversy on Earth because of images taken of the area by probes showing a "face" and other nonnatural shapes on the surface. They indeed turned out to be not natural—an Airlia base where Aspasia had been exiled after Atlantis was destroyed. He, his fleet, and most of his followers were killed when Turcotte booby-trapped the Area 51 mothership in space and exploded it as Aspasia and his followers tried to board.

The remaining handful of Airlia living at Cydonia were cut off not only from their home world but from Earth as Aspasia's Shadow ignored them, retribution for millennia of being cut off from them and battling on Earth without their support as they slept.

In a long path from Cydonia to Mons Olympus, a line of mech-carriers was moving, their claws, gripping debris uncovered from the ruins of the "face." The movement had been noticed on Earth and was being tracked by Larry Kincaid, a NASA specialist who was part of the Area 51 team. The purpose of the movement and what was planned on Mons Olympus, however, remained a mystery.

DIMONA, NEGEV DESERT, ISRAEL

Simon Sherev nodded at the four guards behind the bullet-and blast-proof glass as he passed their station. The four men watched him with cold eyes, muzzles of their Uzis stuck through portals following him even though they knew who he was and around his neck was the proper access card. The men took their jobs very seriously for behind the large steel vault doors to their rear lay the true might of Israel: two dozen atomic warheads.

That vault, while it was the most important charge in Sherev's command at Dimona, was not his destination. Instead he continued down the underground corridor until he came to a second vault. It held objects that had power of a different kind. Sherev showed his pass to the soldiers guarding this bunker, then pressed his face against a retinal scanner. The bulletproof clear door opened with a loud click.

Sherev stepped through, passed the guards, then repeated the process with the vault door. It slowly swung open, lights automatically going on inside. Sherev went inside and hit the control shutting the door behind him. The vault was about forty feet deep by twenty wide, with a high ceiling. Three rows of tables went from front to rear. On them were various artifacts, some human, some they had found to be Airlia.

His focus, however, was on the closest table and the most recent addition to the state of Israel's secret archives. Taken from the Mission's base under Mount Sinai, the Ark of the Covenant rested on a cloth-covered platform. Sherev stopped just short of the table, getting his first good look at the artifact. The Ark was three feet high and wide and about four feet long. The surface was gold-plated. On the lid were two sphinxlike figures with ruby-red eyes. From the reports he'd received, Sherev knew that when the Ark had contained the Grail, the eyes had been an active security system, killing any who approached unless he wore a special garment that lay next to the Ark on the same table. It appeared that removing the Grail had deactivated the system.

Sherev ran a hand along the top of the Ark of the Covenant. Even he who had grown cynical during his decades fighting Israel's covert wars was touched by actually being in the presence of something so essential to his country's faith. Even though he knew it was an Airlia artifact, he could still envision it being carried across the desert by his ancestors.

Since recovering the Ark of the Covenant from the Mission, Sherev had spent much time reflecting on the faith his parents had raised him in. Sherev swallowed hard as the implications struck home with full force, here in the presence of the Ark. The Ark of the Covenant—but what covenant? Was Moses the man whom his countrymen believed in, or, as now appeared, someone very different? Had Moses been a Guide under the influence of an alien guardian, a pawn in the civil war between the factions? Or had he acted of his own free will? And even if he had, did it make any difference if the Ark was an Airlia artifact and his trip up Mount Sinai had not been to speak to God, but to speak with Aspasia's Shadow?

Sherev had seen many of his countrymen die for their faith even as he had killed those of other countries who'd fought for their beliefs. If all were lies— Sherev was startled as the phone on the wall near the door emitted an irritating buzz. Reluctantly he went over to it and lifted the receiver.

"Sherev," he snapped.

"Sir." He recognized the voice of his senior aide. "Intelligence reports that Jordanian, Syrian, and Egyptian forces are mobilizing."

Sherev was not surprised. The Iraqis and Iranians had been on full wartime footing since the moment it was announced that Saddam Hussein had been assassinated.

"We have been ordered to prepare to go to stage three," the aide continued.

Sherev's eyes went to the wall of the chamber, as if he could see into the next one, where the bombs rested. Stage three meant the warheads were to be moved to the surface in preparation for deployment to their various delivery platforms. In his years there they had never gone to stage three, not even during the Gulf War, when Saddam had fired Scuds at Israel. But again, Sherev was not surprised. Recent events were propelling the world into a path not seen since 1939.

"And, sir—" The aide hesitated; making Sherev wonder what could be worse than the news he had just received.

"Yes?"

"Hasher Lakur is here."

Lakur was an influential member of Parliament and the one who had gotten the government to trade the thummin and urim to Al-Iblis—who they now knew was Aspasia's Shadow—in exchange for Saddam's assassination. It had been a deal with the devil that Sherev had opposed.

"What does he want?"

"The Ark."

Sherev turned back to the table on which the artifact rested. He didn't need to ask. He knew why Lakur wanted it—as a symbol to the country, to unite them in the coming war. But it was an empty symbol, Sherev knew, both literally and figuratively.

"He has authority from the Parliament to claim it," the aide added.

Sherev hit the open button and the vault door slowly swung wide. He could see soldiers in the corridor, already moving to get the nukes. He almost laughed from the insanity. Nuclear warheads and the legendary Ark of the Covenant. An interesting combination for Armageddon.

CHAPTER 5: The Past

TUNGUSKA
1908

The scout ship had followed the previous ship's trail for over four thousand Earth years. Time meant little to those who crossed the vastness of space, and especially the creatures inside the ship. Owing to their life span, they viewed time very differently from humans. Also, the crew had been in suspension for most of the journey. They remained in that state as the craft decelerated from interstellar speed, a process that took several years and a long orbit around the system's star.

The crew was awakened as the ship approached the inner planets. Knowing the first ship had disappeared somewhere in the vicinity of this star system, the crew maneuvered with more diligence. They picked up signs of civilization on the third planet and headed toward it.

The scout ship entered the atmosphere of the third planet, searching for any sign of the first craft and scanning the civilization. It was passing above the world's largest landmass when it was struck by an unexpected bolt of power from below and exploded.

The craft was seriously damaged and the crew tried desperately to retreat to the safety of space, but to no avail. It lost altitude, screaming through the atmosphere over the planet's largest landmass. An escape craft holding some of the crew popped out of one side, while a few members tried to bring the crippled scout in for a landing.

They failed, and it smashed into the planet, the explosion devastating the countryside, on a scale not seen since meteors had hit the planet many millennia earlier.

The escape craft raced around the planet, settling in to land underwater, as far away from the crash site as possible. Sensors on the fourth planet picked up the escape craft, but also the lack of any signal from the main ship before destruction.

All went back to the status quo.

In the submerged escape craft, the few survivors slowly began to study the planet on which they had landed, prepared to spend many years doing so before settling on a course of action.

CHAPTER 6: THE PRESENT

EASTER ISLAND

Aspasia's Shadow lay perfectly still. His eyes were closed and his chest was barely moving. His body was bathed in the golden light of the guardian. The Grail was on the table next to him.

There were two things happening in the chamber.

Kelly Reynolds's wasted body was twitching and vibrating as her mind struggled to find a way to send out a message of warning and information. She had picked out the critical parts of Aspasia's Shadow's plan and knew she had to get the information out. And she was quite close to accomplishing that very thing.

And at the end of Aspasia's Shadow's right arm, at the severed wrist, where raw flesh and bone met the air, there was a black-and-red foam bubbling up. And millimeter by millimeter, a new hand began to grow.

BEIJING, CHINA

The Chinese president held a videotape in his hand as he entered the hall of the National People's Conference. The buzz among the delegates about the suddenly called Assembly fell away to respectful silence as the president made his way to the front of the hall.

Just before he mounted the podium, he handed the video to a technician. He took his place behind the microphone.

"The videotaped message I am about to show you was just received by my office. It was transmitted from Qian-Ling."

He gestured and the room went dim. The large screen behind him flickered. A short Chinese man in a golden robe appeared. Behind him was a seven-foot-tall alien with red cat eyes and red hair. There was absolute silence in the hall. The creature—an Airlia they knew from news reports from the West—began speaking in a singsong voice. The man in front translated in Chinese.

The speech went on for ten minutes but the summation was simple: join Artad or be his enemy. And Artad's Shadow had been ShiHuangdi, the Yellow Emperor, the founder of China as they knew it. They had less than one hour to vote and make their decision.

When the screen went blank the hall exploded in pandemonium.

AREA 51

Turcotte cursed. A buzzing noise had been sounding for the last minute. He reached into his pocket and pulled out his SATPhone. He cocked his arm back to throw it away. He was about a hundred meters away from the runway, a kilometer away from Area 51 and still walking into the desert.

Turcotte sat down in the sand. The phone continued to ring. Decades of training fought with his emotions. Discipline versus feeling. He flipped the phone open.

"What?"

"It's Quinn. The Chinese have been issued an ultimatum by Artad. Join him or fight him. The *Stennis* and the *Washington* along with the *Jahre Viking* are headed toward Hawaii and the ships are shielded. The Navy's tried attacking the Alien Fleet—as they're calling it—and lost an attack sub in the process."

Turcotte lay on his back, staring up at the blue sky. His anger was gone. He felt so tired all he wanted to do was close his eyes and sleep. To forget about it all. "And? Nothing I can do about any of that."

"Kelly Reynolds has sent us a message. Text. Forwarded through Pearl to us."

Turcotte sat up straight. "Kelly?" The thought of the reporter stranded on Easter Island stirred him. She'd hoped the aliens could bring good to the human race and he knew that her current situation made him seem like a whining child.

"Yes."

"How did she get it out?"

"She piggybacked it via the guardian SAT-link to the fleet they've captured. I can display it on your phone."

"Do it." Turcotte pulled the phone away and read the lines on the small screen.

```
THE GRAIL IS HERE
ASPASIA'S SHADOW HAS PARTAKEN
HIS FLEET WILL ATTACK HAWAII
CONSOLIDATE, THEN ASSAULT US WEST
   COAST
THEN WORLD
FLEET IS PROTECTED WITH SHIELD
EASTER ISLAND PROTECTED WITH SHIELD
FIND MASTER GUARDIAN TO DROP ALL
   SHIELDS
AND DEPROGRAM NANOVIRUS
LOCATION MASTER GUARDIAN
LOCATION MASTER GUARDIAN
```

```
IN MOTHERSHIP
IN MOTHERSHIP
BUT MASTER GUARDIAN NEEDS KEY TO BE
   FREED TO WORK
BUT MASTER GUARDIAN NEEDS KEY TO BE
   FREED TO WORK
KEY IS EXCALIBUR, MUST BE FREED
   FROM SCABBARD
KEY IS EXCALIBUR, MUST BE FREED
   FROM SCABBARD
ASPASIA'S SHADOW SEEKS EXCALIBUR
ASPASIA'S SHADOW SEEKS EXCALIBUR
ON SAGAMARTHA
ON SAGAMARTHA
```

Turcotte read the message one more time, then put the phone back to his ear as he got to his feet. "What else?"

"Mualama has something on the second mothership. Also, Yakov's been going through the German archives and has found some interesting stuff."

"What about Excalibur?"

"Mualama thinks the Watchers had it but then it disappeared." Quinn paused. "I don't know, sir, but I think this is all connected. The second mothership, the Master Guardian, Excalibur, and the shields."

"What is Sagamartha?"

"I'm checking on that."

There was a lot in the message that Turcotte turned over in his mind. "What else?"

"Someone else must think we know something, too," Quinn said.

"Who?"

"I've got the CINC-PAC on the line. He wants to talk to you."

"Why?"

"How the hell should I know?"

The explosion from the usually mild and meek Major Quinn caused Turcotte to smile for the first time in a long while.

"I think he wants your advice about the Alien Fleet, considering you had me send the warning about the shield," Quinn added in a milder tone. "Given that we're the 'experts' on the Airlia."

"Put him through," Turcotte said.

PACIFIC OCEAN

The entire Alien Fleet slowed to a halt. The maneuver took a while as the mass of the three capital ships was enormous and, even with their screws turning at full-thrust reverse, it was over twenty minutes before they became still. The massive doors the nanomachines had built into the bow of the *Jahre Viking* slowly swung open.

Inside, two submarines, identical in appearance down to the name stenciled on the sail—USS *Springfield*—floated side by side. One was the original, captured by Aspasia's Shadow's forces off the shore of Easter Island. The other was the copy, made by the nanomachines.

Both powered up and sailed out of the bow, slipping below the waves, taking their place in the fleet. All the ships began moving again, picking up speed. Inside the massive open area in the front of the *Jahre Viking,* two more copies of the attack submarine *Springfield* began to materialize molecule by molecule.

The two in the water were different from the original *Springfield,* Los Angeles class, though. Near the bow on either side were newly constructed intakes. As the two submarines cleared the *Viking,* water was sucked in, passed along a series of baffles that increased the pressure and speed of the flow, then ejected it through two openings just in front of the rear fins.

A standard LA class sub was rated at almost thirty-five knots, very fast indeed for a submarine. With the added propulsion system, the two subs began accelerating away until they were slicing through the water at over sixty knots.

AIRSPACE CENTRAL PACIFIC OCEAN

The F-14 carrying McGraw and Olivetti edged behind the S-3 Viking airborne tanker. A refueling probe extended downward and latched onto the intake on the F-14. Fuel from the large pods underneath the wings of the Viking flowed through the probe and into the nearly empty tanks of the F-14. The transfer continued for over two minutes until both pods were empty, then fuel from the rest of the Viking's tanks were tapped until they were drained and the F-14's full.

The probe disconnected. The Viking's engines coughed, sputtered, then died. The plane nosed over and fell toward the ocean. The infected crew made no attempt to make an emergency water landing. It smashed into the ocean killing all on board and shattering into pieces.

In the sky above, the F-14 continued on its way across the Pacific on the mission assigned by Aspasia's Shadow. Inside the cockpit, the nanovirus was at work on both men's lungs, rearranging cells.

"Popeye" McGraw stirred in his machine-induced coma, crying out, almost like a dog having a bad dream, his hands weakly reaching out and pawing for the ejection seat handle. The cry turned to a yelp of pain as the Guide imprinting took charge, and punished the part of his brain that was still "free." McGraw's body was silent once more.

BEIJING, CHINA

The vote in the Chinese Assembly in Beijing was swift and overwhelmingly in favor of siding with Artad. Several factors weighed in that decision.

First, was the fact that Artad's Shadow had been ShiHuangdi. The first emperor in a country that, despite almost a half century of Communist rule, still revered the days when it was the Middle Kingdom and the center of the world. Here was an opportunity for China to return to its place as the leader of the world with the alien's help. This was the deciding factor for the more emotional of the Chinese legislators.

Second, was the fact that the nuclear strike on Qian-Ling had been defeated. The more practical legislators saw it as a case of it you can't beat him, join him. Even if the "him" was an alien.

Third, were the reports of what had happened to the American ships around Easter Island. A war was shaping up between the alien factions and there had been no offer of alliance from Aspasia's Shadow on Easter Island. While the Chinese cheered the defeat of the Americans fleets, they also realized that the United States might just be the first domino to fall before Aspasia's Shadow's forces.

Fourth, Chinese forces were already massing on the coast across from Taiwan and along the borders with North Korea and Vietnam. The world was in turmoil, the dreaded American fleet in the Pacific was for the moment not a factor, and the Chinese military was clamoring that it was time for China to strike. An alliance with Artad would undoubtedly help all their planned moves.

Fifth, Qian-Ling was in western China, where ethnic Muslim forces were revolting. With Artad's help, the Chinese politicians believed they could regain firm control of the area and put down the rebellions.

In the end, only six of three hundred voted against the alliance.

The agreement was messaged to Qian-Ling.

The six were taken out of the parliament into the Square and summarily executed with a bullet to the base of their skulls. Their bodies were strung up to lampposts with cardboard signs hung around their necks proclaiming them traitors to the new Middle Kingdom.

The orders for the various military forces to prepare to attack both Korea and Taiwan were also sent.

And special orders, as dictated by Artad, were sent to military detachments stationed in western China.

KASHGAR, CHINA

Over two thousand miles away from the capital in Beijing, Kashgar was the provincial capital of the Xinjiang Uygur Autonomous Region. As such it was far removed from much of the political maneuvering that occurred in the east. However, despite the distance, the Chinese military remained firmly in control in Kashgar.

When the commander of the garrison received the order from Beijing to prepare a special operations team for an assault to the west there was no questioning the command. The aircraft and troops were alerted. However, the orders stated they were not to move until some special envoys arrived.

QIAN-LING

A Chinese helicopter landed on a dirt road just outside the black shield wall protecting Qian-Ling. A crew chief jumped off, sliding the door to the cargo compartment open, then waited. The land was scorched from the nuclear weapon, which the Chinese had detonated in an attempt to destroy Qian-Ling and the aliens inside.

That things had changed was obvious as the shield wall flickered off for a few seconds and three figures walked out. The shield returned as they approached the helicopter and got on board. The aircraft was off the ground in a hurry, the pilots not wanting to be in the "hot" area or near the strange shield longer than needed.

In the rear of the chopper, Lexina and her cohorts, Elek and Coridan, were on the first leg of the mission they had been given by Artad.

PEARL HARBOR, HAWAII

Admiral Kenzie shut off his SATPhone. What Turcotte had just told him confirmed his worst fears. He looked at the satellite imagery once more. There was no mistaking the two carriers flanking the massive tanker. The last message from the *Norfolk* lay crumpled on his desk. Kenzie was CINC-PAC, Command in Chief, Pacific Area Command. The last month of his tenure had been a disaster on a scale exceeding the worst in American military history. The two captured carriers and assorted escort ships in the photo pictured two-thirds of his naval might.

He had one carrier group left in this hemisphere—the USS *Kennedy*. It was anchored less than a mile away in Pearl Harbor. And the Alien Fleet—his own ships—were less than a day away, steaming at flank speed.

Through the windows of his office, Kenzie could see Honolulu to the east, all the way to Diamond Head. There were a million people on Oahu, with another half million on the other islands in the chain. A million and a half people. Never, not once since taking this position, had Kenzie ever thought those people would be threatened. He never dreamed that he would have to make the decision facing him today.

His phone buzzed and his secretary's voice came out of the box. "The president is on the line, Admiral."

He stared at the phone for a moment, then picked it up. "Mister President, Admiral Kenzie here."

"I've been listening to my National Security Council, Admiral, about the various options. None of them sound good to me. You're the man in the hot seat. What do you say?"

"Mister President, I recommend Task Force Eighty put to sea."

"And?"

"Sir, we can't penetrate the shields surrounding the ships in the Alien Fleet. I believe that fighting it out will only end the same way the last several confrontations with the Airlia fleet have been resolved—with Task Force Eighty becoming assimilated into their forces. And Eighty is the last line of defense not just for Hawaii but for the West Coast of the United States."

The president's voice rose. "So you're just going to turn tail and hide?"

"No, sir." Kenzie turned his chair so he could look out of his office to the west. Like a forest of gray, he could see the masts of the ships anchored in Pearl. "I want permission to take the fleet to sea, swing westward around the Alien Fleet—which Aspasia's Shadow won't expect—and prepare to attack Easter Island when the shield is turned off."

"And who is going to turn off this shield?" the president asked.

Kenzie realized he had to phrase this most carefully. "I am under the impression that various covert units are working on that very problem."

There was a long silence, then the president's voice came back. "That is the advice I am receiving here. God help us."

CHAPTER 7: THE PAST

LONDON, ENGLAND
Spring 1924

"Because it is there."

The answer took the reporters by surprise. They'd expected a long patriotic speech about why George Mallory was attempting the Everest climb for God, Queen, and country. He was standing on the wharf, next to the loading plank for the ship that would take him and his partner Sandy Irvine to India and it was the last time the English press would have a chance to talk to him.

He ignored the shouted questions and raised his hands, quelling the outburst. "You will have to excuse me, gentlemen, but I must do one last check of equipment before we sail. I would hate to have forgotten something important."

As the reporters laughed, he turned without a smile and walked up the gangplank, his new partner Irvine right behind him. The gear was packed belowdecks and Mallory disappeared through a hatchway. Irvine hesitated, then went toward the rear of the ship once his partner was out of sight. A man in a long black coat waited in the shadows near the wheelhouse.

"Very interesting answer Mr. Mallory gave," the man said as Irvine came up to him. The man's face was lined and his dark hair streaked with gray. His eyes danced with an inner light, darting about manically. He held up his hand and made a strange gesture, a secret sign that Irvine returned with the appropriate hand signal.

"I am Nikola Tesla," the man said.

"I have heard of you," Irvine said. "There are some who say you have harnessed great powers."

"Some will say anything," Tesla said evasively. "What exactly do you think he was referring to when he said 'it'? The mountain? Or—" Tesla paused, then put emphasis on the word: "'it'?"

Irvine shrugged. "Does it matter?"

"Yes!" Tesla hissed. "This is more important than your pride."

Irvine was unfazed by the outburst. "You've never seen Everest. Never stood in its shadow."

"Everest is not the goal. What is hidden there must be protected."

"I will do what is required."

"You must stop him—and the thing inside of him," Tesla said.

"Yes, yes." Irvine was anxious to be off.

"You must be careful," Tesla said. "Watch Mallory closely."

"That is why I am doing this," Irvine said.

"You are doing this because you were ordered to," Tesla said.

"I am doing this, yes, because I was ordered," Irvine agreed, "but also because it will be one of the greatest achievements in history. The North and South Poles have been conquered. Everest is the last, great unknown."

"And that is why *it* is there," Tesla said.

Irvine frowned. "And if Mallory is"—he searched for a word—"corrupted? How do I stop him?"

"Kill the host body high enough, then the Ancient Enemy cannot survive."

"You are certain of this?"

Tesla nodded. "I've learned much. I destroyed their craft years ago, but we know now some survived. The Ancient Enemy is very patient. It has spent years gathering information, learning where it is, and now it is finally taking an action."

"Why now?" Irvine asked.

"Because the peak finally seems within man's capability of climbing *and* coming back down."

"We hope it is," Irvine said.

"I envy you," Tesla suddenly remarked.

"Why?"

"Because you will see it."

"If I make it there," Irvine said. "And find the location."

"That is secondary." With that Tesla strode away.

MOUNT EVEREST
Summer 1924

A hundred-foot-high vertical step blocked the path. It was a rock outcropping from the mountain rising above the northwest ridgeline extending down from the mountain-top. Sandy Irvine stared at it for several moments, then turned to Mallory. The elder climber simply pointed up. Mallory had led on the previous step, and now it was Irvine's turn. He used his ice ax, chiseling out a small step. Then another. Then two handholds. He levered himself up, then reached as far above his head as he could and hammered a piton into a crack in the rock. He put a snap link in, then the rope that connected him with his climbing partner.

Irvine felt the rope tighten around his waist and lift him as Mallory leaned back on belay. There was no way a man could have reached this point on Everest, above twenty-seven thousand feet, climbing alone. This step alone would have been impossible for one man to climb. How much longer would that hold true, Irvine wondered. He could not see the summit from his position on the step so he continued up, ever so slowly.

After almost an hour, Irvine reached the top of the step, his hand scrambling for a hold. He found one and pulled himself up on top of the outcropping. He lay still for several moments, simply trying to catch his breath, knowing he never would at this altitude as the air was too thin. He rolled onto his back and looked up. The summit was only five hundred feet above—he started laughing to himself—*only*? And the top of the Kanshung Face, a mile-high almost purely vertical slab of rock that made up a large part of the north face of the mountain was to his left. That was where *it* was.

Irvine slowly got to his feet. He finally knew he could make it the rest of the way without help. When he felt a tug on his waist, Irvine looked down. Mallory was waiting, his face hidden behind oxygen mask and goggles. Mallory began to climb, putting pressure on the rope. Irvine belayed. Mallory made quick time and was within ten feet of the top when Irvine pulled out a knife and held it against the rope.

Mallory paused when he noted he wasn't being helped on the belay and looked up. Irvine couldn't see his partner's face behind the goggles and mask, for which he was glad. It made Mallory seem like a thing, making what he was about to do more palatable. Still, he didn't cut the rope. They had been together for months, traveling from

England by ship, then overland by train, and then by horse and—finally—for months on foot, steadily higher into the Himalayas. He'd found Mallory to be withdrawn but competent, with little sign of the change Irvine had been told had occurred. It had brought forth doubts about what he'd been instructed to do.

Mallory wrapped one arm around the rope, locking himself in place, then pulled aside his oxygen mask. "What are you doing?"

"I cannot allow you near it."

Mallory reached with his free hands into his parka and pulled out a small glowing orb. "This must be placed on it."

"Why?"

"To destroy it."

"Why?"

Mallory cocked his head slightly, as it was a stupid question. "You have no idea of the truth."

"I know you've been corrupted by the Ancient Enemy," Irvine said.

Mallory nodded slightly. "It is part of me. But it is here to save you."

"That is not what is written."

Mallory didn't reply. He reached up for a handhold. With that, Irvine cut the rope.

Mallory desperately clung to the side of the mountain. He didn't speak again even though his mouth opened up, farther and farther. Irvine could hear bones cracking and ligaments tearing. Something gray was now visible in Mallory's mouth, coming forth. Irvine didn't wait to see more. He threw his ice ax at the climber and it hit him in the head. Mallory lost his grip, scrambled for it, then arched backward from the step, free-falling, until he slammed into the base and then began tumbling, picking up speed. Irvine watched as the body smashed into rocks, still rolling, then fell off the first step they had climbed earlier that morning and was gone down the mountain.

Beyond that Irvine knew there was a thousand feet of nearly vertical rock before his partner would crash into rock, ice, and snow. The curious thing was that Mallory had not screamed or made a noise as he slid, as if he accepted and almost welcomed his fate. The memory of whatever had been coming up into Mallory's mouth caused Irvine to shudder, even more than the freezing cold seeping in through his clothing.

Irvine checked the sun, which was well past its apex. He knew if he continued upward his own death was inevitable. He also knew that he could not make it down alone. He looked up at the summit, then across at the top of the Kanshung Face.

The summit? Or the other way? Irvine turned toward the Kanshung Face. It was late in the day and he knew, at best, he would reach the location just before dark, if not after the sun was gone. And that would seal his fate as effectively as a firing squad. And what would be the point of summiting when he was going to die there anyway? No one would know of his feat.

He rubbed his goggles, trying to scrape away the ice that constantly formed on them. He could barely see twenty feet. As had been true for the past week, the ground in front went upward. Ever upward. He was on the roof of the world—higher than any other human being on the planet.

He looked up once more, trying to clear his goggles. The sky was clear and the wind wasn't howling, about as good as weather got on Everest. The ice on the lens was too hard and thick and Irvine gave up on his attempts to clear the goggles and pushed them down so they dangled around his neck. He blinked in the bright sunlight. The sun burned into his eyes, but Irvine ignored the pain as he searched the rock wall for the climbing route to the left.

He was on the north face of Everest. On Mallory's first trip years earlier he had proclaimed the north face impossible to climb. The only possible way up Everest, Mallory had so boldly pronounced, would be via the less steep southern approach. Those words had been one of the indicators of trouble when Mallory announced this expedition and indicated he would use a north side route. High peaks were visible, all below him, and beyond them the brown plateau of Tibet. He could even make out the curvature of the Earth in the far distance.

The terrain grew steeper as he moved away from the ridge that he would have followed had his primary goal been summiting. He paused as the crampons on his left foot hit something solid. Rock was his first thought. He looked down. There was something brown. He reached down with one mittened hand and wiped away snow. A frozen face looked back at him, the skin etched where the steel had dug in.

As far as Irvine could tell, the man was dressed in leather. How long he had lain there, Irvine didn't know for sure but he could make a guess. This was one of the party that had put Excalibur here millennia ago. Rather than discouraging him, the presence of the body gave Irvine a boost of energy. If men like this, with ancient equipment, had conquered the mountain so long ago, surely he could go farther. One of the man's hands was clutched to his chest and on a finger Irvine could make out a large ring, with an eye carved onto the surface.

Irvine reached the edge of the ridge. Beyond was the top of the Kanshung Face. Irvine blinked, trying to clear his eyes. There was a thin ledge, less than six inches wide, leading out onto the top of the rock wall. It went straight for about fifty meters, then disappeared around a rock-and-ice cornice. Below was a vertical drop as far as he could see. The wind was sending plumes of snow off the summit, whipping the white flakes around.

Irvine stepped onto the ledge, arms spread wide, the weight of his pack like a hand trying to pull him off the mountain. He shuffled his feet, slowly making his way along the edge. It took an hour to reach the spur, all the while the wind and the pack striving to separate him from the rock face.

The cornice was the worst. Reaching around, Irvine could tell it was two feet wide. The ledge disappeared completely and the rock was smooth. He couldn't tell if the ledge continued on the other side. He had to trust that it did. Below was air.

Irvine took several deep breaths, only to realize there was very little oxygen flowing into his mask. He tried to remember when he had switched over to the last bottle, but his mind couldn't compute the time.

He swung his left leg around the cornice, feeling the momentum take his body. He was committed as he followed through with his left hand. His left boot scrabbled for a hold, but his foot was so frozen he couldn't tell if it had found purchase or not as he lifted his right foot and let go with his right hand, his body sliding around the cornice. He fell, was convinced he had failed and would continue falling, when a shock slammed up his left leg as the boot landed on a ledge. His hands scrabbled to keep his body from tipping over.

He hugged the side of the mountain so tightly, the right side of his face froze to the rock. But he didn't even feel it. His eyes were glued to what was just ahead. The ledge widened to six feet deep, almost a cave. Set in the rear of this indent in the side of Mount Everest, frozen into a sheet of ice almost a foot thick, was Excalibur, sheathed in an ornately carved scabbard.

Irvine moved closer, ripping skin from his face as he pulled from the rock, now unaware of the dangers of falling, his mind and body drawn toward the sword. He stumbled and almost fell, before he noticed that on either side of the sword was a body, frozen to the mountain. Irvine looked down. The one on the right was dressed in brown leather and furs, the same as the previous one he had found. The one on the left also had furs, but underneath was a black robe fringed with silver. The man's face was aged, his hair and thick beard white. In his frozen hand was a long wooden staff.

The two bodies flanked the sword, dead eyes open, staring out over the world. Each man had a ring similar to the previous body's. Strangely, each man's face was twisted with a frozen smile that had endured for millennia.

Irvine turned his attention back to Excalibur. He pulled his mittens off and pressed against the ice. Encased in the ice, the sword's handle glittered in the waning daylight. The metal was shiny, unmarred by the elements. He understood now why legends had grown up around it. He felt an urgent desire to touch it, but the ice denied him access even to the scabbard.

Irvine suddenly realized he had no feeling in his hands. He tried pulling them back, but they were stuck to the ice. With all his will he pulled his arms back. He blinked with almost bemusement as three fingers on his right hand and two on his left simply cracked off and remained frozen to the ice. He felt no pain, just a distant dullness from his elbows down.

With great effort he slid to a sitting position between the two bodies. Irvine slumped back against the ice. The rays of the sun were horizontal and soon it would be gone. The wind, strangely enough, had died down. It was eerily quiet; the only sound he could hear was his own gasping for oxygen in the thin air.

He sat back, totally exhausted. Still he summoned the strength to turn his body ever so slightly so that he was looking at the mountain, at Excalibur. A slight smile touched his blood-spattered lips. And that was how he died.

CHAPTER 8: THE PRESENT

AREA 51

Turcotte ignored Yakov, Che Lu, and Mualama. He walked into the room where Duncan was seated in a chair, a blanket wrapped around her slight frame. His fatigues were dusted with sand from his sojourn into the desert and where sweat had soaked through the camouflage material, the sand was crusted in place.

"You're back," Duncan said, a hesitant half smile on her face. She started to get up. "Mike, I'm telling you the—"

"Shh—" Turcotte said as he lightly put a hand on her shoulder and pushed her back into the chair.

But that didn't stop Duncan. "I'm telling you the truth as far as I know it."

"I know. I think I've got an idea what was done to you. When we infiltrated Majestic-12's base at Dulce," Turcotte said, "we found that they were conducting experiments on abductees, including Kelly Reynolds's friend Johnny Simmons. Mind experiments using Airlia technology."

"Dulce was destroyed," Duncan said.

"Yes, but they got the basic technology from the Airlia. They were working on EDOM—electronic dissolution of memory. Majestic was using it on abductees to wipe out their real memories of being captured by Nightscape, and then implanting false memories of disinformation."

Duncan frowned. "Are you saying my memories are

false? That everything I know is a lie? Electronic signals implanted in my brain?"

Turcotte tapped the CIA folder. "We know your memories are a lie, Lisa."

A nerve twitched on the side of her face. "I don't have a son?"

"I'm afraid not."

Duncan was shaking her head. "It can't be. It just can't be. I remember him. I remember all of it. Damn it, Mike, I remember giving birth to him. The pain. I watched him grow up. Maybe some of my memories are false, but others true? All of it can't be a lie."

Turcotte remembered how Johnny Simmons, Kelly Reynolds's friend who had gotten her involved in the whole Area 51 mess, had killed himself after they'd rescued him from an EDOM pod at Dulce. To have one's past taken away and replaced with a set of lies was undoubtedly devastating. It took away a person's sense of self. Duncan had just learned that her family was not only dead, they had never existed.

"It doesn't make sense," she finally said. "Why would Majestic have done this to me? I ended up putting in motion the forces that destroyed them."

Turcotte shook his head. "I'm saying the technology and techniques used on you are similar to the EDOM Majestic used. I'm not saying Majestic was behind it."

"Who, then?"

"That's a very good question," Turcotte said. "If we can figure that out, maybe we can figure out who you really are."

Turcotte went to the door and motioned for Quinn to come in. "How far has Dulce been excavated?" he asked the major.

Quinn checked his PDA, accessing the CUBE mainframe. "They're down to the bottom level."

"So they've uncovered the EDOM pods and research area?"

Quinn nodded. "And the guardian that corrupted Majestic. It's being held under heavy guard but it doesn't seem to be active. Just like the one in the Mission under Mount Sinai seems to be off-line."

"Where are those guardians now?" Turcotte asked.

"I don't know. UNAOC has taken over all Airlia artifacts. Most likely they are still where they were found."

"Do you think it would be possible to reverse EDOM?" Turcotte asked him. He saw Duncan lift her head, listening intently now.

Quinn shrugged. "I have no idea. That's not my field of expertise."

"Find someone whose it is," Turcotte ordered. He nodded toward the door. "Tell the others to come in."

Che Lu, Mualama, and Yakov entered the conference room and sat around the table. Turcotte quickly updated them on what he thought had been done to Duncan.

"But we don't know who did this to her," Yakov said when Turcotte was done. "It could have been Artad's side; it could have been Aspasia's Shadow's."

"Well, we can assume it wasn't Majestic," Turcotte said. "Which means someone else has or had access to the same technology."

"Most likely garnered from Airlia artifacts," Yakov said.

Che Lu was rubbing her chin in thought. She looked at Duncan. "This means you cannot trust any memory prior to ordering Turcotte to infiltrate Area 51."

"I can't trust my memory and I don't know what has happened to me." Duncan held her hands up in defeat. "What now?"

"We need the Master Guardian," Yakov said. "And Excalibur. And we do not have much time."

"How long until Aspasia's Shadow's fleet is in range of Pearl?" Turcotte asked Quinn.

"A couple of days."

"Should she be listening to this?" Yakov asked, nodding toward Duncan.

"You want to shoot her again?" Turcotte snapped.

"We don't know who she is," Yakov pointed out. "*She* doesn't know who she is. And more importantly, we don't know who did this to her or why."

Turcotte rubbed his forehead, trying to relieve a pounding headache. "Let's keep it simple—we've got to do two things. Recover Excalibur and find the Master Guardian, which, according to Kelly, is in the second mothership. Does anyone disagree with that?"

There were no objections.

"I think we all understand the gravity of the situation," he continued. "It's not just the fleet that is approaching Hawaii or Artad's ultimatum to the Chinese government. I want you to think about what will happen if Aspasia's Shadow combines the Grail with the nanovirus he is using to control all those people. He will have an army of unkillable slaves that he can increase exponentially with every battle he wins. On top of that, imagine the horror of being controlled by the nanovirus while being immortal—it would be an eternal hell."

Turcotte placed his hands flat on the table and looked each of the people in the room in the eye, uncertain whether he could trust a single one of them and forced to accept, for the moment, that he had no choice. "So. First. Where is the second mothership that holds the Master Guardian?"

Quinn pulled another folder from his briefcase. "The

Germans were also searching for a mothership. They zeroed in on the legend of Noah's Ark."

"And?" Turcotte prompted.

In response, Quinn threw a black-and-white photograph of a mountain on the table. "They finally focused their search on Mount Ararat. It's the legendary location for where the biblical ark ended up. And we've learned there's a lot of truth to legends, haven't we?"

Turcotte picked up the photo. "How come no one's found it? Ararat's not exactly the most remote place in the world?"

"It is somewhat remote," Quinn said, "but more importantly, Ararat has always been in the center of political and ethnic turmoil. It's located awkwardly in a part of Turkey that juts between Iran, Armenia, and Azerbaijan. And the locals in the area are mostly Kurds, who have been fighting the Turks for centuries."

"Still—" Turcotte began, but Quinn interrupted him.

"The mothership we found here was hidden in a cavern," Quinn reminded them. "While there have been a few expeditions that have searched for Noah's Ark on Ararat, they all assumed it would have grounded on the surface after the Great Flood. At worst, they figured it might be covered by several feet of soil or caught in a glacier, not hidden in a cavern deep inside the mountain itself, like the mothership here was hidden."

"All right." Turcotte put the photo down. "Let's say the mothership and the Master Guardian are hidden under Ararat somewhere. What about the key—Excalibur? What was this stuff about Saga-something or another?"

"Sagamartha," Quinn said. He pulled out another photo. Again of a mountain and tossed it on the table. "That's what the Nepalese call Mount Everest."

Turcotte picked up the picture, recognizing the world's highest mountain. "Great," he muttered.

"A bouncer ought to be able to go anywhere on the mountain safely," Quinn noted.

"Why do I have a feeling it won't be that easy?" Turcotte said. "Yakov. The ark is yours."

"By myself?"

"Afraid of a challenge?" Turcotte didn't wait for an answer. "I'll see if I can get you some help. One thing to keep in mind—I don't think Artad has forgotten where he parked the damn thing."

"Understood," Yakov said.

"And Excalibur?" Mualama asked.

"I'm going after it," Turcotte said.

"I will help you," Mualama said.

Turcotte's instinct was to decline the offer, but he didn't want to leave Mualama alone. "All right. And check Burton's manuscript to see if that sheds some light on any of this. It would be nice to have an idea where exactly on Everest it is." He turned back to Quinn. "How soon can you have a bouncer ready for me?"

"Thirty minutes."

"OK." Turcotte looked around at the small group. "The plan is Yakov gets to the ark and the Master Guardian. I get to Excalibur and free it so that Yakov can use the Master Guardian to shut down Artad's and Aspasia's Shadow's guardians." He focused on the Russian. "You should be able to drop the shields and stop the nano-virus."

Yakov laughed. "That is all you want me to do?"

Turcotte slapped the Russian on the shoulder. "Hey, I only have to climb Everest. Want to swap?"

Yakov pretended to consider the proposal seriously for a few seconds, then shook his head. "I am much heavier than you. It is best you do the climbing."

"Always the practical one," Turcotte said.

• • •

Down the hall, Larry Kincaid was doing something he had
spent a career at NASA and JPL doing: looking at imagery
of an object in space. In this case, the object was Mars as
viewed through the Hubble Space Telescope.

The deeply rutted track in the red surface of Mars going
from Cydonia to Mons Olympus was obvious. He had taken
the time to count the number of mech-robots and come up
with over three thousand, but the amount seemed to be
growing hourly—more were leaving Cydonia than returning.

He could see the massive cut in the Mons Olympus escarpment. And now he saw the destination as the first of the
carriers began dumping their black cargo high up the slope
before turning to head back. The site was less than a mile
from the volcano's crest.

Other mech-robots were digging into the side of the volcano, excavating.

"What the hell are they building?" he wondered out loud
as the printer spit out the latest picture.

PACIFIC OCEAN

As the two attack submarines headed northwest toward
Hawaii, they increased speed. The nanotechnology was monitoring performance, transmitting the information back to the
guardian on Easter Island. The alien computer then sent back
the new design orders increasing the submarines' maximum
speed.

The changes increased the subs' speed to over seventy-
eight knots.

AREA 51

Turcotte looked up from the computer screen as Quinn appeared next to him. He had just finished typing in a brief query to Kelly Reynolds and was ready to hit the enter key, sending it through satellites into the stream of traffic going between the Alien Fleet and Easter Island. The US military was in a quandary about the message flow because if they cut off the Alien Fleet's access to the MILSTAR communications system, they would also have to cut off all their other forces, thus making the system useless. So far, they had elected to keep the system running and send messages to forces using ground encryption.

Turcotte hesitated because he was afraid the message might get noted by the guardian or Aspasia's Shadow, who might retaliate against Kelly. He'd phrased his query in a way that he thought only the reporter would understand and would seem innocuous to any sniffer program, but he understood he was risking her life with the message.

"What's up?" Turcotte asked.

The major pointed toward the status board at the front of the room. "We've got a dozen inbound choppers along with a large fixed-wing plane."

"Reinforcements?" Turcotte asked. Area 51 was operating at below bare minimums as far as personnel went, as orders from Washington had stripped most of their personnel. They had a half dozen people left from a regular staff of over three hundred.

"I've been trying to get us people," Quinn said, "but I haven't received any acknowledgments from the aircraft. They aren't responding to hails."

"Range?" Turcotte's attention was torn away from the message he'd been composing.

"Ten klicks and closing fast."

Turcotte was surprised to feel a kick of adrenaline, similar to what he had always felt before going into action. He knew that Washington—every government—was infiltrated by both alien groups in various ways. And even worse, there were the various human factions inside of each government now lining up in one of four ways: to side with Artad; to ally with Aspasia's Shadow; to try to be neutral; or to fight both alien groups and their minions.

Three out of four options did not bode well for what they were trying to do there at Area 51, Turcotte thought. Not good odds.

"Have you copied everything onto CD-ROM?" he asked Quinn. "The archive material, Burton's manuscript, all the Majestic records? Everything?"

"Yes."

Turcotte could see the small dots on the large screen closing. The choppers were over the lake bed.

"Take the disks, get the others, and go to a bouncer," Turcotte ordered.

"What do—" Quinn began, but Turcotte cut him off.

"Do it now!"

Quinn still paused. "The doctor took Duncan to the medical hangar on the surface to run some tests," Quinn said. "I can get Che Lu, Kincaid, and Mualama."

"Then do it!" Turcotte yelled as he hit the send key for the message, then ran for the surface elevator.

Five Apache helicopter gunships led the way, followed by five UH-60 Blackhawk helicopters carrying troops. They were low over the desert floor, less than twenty feet up and moving fast.

Ten miles behind them was a specially modified C-130

transport plane with large red crosses painted on the wings and high tail.

Turcotte could hear the choppers as he ran across the sand toward the medical building. It was about a quarter mile from the hangar doors and next to the runway tower.

An Apache helicopter swooped in front of him, 30mm cannon aimed directly at him. Turcotte ignored it, trusting that American soldiers, regardless of their orders, would not fire at an unarmed man. He reached the door of the medical building as a Blackhawk landed fifty meters away in a swirl of blowing dust. A dozen men dressed in camouflage jumped out.

Turcotte threw the door open. "Lisa!"

There was no response. He ran down the hallway and twisted the knob on the lab room. It was locked. Turcotte slammed his boot into the door, right above the knob. The wood splintered. He shoved it open and stepped inside. Duncan was on the examining table, her eyes closed. Turcotte rushed to her side.

"Lisa?"

He started as he felt a sharp jab in his right arm. He spun, open left hand slamming into the doctor's chest. The white-coated figure flew backward, syringe falling from his fingers. The doctor tried to get up and Turcotte hit him hard on the side of the head, knocking him unconscious.

Turcotte turned back to the table, trying to scoop Duncan up, but his arms were weak. He couldn't lift her. Turcotte strained, putting every ounce of effort he could muster into it. He slumped to his knees, leaning against the table.

He sensed people behind him. He collapsed, body turning as he did so. He was seated on the floor, his back against the table, unable to move at all. He couldn't even move his eyeballs. He could see a half dozen soldiers fill the room. Two of them picked up Duncan and carried her out. An officer knelt in front of Turcotte. The officer checked his pulse, then looked over his uniform, noting the various patches. The man bit his lip with indecision. Then he stood.

"Let's go," the officer ordered.

"But, sir, we're supposed to arrest all—" one of the men began.

"That's an order," the officer said.

The men and doctor exited the room, leaving a helpless Turcotte.

"Come on." Quinn ripped the laptop computer out of Che Lu's hands to lighten her load as they ran across the hangar floor toward the waiting bouncer. Yakov, Mualama, and Kincaid were already climbing up the side of the bouncer. The massive doors were partly open and they could all hear helicopters close by.

The snout of an Apache helicopter poked through the empty hangar doors. The multibarreled 30mm chain gun under the nose of the craft snooped about, linked to the sight flipped down in front of the gunner's eye. Wherever the gunner turned his head, the barrel of the chain gun followed. And the gunner was obviously now watching the five members of the Area 51 team scurry onto the bouncer.

Balanced precariously on the top of the bouncer, Yakov pulled a pistol out and aimed it at the gunship.

"No!" Quinn yelled as he reached the side of the craft.

Yakov's finger was on the trigger, but he hesitated.

Inside the Apache the gunner had Yakov square in the reticles of his HADSS—Helmet and Display Sighting System—a monocular just inches from his right eye.

"Warning rounds," the pilot ordered over the intercom.

The gunner turned his head slightly and squeezed the trigger. A burst of 30mm rounds—each the size of a milk bottle—ripped through the air and hit the skin of the bouncer five feet to the right of Yakov, ricocheting off.

Major Quinn was knocked off his feet onto his back as Che Lu slammed into his chest. He blinked and tried to get up, but the Chinese scientist was on top of him. He felt something wet soaking into his chest and when he looked down saw that a round had punched through the old woman's slight frame.

"Oh, God," Quinn whispered as he slid her to the floor.

Yakov slid down the bouncer and joined him, kneeling next to Che Lu and tenderly placing a large hand around her neck, searching for a pulse.

"She's gone," Yakov said.

"It can't be," Quinn whispered.

"Get on board," Yakov stood, the pistol in his hand. He brought it up and aimed at the cockpit of the Apache. He squeezed off six shoots in rapid succession. They impacted harmlessly on the armored cockpit.

Quinn tried to ignore the blood soaking through his uniform as he climbed onto the side of the bouncer, reaching up and taking Mualama's outstretched hand. The African literally pulled him up and tossed him into the open hatch. He quickly slid into the pilot's depression, taking the controls into his shaking hands.

Mualama was down next, followed by Yakov. Kincaid was strapping down gear as Quinn lifted the bouncer off the floor of the hangar. He accelerated directly toward the Apache blocking the opening. It bobbed left, narrowly missing getting rammed.

Two other Apaches made gun runs at the bouncer as it exited the hangar, firing just in front of the alien craft. Quinn ignored them, pressing forward on the control stick.

Everyone flinched as the Apaches circled back and fired

once more, rounds slamming into the side of the alien craft, the impacts visible via the strange ability of the skin to act like one-way glass.

Quinn accelerated the craft and they were moving over six hundred miles an hour within ten seconds, leaving Area 51 and Che Lu's slowly cooling body far behind.

Squads of soldiers entered the CUBE, arresting all those who had been left behind. They planted small explosive charges on every computer and communications device. As the red digits slowly counted down to detonation the men expeditiously exited the complex.

On the surface, the C-130 rolled down the runway and came to a halt, where the squad of soldiers waited with Duncan. The back ramp came down and touched the concrete. Four white-coated figures rolled a gurney off the ramp and up to those waiting. They put Duncan on the gurney and strapped her down. Standing inside the cargo bay was a fifth white-coated figure, a tall man with shockingly white hair and piercing blue eyes.

When they rolled the gurney onto the plane, he leaned over Duncan, checking her vital signs, even as the ramp began to close and the aircraft began turning.

As it roared down the runway, the charges inside of Area 51 detonated.

Inside Hangar One lay the body of Che Lu. From the Long March in 1934, through the agony of World War II and the subsequent Communist regimes, to watching her students die in Tiananmen Square, to the thrill of entering Qian-Ling, her journey was finally over in the most unlikely of places.

CHAPTER 9: THE PRESENT

PEARL HARBOR

Roberta Lockhart wore with pride the four stripes on the cuff of her blue jacket that indicated she was a United States Navy captain. From the streets of south-central Los Angeles, through the rigors of the Naval Academy, to the subtle racism and sexism of the active Navy, she had followed two rules her mother had taught her with unswerving obedience: Do your job better than anyone else and treat everyone with respect.

At the moment she was standing behind another black woman, twenty years her junior, a new rating assigned to SOSUS-PAC, Lockhart's command. To Lockhart the new sailor's sex or race made no difference—she was doing her job making sure the newcomer was trained as well as possible.

SOSUS stood for sound surveillance system. The first SOSUS systems were put together in the fifties and the sixties and laid along the Atlantic Coast—SOSUS-ATL. Then the Navy emplaced Colossus, which is along the Pacific Coast. Both were linked lines of passive systems submerged in the ocean, designed to listen for the movement of submarines through the water.

Those first two systems guarded both coasts of the United States, but as the Soviets deployed ballistic missile submarines that could stand far off the coast and lob their nuclear warheads into the heartland of America, it was realized they weren't enough.

In response the Navy emplaced systems just off the Russian coast, near the two major Soviet sub ports at Polyarnyy and Petropavlovsk. Since then, the Navy continued to add to the worldwide SOSUS web. A line of devices was emplaced off the Hawaiian Islands. Each receiver consisted of a cluster of hydrophones inside submerged tanks as large as the oil storage tanks just outside of Lockhart's command. The tanks were sunk to the bottom, anchored, then linked by cable. The cables were buried as the Soviets—and the Russians afterward—had a tendency to send trawlers dragging cable cutters near the systems.

All the systems were coordinated so that not only could SOSUC detect movement, but by comparing pickup timing from various sensors, Lockhart's people could draw at least two lines and pinpoint the emitter's location.

There was only one problem with the system: differentiating between friendly and enemy submarines. As part of their security, American ballistic submarines patrolled within large assigned areas at the discretion of their commanders, where it was more than likely that a potential enemy submarine would be in the same area.

The solution was simple but effective. Every friendly submarine had an ID code painted on its upper deck with special laser reflective paint. SOSUS could pinpoint a sub, then a FLTSATCOM satellite could fire a laser downlink toward the indicated spot using a high-intensity blue-green laser, which could penetrate to submarine depth and read the code.

Lockhart had been in Admiral Kenzie's office earlier in the day along with all the other senior military commanders on Oahu. The information that the fleet would sail the next day and essentially leave the islands undefended by sea had been met with shocked silence.

Even the Army's main unit on the island, the Twenty-fifth Infantry Division at Schofield barracks was on the move. All day she'd watched truck after truck of soldiers come into the port and troops walk up gangplanks onto the Navy ships.

Absolute secrecy had been Kenzie's number one directive. Only those in the room knew what was to happen but the media had picked up the activity and over the entire island there was a sense of near panic. Despite a blackout on news, rumors were rife of naval disasters and pending doom.

Lockhart knew she and her people would not be with the fleet when it sailed. She also knew what had happened to Task Forces seventy-eight and seventy-nine. Along with an Air Force AWACS flying patrol to the southeast, her people were the warning line for the island chain.

In Hawaii, particularly at Pearl Harbor, early warning was something on the order of a religion. Despite being over sixty years in the past, no one forgot what had happened on December 7, 1941. The *Arizona* Memorial was a daily reminder in sight of every person at Pearl.

"Anything?" Lockhart asked. It was a sign of the stress of the times that she asked. She knew her sailors would report anything out of the norm. She also knew the report from the satellites was that the enemy fleet was slightly more than two days out. Still.

"No, ma'am," the rating replied.

Lockhart walked across the dimly lit room to the other occupant, her senior enlisted man, Markin, and best "listener." She leaned close so the rating wouldn't hear. "Anything?"

"Pod of whales here." Markin tapped his screen, indicating a spot southwest of Maui.

"Maybe you should get some rest," Lockhart said. "There should be nothing—" Her mouth snapped shut as Markin held up a finger, indicating the need for quiet.

She waited.

After five long minutes, Markin slowly pulled off his headphones. "There's a strange sound southeast."

Southeast. Where the enemy was coming from, Lockhart thought. "Range?"

He checked his computer. "One hundred seventy-five miles, ma'am."

Too close, she thought. Too close. "What is it? Submarine?"

"I've never heard this before," Markin said. "Give me a minute, ma'am." He put the headphones back on and closed his eyes.

Lockhart walked over to her new rating. "Anything strange?" she asked.

The young woman hadn't heard the exchange with Markin, but she had seen that something was up. Her face tightened as she listened.

"There's something, ma'am," she finally said.

Lockhart noted that Markin had taken off his headphones and was looking toward her. She was torn. "What do you think it is?"

"Water, high pressure," the rating said.

Lockhart frowned, then went over to Markin. "What do you hear?"

"I've never heard anything like this before," he said.

"Water under pressure?" she asked loud enough to be heard by the rating.

Markin nodded. "Yes."

"Ma'am," the rating called out. "I heard something like this in school in Orlando."

"And?" Lockhart and Markin waited.

"The instructors had a tape of what they called prototype sounds. They said the Russians had a new type of sub on the boards that would utilize water-pressure propulsion. This is a very similar sound."

Lockhart frowned. "Range?"

"One hundred and sixty-five miles," Markin said.

"You just said 175," Lockhart said.

"And now it's 165, 164," he corrected.

"What can move underwater that quickly?" she demanded.

"Nothing man-made," Markin said.

"How fast is the contact?" she asked.

"Almost eighty-seven."

"Oh, my God," Lockhart muttered under her breath so no one could hear. "Any satellite scan?" she called out.

"Positive scan on both targets," another sailor responded.

Lockhart waited. "Report," she finally ordered when he didn't say anything further.

"Uh—ma'am, both have the same ID tag. The *Springfield*. But—" he paused, then blurted out—"the *Springfield* can't move that fast. And how can there be two?"

Captain Lockhart's face was hard as she picked up the hot line that connected her to fleet headquarters.

AREA 51

Feeling had been returning to Mike Turcotte's body for the past hour, from his extremities inward. He'd already tried getting to his feet a dozen times to no avail. He reached up and grasped the edge of the table and tried once more. He managed to pull himself up so that he was leaning against the table.

He felt hungover, his head pounding, his body unsteady. He looked about the examining room. A clipboard was next to the sink and he went over to it. Flipping it open, he noted several medical forms—results of tests the doctor must have run, along with two pages of notes in handwriting he could hardly read. There were also several X rays clipped to it. Turcotte ripped the papers and X rays out of the clipboard and shoved them in the cargo pocket of his pants.

He went to the door, carefully opening it, and peering

outside. As expected, no one was about. He moved as quickly as his pounding head would allow to the outside exit. He shoved open the steel door. It was night, a cool breeze blowing in from the surrounding desert.

A full moon had just risen above Groom Mountain and he could see relatively clearly. He saw the massive hangar doors set into the side of the mountain. Turcotte walked over and entered the hangar. A bouncer was missing and he felt a moment's relief, knowing the others had most likely escaped, then he saw the dark form lying still on the concrete floor. Not wanting to, he forced himself to go over. A pool of blood had spread out beneath the body.

Turcotte ignored the blood as he knelt and turned the slight figure over, knowing who it was before he saw her face. He scooped Che Lu in his arms and walked out of the hangar, across the runway, and into the desert.

EASTER ISLAND

Aspasia's Shadow slowly sat up and looked about the guardian chamber. The golden glow from the guardian bathed the entire area with its light. Six motionless Marines stood guard in the shadows near the tunnel. He lifted his arm and put his new hand in front of his face. He flexed his fingers, stretching the new skin.

He laughed, the sound echoing off the walls. He reached up and removed the *ka* from around his neck. He would never need it again. Millennia of dying and being reborn were over. He was immortal and this body would be his forever. The Grail, the carrot that the Airlia had held in front of humans from the very beginning, was his to do with as he willed.

He went to the guardian and made contact, checking the status of his forces. All was progressing well with the fleet. And there was an acknowledgment from his man in Iran, indicating preparations were going forth to seize the second mothership and Master Guardian. His team heading toward Everest was on schedule.

Perfect. It was time to let the humans know their options. He went to the tables holding the equipment that had been abandoned by the United Nations when they evacuated the island. He turned on a computer that had direct satellite contact with the UN.

AREA 51

Turcotte rode the elevator into the underground bunkers. His fatigue shirt was soaked with sweat and his hands covered with sand that had stuck to the perspiration. Dried blood encrusted the lower part of his pants.

A few lights were still working, flickering, showing the destruction that had been wreaked. The silence was unsettling. As he expected, the place was abandoned and Turcotte quickly retraced his steps to the surface.

Turcotte went to the runway tower and broke into the supply area. He grabbed a survival vest, checked the small radio to make sure it was working, ensured his SATPhone was still in his pocket, loaded up on a half dozen full canteens, then left Area 51 and headed out into the desert.

UNITED NATIONS

The men and women chosen for UN Alien Oversight Committee (UNAOC) had done little in the last several months other than observe. This was not because they lacked the will, but more that they lacked the knowledge of what was really going on in order to make a coherent decision. Added to that indecision was worry over the infiltration of their governments and the influences of Guides, Ones Who Wait, and the various human contingents that proclaimed one side or the other of the Airlia civil war to be the one to support.

While every member country of the United Nations had signed an agreement to abide by the decisions of the committee, the reality was that, as had been true for the history of the United Nations, countries only followed the agreement when it suited their interests.

Every country was supposed to surrender any alien artifacts they had in their possession to the UNAOC. So far, not a single item had been turned over. A large row had already erupted over the refusal of the Israelis to release artifacts, including the Ark, that they had taken from the Mission inside Mount Sinai.

Additionally, the militaries of all countries were ordered to coordinate with the UNAOC security panel. A few token phone calls had been made, but not a single troop, plane, or ship had been placed under UN command. All eyes were on the Pacific and the surviving American fleet there.

Given that the previous head of UNAOC had been assassinated by a Guide, the committee members not only felt powerless, they also felt threatened.

As they gathered at the conference table to listen to Aspasia's Shadow's message, the absence of the Chinese member was noted.

The screen on the laptop in front of each UNAOC member came alive with Aspasia's Shadow's pale face. He wasted no time on pleasantries.

"You have called me Al-Iblis. You humans have called me many names over the millennia in many places. I am Aspasia's Shadow, but I am more than he ever was. You killed him and stopped his space fleet, but you cannot stop me. You can only join me and reap the benefits I offer. Despite your transgressions I will forgive you. I am going to tell you the truth so that you know the reality of your tenuous situation.

"I possess the Grail. It holds the secret of immortality. I offer that to those who join me. I offer the might of my fleet and my other forces to those who join me. You know you cannot penetrate my shields or defend against my nanovirus or my Guides. You are powerless. Report back to your governments. Tell them to face the truth.

"You have a choice now. Join me or fight me or stand aside. But realize that your time is short. And Artad is awake. He has already contacted the mainland Chinese government. They have chosen to side with him. They will die because of that decision.

"Artad cares nothing for humans. His Shadow created the Black Death in the Middle Ages and almost wiped you off the face of the planet. Only I was able to stop it and save you as only I can save you from him now."

There was a pause, then Aspasia's Shadow continued. "And there is something else you must know. Something that Artad will not tell you. The reason why the Airlia came here to your planet so many years ago."

There was absolute silence in the hall now as everyone unconsciously leaned forward to hear what was about to be said.

"They—we—came here to protect you," Aspasia's Shadow said. "You humans are like newborns when it comes to the larger reality of the universe. There are many species among the stars. And some of them hate any life-form not their own. In this galaxy, there is a life-form we call the Swarm. They are a race of parasites unlike anything you could imagine in your worst nightmares. They were, are, the Airlia's Ancient Enemy."

Aspasia's Shadow grimaced as if remembering something particularly bothersome. "The Swarm have conquered many planets, destroyed many species, and long ago we came into contact with them. Even we don't know where their home world is. Some have said they have no home anymore, but just expand outward, consuming intelligent life wherever they find it. There is no communicating with them or negotiating. They exist to destroy."

Aspasia's Shadow pointed down. "They have been here, humans. On your planet. Scouts. I have protected you, destroyed their scout ship, and prevented them from communicating back to let their fleet know of your planet. If their fleet comes here, not even the Airlia can protect you.

"Their scouts can infiltrate any intelligent species, become part of them so that no one knows they are there. And when their fleet arrives, they destroy every living thing, consuming it so that their own forms can go on.

"Aspasia's mission was to protect you and help you. And he did so for many years. Your people were in caves when he arrived. He built Atlantis, brought civilization to humanity. It was a golden time.

"But then Artad came along with others—all cowards and deserters from the war against the Swarm. They wanted to hide here, to cut us off from our home system. There was civil war and then there was a truce. But still Aspasia stayed nearby to help defend you and you thanked him by destroying him.

"I am taking his place. I will continue to help defend your planet but you must join with me. It is in both our best interests to work together.

"Fight me and die.

"Stand aside and eventually you will be mine anyway and I will remember your lack of commitment.

"Join me and reap the benefits and be protected."

The screen went dead.

SEOUL, SOUTH KOREA

The South Korean president's hand shook as he took a sip of tea. The conference room was dark and slides appeared on the far wall, one after another, without a single comment from the American officer waiting close by.

General Carmody was the Eighth Army commander, the senior American officer in South Korea. The images he was showing President Pak had just been given to him by his G-2, intelligence officer. They were from a KH-14 Keyhole spy satellite that was on permanent station over the Korean peninsula. They showed something that hadn't happened in almost fifty years: Chinese troops crossing the Yalu River into North Korea and heading south. Tanks, armored personnel carriers, and thousand upon thousands of infantry were on the move. All heading south. Then the locations of the photos changed. Pak recognized the DMZ. There was no mistaking the fact that North Korean forces were mobilizing.

Finally, the last shot was displayed and Carmody turned the lights back on. They were the only two people in the room. The general sat down across from Pak. "We estimate at least two corps of Chinese troops have already entered North Korea with another three corps to follow on. Over a half million men."

"And the Seventh Fleet?" Pak asked. For decades South Korea had lain under the umbrella of protection provided by America's military. While most of the world had forgotten that the Korean War had never officially ended, it was never far from the minds of the people who inhabited the southern half of the peninsula.

"The Seventh is"—Carmody seemed to search for a nice way to put it, then he simply shrugged—"gone. We're abandoning Hawaii. That tells you where things stand."

Pak had already known that from his spy network. "So? What now, General? You have reduced your troop strength in my country to the point where your presence is merely a trip wire. Several thousand Americans whose death would be avenged. But there is no avenging force now."

An aide entered the room and handed a piece of paper to the president before withdrawing. Pak read it. "The UN has been issued an ultimatum by Aspasia's Shadow from Easter Island. Join him or fight him."

"What will the UN do?" Carmody asked.

"A vote is scheduled." Pak laughed bitterly. "In two days' time. Much too late for us."

"Aspasia's Shadow can't help us here," Carmody said.

Pak crumpled the paper and tossed it in the wastebasket. "Evil is evil and I believe these aliens are evil, whatever face they present."

"There is one possible course of action," Carmody said.

"And that is?"

"Tactical nuclear weapons. A preemptive strike into North Korea. Along the axes of advance."

Pak stared at the general. "Your government would authorize that?"

"I doubt it."

"Then why do you bring it up?" Pak asked. Carmody had been Eighth Army commander for two years. He was unique in that he was half-Korean, his father an American soldier, his mother a Korean his father had married during a tour of duty in the country. Carmody had grown up in the United States, attended West Point, and served all over the world, before returning to his mother's country to command his father's forces there.

"My government..." Carmody paused, searching for words. "Let me put it to you plainly, Mister President. There is great concern among my fellow officers about the integrity of my government. About how much the aliens and their followers have compromised the chain of command. This vote—I don't know how the United States will vote, but I agree with you that these aliens are evil. The Chinese have allied with Artad and I see nothing good coming out of that."

He paused, then continued. "I do not think that South Korea is very high on anyone's priority list in Washington right now."

"Detonating nuclear weapons against another nuclear power would be on Washington's priority list," Pak said.

"That's true," Carmody acknowledged. "But, Mister President, I think—" He was interrupted by a loud buzz that caused both men to start.

"It is the line to the North Korean president that we established last year. It has never rung before." Pak turned his chair and picked up a red phone, putting the receiver against his ear. Carmody got up and went to the far side of the room out of earshot and waited. When he heard Pak hang up he went back to his chair.

"The North Koreans are making an offer. They have allied with China, who have allied with Artad. We have the choice of joining them or dying. It seems our vote is here now."

"Your decision?" Carmody asked.

"I gave him my answer. We will fight."

PACIFIC OCEAN

With the shield turned off for the moment, the carriers *Stennis* and *Washington* adjusted course twenty degrees to the starboard so that their flight decks were facing directly into the wind. They were still a two-day sailing from Hawaii, over twelve hundred miles away, equaling a round trip of twenty-four hundred miles. Given that the range of the planes they were launching, F-14 Tomcats, even with external tanks, was only slightly over two thousand miles, the maneuver did not seem logical. And, the external tanks on the sixty planes gathering in formation and heading toward Hawaii did not contain fuel, which meant they had an effective range of only fifteen hundred miles.

The sixty planes also weren't flying at a rate to conserve fuel. With afterburners kicked in, they were flying at over Mach 2, fifteen hundred miles an hour so that they would arrive at Hawaii just as their fuel tanks ran empty.

Behind the planes the shield came back on and the carriers headed toward Hawaii.

THE STRAIT OF TAIWAN

Archaeological evidence indicates that humans have inhabited Taiwan for as long as ten thousand years. There were also signs that Japanese forces occupied part of the island in the twelfth century. The first Europeans to visit the island were the Portuguese in 1590, calling the island Formosa, which meant "beautiful" in their language. The Spanish attempted some settlements but were kicked off the island by the Dutch, who occupied it and neighboring islands in 1622.

In 1644 the defeated followers of the Ming dynasty retreated to Taiwan and expelled the Dutch, establishing a Ming enclave and also the precedent of the island being a refuge for those out of favor with the ruling force on the mainland.

After the British victory over China in the Opium Wars, the Treaty of Tientsin in 1860 opened two ports on Taiwan's west coast to foreign ships. Missionaries, both Roman Catholic and Protestant, weren't far behind.

At the end of the first Sino-Japanese War, China was required to cede Taiwan to Japan. Given their tenuous ties with the mainland, the inhabitants refused to be trade bait and rose against the occupying Japanese. This rebellion and the brutal attempts by the occupying forces to "Japanize" the inhabitants went on for over fifty years until the end of World War II and the defeat of Japan. Taiwan was returned to mainland control, but that was viewed by the inhabitants as negatively as the Japanese occupation had been. Once more they rebelled, and once more they were brutally handled, this time by their own countrymen.

However, on the mainland, things were not going well for the ruling Kuomintang (KMT) forces led by Chiang Kai-shek. Like those of the Ming dynasty before, the KMT retreated from the Communist forces to Taiwan. The Communists planned to invade the island, but these plans were put aside when American naval forces were sent to the strait between the mainland and the island. Subsequent to that, America poured over four billion dollars of aid into the country, viewing it as a bastion of "freedom" in a dangerous part of the world, and turning a blind eye to Chiang Kai-shek's and the KMT's depredations.

Gradually, rule on Taiwan shifted toward real democracy, just as the United States was shifting its focus from the island to the mainland. When Nixon visited Beijing in 1972, those on the island saw the handwriting on the wall. Formal ties between the US and Taiwan were broken in 1979 and in 1980 the formal defense treaty between the two countries lapsed and was not renewed.

The flagship of the Chinese Eastern Fleet was the destroyer *Qingdao*. It had engines made in Ukraine, a British combat control computer to aim its weapons, French helicopters, and weapon systems purchased from a half dozen other countries. The crew, however, was one hundred percent Chinese.

The *Qingdao* was in the Straits of Taiwan, a hundred-mile-wide stretch of water that separated mainland China from what it considered a wayward province in Taiwan. The strait had seen decades of posturing and bluffing between the navies of the two countries but all that changed as the targeting radar on the flagship located a Taiwanese frigate thirteen miles off its port bow.

The word had come from Beijing just ten minutes earlier. No choice was offered for Taiwan. The bitter blood between mainland China and the small island nation off its coast allowed for no resolution other than annihilation. Accordingly, the *Qingdao* launched a half dozen antiship missiles toward the Taiwanese ship. Two struck, causing massive damage and killing many sailors.

On both sides of the strait, the respective militaries geared up for all-out warfare.

THE GULF OF MEXICO

Lisa Duncan slowly opened her eyes. Her head felt heavy and she knew she'd been drugged. She was lying on her back, a pillow under her head, a white sheet covering her body. Looking up, all she could see was a steel ceiling with numerous pipes running across it. She swallowed and her ears popped, equalizing pressure. She could feel something around her arm and several leads taped against other parts of her body.

She heard a noise to her left and turned her head. A white-coated figure walked in. The man was tall and distinguished-looking, with silver hair and a short white beard. He pulled a stool out from a desk and slid it next to the table she was on.

"How are you doing?" he asked as he checked the readout on a medical monitor next to the bed.

Duncan's throat was dry and she tried to talk but only a croak came out. The man went over to a sink and returned with a small paper cup of water, which he carefully pressed against her lips. Duncan drank the entire cup, and then he pulled it away and retook his seat.

"Who are you?" she managed to get out.

"Dr. Garlin. The more interesting question is who are you?"

"Where am I?"

"The new Area 51."

"And you're the new Majestic." Duncan swung her legs over the edge of the table and sat up, holding the sheet tight around her body. The pounding in her head was fading rapidly. Looking down, she could see that the various leads attached to her body went to the monitor and there was a band around her arm with an IV pressed through it.

"Yes. That was a good guess."

"No guess," Duncan said. "It makes sense." She was looking about. "What kind of doctor are you?"

"An MD. Specialization—cellular structure."

"You want to find out what happened to me."

"Yes."

She nodded slowly, her head pounding with pain. "So what happened to me?"

"We have some ideas, but some of the data is still being processed."

"What's the charter of the new Majestic?" she asked. She was shaking her head back and forth, trying to work out the lingering effects of whatever drug she'd been given.

"The same as the old one," Garlin said.

"The old one didn't work too well."

"It worked well enough for almost fifty years," Garlin noted.

"Where are the others? Turcotte? Quinn? Yakov?"

"We don't know. We had to"—he paused, as if searching for the right words—"shut down the old Area 51."

"Why?"

"When Major Quinn had the CIA do a check on you, we were copied on the results, as we've been copied on everything going into Area 51. And you ask why we shut down Area 51?" He held up his hand as he ticked off reasons. "You've got Professor Mualama, who turns out to be a former Watcher—or is he former?

"Yakov. A Russian. Section IV was destroyed—all except him. Pretty convenient. And he came back from Moscow with a bug planted on him.

"Che Lu. Chinese. A country that now appears to be siding with Artad and preparing for war against both South Korea and Taiwan. And she just happened to be the first person to enter Qian-Ling in many centuries. How did she get permission from Beijing to do that when every other request was immediately turned down?

"Major Mike Turcotte. Involved in a questionable incident while working counterterrorism in Europe. He was then recruited by you to spy on Majestic; which bring us to you. You didn't even really know who you are, did you? And now you don't know what you are."

When Duncan tried to stand, he politely but firmly pushed her back onto the table. "Not yet. You need to know what's going on, so you understand what is at stake."

"I know what is at stake," Duncan said.

"Do you?" Garlin asked. "You don't even know who you are or where you come from." He leaned back slightly on the stool. "Do you know why the Airlia came to our planet in the first place so long ago? Why they fought, and continue to fight, a civil war? Why they were stranded here?"

"Do you?" Duncan threw back at him, but her voice was less combative as she contemplated his questions.

"Not yet, but we're working on it. Aspasia's Shadow just made an announcement to the UN. He claims the Airlia came here to help and protect us from another predatory alien species. Or at least Aspasia did. He says Artad is a deserter."

"Is that true?"

"Are you willing to believe Aspasia's Shadow?"

"Not really."

"We're taking a bigger view than the previous Majestic, especially as we know so much more than they did. We think understanding the Airlia would be pretty helpful in the current situation. Allowing us to act, rather than constantly react."

"How did you come into existence?" Duncan asked.

Garlin briefly stroked his short white beard as he considered her question. "We want you to understand the situation. We want you to cooperate. So far your actions have appeared to be loyal to our country, so we hope that if you believe what you hear, you will continue to be loyal to the best of your abilities.

"When the primary Majestic-12 was compromised by the guardian they discovered in South America at Temiltepec and the security of Area 51 breached, a plan that had been prepared over forty years previously was put into effect. For every member on the Majestic-12 committee, there has always been a backup selected. We"—he tapped his own chest—"had no idea we filled these positions, but apparently we were picked by the twelve primary Majestic members from within their own organizations based on detailed psychological profiles that practically assured we would be willing to step up and assume the primary roles once we were informed. The fortunate thing was that we were picked *before* the primary Majestic-12 was compromised by the guardian computer, so those chosen were chosen because they were projected to be loyal to the original charter for Majestic.

"It has worked as planned. Even as Majestic was being broken apart, with members dead or under indictment, twelve of us received a top-secret CD-Rom by special courier sent from the NSA vault. On each disk was a detailed report of Majestic's formation by presidential decree during Eisenhower's administration and a summary of its subsequent actions over the years along with all that had been discovered about the Airlia and their artifacts.

"Of course, there was no information about Majestic's

corruption after uncovering the guardian computer at Temiltepec in South America and bringing the alien computer back to Dulce. Still, the basic decree Eisenhower had given the original MJ-12 rang true to those of us who received the CDs—protect America at all cost from alien influence."

Duncan was silent, listening.

"We gathered a week ago at the designated time and location indicated on the CD—a small airfield outside New Orleans. A tilt-wing Osprey landed, and the back ramp opened up. There was no one in the cargo bay and the door to the cockpit was locked. We got on board and the plane immediately took off. It flew out over the Gulf of Mexico, staying just above the waves to stay off radar. The engines rotated up and we finally landed on board what appeared to be an abandoned oil rig, about a hundred miles from the nearest shore. The ramp opened, we got off, and the plane was back in the air and flying away.

"There was no one there. But we followed the directions on the CD, punched in the correct code on a keypad, and got into an elevator on one corner of the rig. It went down the one leg of the rig to the ocean floor, where an undersea habitat—this place—was attached. The new Area 51."

"How far down are we?"

"Three hundred feet."

"And you have contact with the outside world?

"A secure contact via satcom up top on the rig to the NSA. However, we're keeping quiet so far, just listening. We want to determine a valid course of action before we do anything."

"How come you didn't contact us at the old Area 51?" Duncan asked.

Garlin shook his head. "You still don't understand, do you?" He pointed at her. "We don't know who you are. We don't know whom at the old Area 51 we could trust. We're starting over with a clean slate.

"So far, we've done little other than try to keep track of the rapid flurry of events around the world. But when we received a report from the old Area 51 about what had happened to you, we acted swiftly, issuing orders with our presidential authorization."

"So you've kidnapped me," Duncan said. "Seems like something the old Majestic would do."

"The old Majestic protected America for almost fifty years," Garlin said. "Now it's our turn. And we want to be very careful that we don't get compromised like they did. We might be the last best hope for mankind."

"Why haven't you done anything?" Duncan demanded. "Why have you been hiding here while we fought the aliens?"

Garlin tapped her on the knee. "Because we were waiting for you. You're the key. You're immortal now. If we can figure out what happened to you, we think we can win this war and not just the next battle."

JERUSALEM, ISRAEL

The holiest city in the Christian world had never known such a gathering of people in the streets. The route had been announced on the news the previous evening and people had begun staking claim to a spot immediately, the numbers swelling through the night. Tens of thousands came in from the surrounding country as word spread.

Jerusalem was, in reality, several cities with a clear distinction between sections. The Christians flocked to the northwest, where the Church of the Holy Sepulchre was located, built over the site where Jesus was executed and the holiest place in Christendom. The northwest was Muslim territory, where the Dome of the Rock was located, the third most holy place in Islam, where the Prophet Muhammad made his ascent into heaven. In the southwest corner of the city were the remnants of the temple built by Solomon. Called the Wailing Wall by outsiders, the Jewish people preferred to call the area the Temple Mount. Ironically, on top of the mount is the al Aqsa mosque.

Like many others, Simon Sherev had traveled to Jerusalem when he heard the news. His duties at Dimona were minimal now that the nuclear weapons were staged forward. The country was on a war footing, like most in the world, and security was tight in the city. Sherev's clearance allowed him to get close to the open area in front of the Wall. The massive stone blocks towered above him and he noted that in keeping with tradition the women were on the right side, the men on the left. Sherev remembered the first time he'd been on that very spot, many years previously. It was a tradition that new recruits in the Israeli army made a forced march of over one hundred miles, ending at the Wall. That day Sherev had been profoundly moved, but looking back, he wasn't sure whether it was reaching the Wall or the fact that his training had been over.

To the left of the Wall was a stone gallery. He could see elite members of a counterterrorist unit guarding the entrance to where the Ark of the Covenant was being held. He could also see a large cluster of television reporters and their cameras nearby. Hasher Lakur was standing in a bright circle of lights, being interviewed. The fool, Sherev thought. Publicizing the Ark was one thing, but doing it there, in the most divided city in the world, was insanity.

He wondered how Lakur was explaining the Ark. Was he claiming it truly was the Ark of the Covenant that Moses had carried out of the captivity? In a way, that was true, but it was also true the Ark was an Airlia artifact. How would that go over? Sherev wondered. It was a desperate gambit at a desperate time. Sherev had seen the intelligence reports about the various Arab countries mobilizing. Could they finally bring together the *jihad* they had always failed to complete? Or would they fall on each other like jackals? Would showing the Ark unify long-suffering Israelis or sow fatal doubts?

The media circle around Lakur broke up and he went through the narrow gate into the holding area. Sherev estimated there were at least a hundred thousand people watching and he knew the video was being beamed to millions more. The security personnel had to link arms to keep the crowd back. Sherev noted the snipers posted along the top of the Wall scanning the crowd. He could hear the sound of helicopters in the distance and he imagined that several Cobra gunships were on standby.

A hush ran over the crowd as several rabbis came out of the gate. They were followed by a man dressed in the high priest's robes they'd recovered from the Mission in Mount Sinai. A ripple of excitement ran through the crowd as many recognized the garb: a white linen robe underneath a sleeveless blue shirt—the *meeir*—on top of which went a coat of many colors; a breastplate encrusted with precious stones, and on his head a crown of three metal bands. It was an impressive uniform, but everyone's attention shifted from the priest to the next group coming out of the gate. Four men stepped forward, two on each wooden pole, and between them they carried something large covered in a white cloth.

Even Sherev, an avowed cynic who had seen the Ark of the Covenant, was impressed. Maybe Lakur was right. He could feel something in the crowd as they watched the men carry the covered Ark to a table set just in front of the Wall. They set it down, then pulled the poles out of the metal loops. The priest stood in front of the Ark, arms raised, saying prayers.

Sherev frowned. A helicopter was coming closer, the sound intruding on the absolute silence of the crowd, the echo of the priest's words off the Wall. The priest reached out and slowly pulled the cloth off.

The Ark was three feet high and wide, by four feet long. The surface was gold-plated. On the arched lid were two cherubim-sphinxes shaped exactly like the Great Sphinx and the Black Sphinx that was hidden underneath it. Sherev knew they were part of the Ark's security system, but they only functioned if the Grail was inside. Since Aspasia's Shadow had taken the Grail to Easter Island, the ruby-red eyes remained dark.

The damn helicopter was getting even closer, somewhere just over the Temple Mount, Sherev's experienced ears told him. He looked up. A Cobra gunship came sweeping in, just clearing the top of the wall, then nosing over.

The pilot made no attempt to pull out of the dive. It slammed into the space just in front of the Wall. The Ark, the priest, the rabbis, all were enveloped in the fireball.

Everyone within a hundred meters of the crash site was killed. Sherev was knocked backward by the blast as he struggled to his feet. He ran forward shouting orders, passing dismembered bodies, a sight he had seen before many times in Jerusalem. He pulled a radio off one of the bodies and began issuing orders.

His Blackhawk helicopter appeared over the Temple Mount and descended, blades blowing the flames outward and clearing a space right over where the Ark had been—and still remained, Sherev realized, the artifact lying unscathed on the ground. He issued further orders and the Blackhawk landed next to the Ark. The side door slid open and the crew chief jumped out with a survival blanket in his hands, joining Sherev next to the Ark. Together they threw the blanket over the Ark, then carried it on board the chopper. Another crew member ran over to the body of the priest. The man was dead, exposed flesh burned, but the garments were untouched. He grabbed the body and dragged it to the chopper, wrestling it on board.

"Take off. Now!" Sherev ordered the pilot.

PEARL HARBOR

Captain Lockhart was in the shore command and control center of Pacific Fleet Command and could see on the large display radar the ships rapidly leaving Pearl Harbor in response to her warning. She glanced at the red dot moving swiftly on the screen to the southwest. Numbers below the dot indicated twenty minutes before the strange contact arrived. She knew the capital ships, including the carrier *Kennedy*, had been the first through the channel and into the open sea, turning west at flank speed as soon as they were clear.

Admiral Kenzie had given shore command to her. She'd almost laughed when he'd told her that before catching his helicopter ride out to the *Kennedy*. The glass ceiling against both her color and her sex had suddenly disappeared so that she could take charge.

"We have air contacts, rapidly closing," one of the radar personnel announced. A second later, another red dot appeared on the screen, farther to the southwest, but moving more quickly than the submerged contact.

"I thought the carriers were out of range?" she asked. The markings in the bottom right corner of the status board indicated how far away the two captured aircraft carriers were and Lockhart knew the basic statistical data for the planes those ships carried.

There was no answer. Lockhart realized that it was a foolish question. The alien forces were beyond the bell curve of normal military action.

"Launch what we have to interdict," she ordered.

From Wheeler Air Force Base, Kaneohe Marine Air Base, and other fields around the island, all the planes that couldn't be loaded onto the *Kennedy* scrambled and headed to the southwest. There were thirty-five planes in the makeshift squadron—a mixture of F-15s, A-6 Corsairs, and a few F-16s and F-18s.

Lockhart sat down in the command chair and watched war being played out on a large computer display.

AIRSPACE, PACIFIC

The two groups of planes closed on each other faster than four times the speed of sound. The encounter was brief and brutal. Each side had one shot and at the speeds they were flying, they were in range and then past each other in less than a minute. Twelve American planes were destroyed and twenty Alien craft.

As the remaining twenty-three American planes turned, the Alien squadron was already a hundred miles past them and closing on Hawaii.

PEARL HARBOR

Lockhart could see the red dot closing, the blue giving futile chase. The other red symbol representing the submerged contact was less than twenty-five miles off the coast. The last ship of Task Force Nimitz had cleared the harbor and was heading west.

She realized that both Alien forces—submerged and airborne—would arrive simultaneously. She felt as if she were in a dream—a nightmare—watching the dots approach on the screen. She got out of the chair and headed for the stairs.

She went up to the roof of the PAC-FLEET command building, overlooking Pearl Harbor.

There was a tinge in the eastern sky, indicating dawn was approaching. She blinked as two dozen Patriot missiles roared out of their silos from mobile launchers parked less than a mile away along the edge of Wickam Field.

She watched the long, bright rocket tails of fire race to the southeast. There were several flashes on the horizon as a handful of the Patriots struck home. She knew the bogeys were less than a minute out. She glanced toward the harbor. Nothing.

She heard the jet before she saw it. It came in low, less than twenty feet above the rooftop. There was a small flash, as it was right overhead. Lockhart twisted her head to follow the jet as it went inland, gaining altitude. She felt something on her upturned face.

Then she began screaming as the nanovirus tore in through her skin into the bloodstream.

All over the island, at every key military point, the Alien jets dropped their pods of nanovirus. At Wickam Field, four jets blanketed the entire field, then circled around and landed, safe inside the contaminated zone. One by one, the other jets came in from their targets and landed.

In Pearl Harbor, the two modified submarines searched for the fleet, but returned to the main channel without a target. Then they locked onto the only ship they could find in the harbor, transferring nanomachines into it.

CHAPTER 10: THE PRESENT

VICINITY AREA 51

Turcotte sat perfectly still in the shadow of a boulder, watching a rattlesnake slither across the sand ten feet away. He estimated he was eight miles from Area 51. He felt better than he had in a long time. Free of responsibility. His concern over Lisa Duncan's kidnapping was somewhat offset by the fact that he had no real idea who she was. Of course, she didn't either, he realized, as he continued to watch the snake move away. He viewed the abandonment of the underground base at Area 51 as a potential blessing, meaning he might be free of the responsibilities he had assumed since arriving there in an undercover role.

Turcotte had always been a loner and he felt at ease by himself in the desert. His father had been killed in a logging accident when Mike was eight and the next summer he had gone to the same camp to work, doing odd jobs. He did that for the next few years until he was large enough to heft a chain saw and wield an ax. The toughest schools the Army put him through years later—Ranger, Special Forces, Scuba—were nothing compared to his time in the forest. It was rough work among even rougher men and Turcotte brought his check home each month to his mother.

The snake was gone, slithering between two rocks. Turcotte felt his SATPhone vibrating in his pocket. He pulled it out and looked at the small screen. It displayed Quinn's SATPhone number.

Duty.

It was a word beaten into him as a child and reinforced as an adult. He almost laughed out loud as his mind slid to the words he'd been forced to memorize as part of his officer training—the speech MacArthur had made at West Point upon accepting the Thayer Award in 1962: *"Duty, honor, country. Those three hallowed words reverently dictate what you ought to be, what you can be, what you will be. They are your rallying point to build courage when courage seems to fail, to regain faith where there seems to be little cause for faith, to create hope when hope becomes forlorn."*

The damn West Point graduate tactical officer at his college had made all the ROTC cadets memorize it, just like cadets at the Academy were forced to.

Turcotte flipped the phone open. "What?"

THE GULF OF MEXICO

"Do you know why humans die?"

Lisa Duncan was startled by the question. Garlin had been drawing blood, for the seventeenth time, according to her calculations and the number of needle marks in her arms. What was fascinating was that the first needle puncture wound, made just an hour earlier, was gone, all healing at a remarkable rate. She worried about the IV. What was he putting into her? How had they knocked her out? What did they know that she didn't?

"Old age?"

"What is old age?" Garlin went to the door and passed the tube outside, before coming back to sit on a stool in front of her.

"Cells get old," Duncan said. "They stop reproducing."

"Do you know why?"

"No." She gave him a cold smile. "Remember? My past is not real. So maybe my medical knowledge is bogus too."

"Do you know what a telomere is?"

Duncan shook her head. There were no lingering aftereffects of whatever drug they gave her, she realized. She felt fine, better than she could ever remember.

"At the end of each chromosome in every cell in your body are small bits of DNA called telomeres. These bits serve a very important purpose. The telomere acts as a protective cap to keep the chromosome from unraveling at the ends with each cell division. After approximately a hundred divisions a cell runs out of telomeres. After that, the chromosomes begin to degenerate with every cell division. Eventually, the cell dies as the chromosome damage accumulates."

Garlin paused, looking down at his hands. Duncan could almost see him testifying before a congressional committee. Then she had to think for a moment—had she truly testified in such a manner as she had envisioned?

Garlin continued. "You age because as you lose telomeres in your cells, your body is like a clock winding down. Eventually you will not have enough good cells to perform some essential task somewhere in your body and one of your vital systems will fail.

"We first became aware of this about fifty years ago when the geneticists Paul Hermann Müller and Barbara McClintock discovered that the telomeres keep chromosomes from fusing end to end, which could lead to chromosome breakage and loss as cells divide. But not only do they keep cells from fusing, they maintain the integrity of the cell itself. This is vital when you start considering the basic gene structure of the human."

Duncan rubbed her arm over the puncture marks, noting that even the latest one was fading. "Why do we run out of telomeres? If they're so important, it seems that the body would make them in order to protect itself."

"Good question," Garlin said. "And it brings up an interesting paradox. To make telomeres, you need an enzyme called telomerase. Normal cells, however, for some reason after birth, don't make telomerase. In fact, the only time we've managed to discover telomerase synthesis inside the human body after birth is in cancer cells. That's one of the reasons why it's so hard to kill cancer."

Duncan frowned. "That doesn't make sense. The enzyme we need for longer life is only produced by cancer, which kills us?"

"This is still a relatively new field," Garlin said. "We have started at the very basics. In the seventies we first studied telomeres in protozoan ciliates, single-celled organisms that propel themselves with hairlike projections called cilia, rather than in mammalian cells. At that time, ciliates were much easier to work with because they have many more telomeres per cell than do mammalian cells. These organisms have two nuclei, and during the formation of the larger of these, the so-called macronucleus, the chromosomes break up into fragments that then replicate, producing from twenty thousand to as many as ten million pieces of DNA, each of which becomes capped at both ends by telomeres. In contrast, a human cell has only ninety-two telomeres, two for each of the forty-six chromosomes."

"But we've mapped human DNA," Duncan noted. Something about what Garlin had just said bothered her, but she couldn't put her finger on it exactly and she forgot about it as he continued.

"Only very recently," Garlin said. "Bear with me. I want you to understand this. As study in this field progressed, some surprising things were learned. Elizabeth Blackburn of the University of California, San Francisco, in the early seventies discovered something quite strange about the molecular regions around the telomere. She found that the sequence for telomeres was very short and repeated numerous times, around sixty. This was surprising because at that time the only DNA that had been examined closely—in bacteria and viruses—did not have repeated sequences.

"Expanding to other organisms, other researchers found the same thing—a repeating code in the telomeres. Yeast for example. This led researchers to believe all telomeres were like this. When we finally isolated the first human telomere at Los Alamos, we found a repeating sequence TTAGGG— where the T stands for thymine, the A for adenine, and the G for guanine. What was strange was that all other telomeres— the ciliates, yeast, etc., only had thymine and guanine."

"Why are we different?" Duncan asked. She wondered why he was giving her so much information—first about the new Majestic, and now about this. It was as if he felt she had some information that he expected her to give in return. She realized it was a subtle interrogation technique, one Mike Turcotte might have used.

"Good question," Garlin said. "We'll get to that. Not only do telomeres protect cells from degrading and losing chromosomes, we found they did other things, much more subtle. By extending the ends of the chromosomes with repetitive, noncoding DNA, they prevent the gradual loss of genetic information that would otherwise result from a quirk in the way DNA is replicated. The polymerase enzyme that copies the DNA can't reproduce both strands of the double-helical molecule all the way to the ends. As a result, chromosomes would get progressively shorter with every cell division and essential genes would gradually be eroded. This doesn't happen because the cells can add telomeric DNA to the incompletely replicated ends of the chromosomes."

"In other words," Duncan said, "it keeps our gene pool in line."

"Right. The yeast work showed that when linear DNAs

tipped with ciliate telomere sequences are put into yeast cells, they subsequently acquire yeast telomere sequences. This indicated that the yeast was able to add sequences de novo to chromosomes."

Duncan held up her hand as she tried to follow. "Are you saying the telomere changed to adapt to the new cells?"

"Yes."

She knew what Garlin was telling her was unusual and she also knew he was leading up to something about what the Grail had done to her.

"Telomerase," Garlin continued, "is unlike all other enzymes we've studied. In addition to protein, it contains an RNA component, which serves as the template for synthesizing the telomere repetitions and the reproduction of the genetic makeup of the host. This suggests that the enzyme might be an intermediate in the evolution from the RNA world to the current world of DNA and protein."

"That's why unicellular organisms are basically immortal," she said. "Because they have telomerase, they can replenish their DNA that would otherwise be lost every time the cell divided."

"Correct," Garlin said. "And why humans aren't. Since we don't have telomerase, our telomeres shorten every time our cells divide. Sperm and egg cells have the longest telomeres. We start dying the second we are conceived and our cells start dividing and multiplying."

"Why?" Duncan asked.

"That's the thing that's puzzled researchers. If a single cell organism can have telomerase, why can't we? And it's more than just about dying, we're also talking about repairing cell damage."

Duncan's hand went to her lower chest where Yakov's bullet had killed her. There was no sign of the wound even though less than a day had passed since she had been shot.

"Telomeres support the activity of the RAD9 gene," Garlin said. "RAD9 halts the growth of cells whose DNA has been damaged, which suggests that telomeres are part of the cell's damage-sensing system."

"So if we could produce the enzyme telomerase," Duncan said, "we could keep our telomeres active, protect our cells as they reproduce, and be immortal."

"It's not that simple," Garlin said. "Researchers have actually done experiments, trying to make immortal cells. They introduced oncogenes from simian virus 40 into cultured cells to activate telomerase. Many of the cells died, but some survived and continued to divide with active telomerase, which stabilized their telomeres."

"Why the difference?" Duncan asked.

"There were abnormal chromosomes in the cells that survived. The problem with the research so far," Garlin continued, "is that, as we told you earlier, the only cells we've discovered in humans that have active telomerase are cancer cells. In actuality, most of the medical research in this area so far hasn't been focused on immortality but on developing inhibitors to block the telomerase in cancer cells so they'll die.

"Some researchers at the University of Colorado have succeeded in cloning the gene that activates telomerase in human cells. This has led to two hopes—one that we can develop targeted inhibitors that will attack telomerase in cancer while not destroying healthy cells and secondly that we might activate telomerase in healthy cells to slow down aging and cell degeneration.

"We think that telomerase activation may be a necessary step for all tumors. The reason for this is that most cancer cells are immortal. Cancer cells, unlike normal cells, can divide indefinitely in tissue culture if given adequate nutrients. Normal cells have a limit of fifty plus or minus ten divisions, the Hayflick limit, before they grow old in culture and stop dividing. The ability of cancer cells to keep dividing is believed to arise from the activation of telomerase. Therefore if telomerase is inhibited then the telomeres in cancer cells will shorten and will act as a brake on the cancer cell growth."

"And my telomerase?" Duncan asked.

"It's active."

"Do I have cancer?"

"No." Garlin stood. "You're immortal as far as we can tell. Not only that, but you can replace damaged cells rapidly, as evidenced by your recovery from your gunshot wound."

"How did this happen?"

"The Grail did something to you," Garlin said. "We know the end result—your cells actively produce telomerase—but we don't know how the Grail did this." He turned for the door. "But we will discover it."

QIAN-LING

Artad strode through the main cavern of Qian-Ling, noting the various containers, followed by a half dozen of his kind. The shield generator, a spinning cylinder forty feet long, produced a low hum that pervaded the entire enclosure. He stopped in front of one of the containers right next to the large shield generator and placed his six-fingered hand on a panel. One side slid up, revealing a smaller version of the generator, about ten feet long, resting in a black metal cradle with wheels.

He turned and gestured to his followers. An Airlia got on either side of the generator and moved it out of the container. They followed Artad with it as he continued through the cavern. He paused in front of an intricately designed replica of a dragon—ten meters long, half that wide, with a long arced neck ending at a serpent's face with dark red eyes. Short wings extended from each side. The metal skin glittered, as bright as the day thousands of years ago that Artad had captured it from Aspasia's Shadow's forces. It was known in Chinese lore as Chi Yu, the dragon beast from the south.

A ramp, just below the tail, was open, revealing the interior and the pilot's seat. Artad turned to the Airlia behind him and quickly issued orders in their singsong language. Then Airlia and the two pushing the generator went up the ramp. They secured the generator inside and settled down into the seats. The ramp slowly rose and closed.

Using the same drive as the bouncers, Chi Yu rose into the air and turned toward a tunnel that led to the outside world. It disappeared into the tunnel as Artad returned to the room containing the guardian. He turned off the shield wall briefly to allow the flying dragon to depart, then reactivated the wall. He then went over to the guardian and reestablished contact in order to plan the next stages of the war.

IRAN-TURKEY BORDER

Only seventeen miles away. General Kashir could clearly see Mount Ararat directly ahead from his position standing in the top hatch of his armored vehicle. Seventeen miles away and across the border, which was just a quarter mile in front of him. Kashir's vehicles were on the crest of a small rise, the rest of his column hidden behind him. He could see the border post where a handful of Turkish soldiers were on duty. He had no doubts that he could overrun the post quickly. The issue was what would happen in the seventeen miles on the way to Ararat and then on the slopes of the mountain itself.

He knew that his country was gearing up for war, although the enemy had yet to be determined. There was talk of renewing conflict with Iraq. Others said there would be *jihad* against Israel, where all the Muslim countries would set aside their differences and destroy the rogue state once and for all. Kashir thought the first was more likely than the second. His mobilization of a mechanized regiment was lost in all the activity and he knew he would not be missed for a while in his own country. The Turks were a different matter.

Still, he knew he had no choice. He must go to Ararat and do as ordered. He told his driver to move forward while waving his arm to the troops behind, indicating they should follow. Two dozen tanks and twice as many armored personnel carriers lurched forward.

The guards saw the convoy coming and stood uncertainly in the road behind their thin wooden pole. One of them, an officer, stepped up just behind the pole and put his hand up, indicating for Kashir to stop. The general responded with a burst from his fifty-caliber machine gun.

The front of his APC crashed through the barrier. Other vehicles were firing, killing the guards as they tried to run away. Kashir had his driver pull off to the side to let the tanks take the lead.

He put the binoculars to his eyes and looked toward the mountain. So close, yet he knew so much could happen in the next seventeen miles. He keyed his radio.

"Faster!" he ordered.

NEVADA DESERT

Mike Turcotte climbed up the side of the bouncer and slid inside. Quinn, Mualama, Kincaid, and Yakov watched him enter. Turcotte could smell the fear coming off them, no matter how much they tried to control it. They all knew they had been targeted for death and just barely escaped. He'd learned early in his military career that fear was a part of combat and could not be dismissed.

"What happened to Che Lu?" he asked, noting the blood splattered on Quinn's uniform.

"She was killed." Quinn's hollow voice indicated his shock.

"I know that," Turcotte said. "I just buried her. How did she die?"

"Ricochet off the bouncer. Killed her instantly."

Turcotte sat down on the floor of the bouncer feeling the little energy he'd gained drain from him. His earlier suspicious thoughts about the old Chinese professor and her timing of the opening of Qian-Ling had faded away as he dug into the sand with his bare hands. He remembered her concern for him when he had searched for the Mission.

He looked at each of the four closely. Quinn was in the pilot's seat, a laptop extended across him, screen glowing, but his eyes were dull. Yakov, the large Russian, was standing, his presence filling the interior, the top of the bouncer just inches above his head. Kincaid had his own laptop clutched in his hands. And Mualama—Turcotte frowned as he looked at the African archaeologist. His initial impression of fear and anxiety from those inside didn't extend to Mualama, who appeared quite unconcerned about recent events. A metal briefcase was at his feet and Turcotte assumed that it held Burton's manuscript.

"What have I missed?" Turcotte asked. "Major?" he said in a sharper voice, getting Quinn's attention.

Quinn answered. "I've got no contact with anything at Area 51 and—"

"The equipment was destroyed and everyone left there arrested," Turcotte said succinctly. "Area 51 is shut down. Who did it?"

"Uh—" Quinn was flustered. "I don't know."

"They were Americans," Turcotte said. "Were they under the influence of Guides?"

"They were military," Quinn said.

"Acting under whose orders?" Turcotte pressed.

"They had an ST-6 clearance," Quinn said. "I've accessed the NSA and copied some of their transmissions."

"We have an ST-6 clearance," Turcotte said. "Who else has one?"

"We *had* an ST-6," Quinn said. "Not anymore."

"Who else has one?" Turcotte asked again.

"Majestic—and us after them—were the only groups that had one as far as I know," Quinn said. "ST-6 was invented by Eisenhower specifically for Majestic so they could operate in case of alien attack."

Yakov was nodding as if this made perfect sense. "So there's another Majestic."

"Why do you think that?" Kincaid asked.

"Because that's the way covert organizations operate," Yakov told him. "Always have a backup. Which also means if they were willing to destroy Area 51, that there is another Area 51 somewhere where they're operating from and where they've taken Duncan."

Turcotte listened to the Russian and agreed with the logic, but he also thought that would require a hell of a lot of efficiency on the part of the US government, something his years of service had indicated didn't happen often. He was tempted to ask Yakov where the backup for Section IV was, but refrained.

"What is our backup?" Kincaid asked.

No one answered that.

"Aspasia's Shadow sent a message to the UN," Quinn said. He turned his computer around so they could gather and look at the screen. The message played through to the end, then Quinn closed the top.

"Truth and lies mixed together" was Yakov's summation. "The issue is—which was which?"

"It doesn't matter," Turcotte said.

"Why not?" Yakov asked.

"Because Aspasia's Shadow isn't really human," Turcotte said. "And Artad definitely isn't. We could spend the rest of our lives trying to figure this crap out, but that's the bottom line. Even if Aspasia came here long ago to protect the planet, it might be a case where the cure was as bad as the disease. He certainly hasn't been a friend of mankind over the millennia. Nor has Artad." Turcotte remembered something. He reached into his pocket and pulled out the medical papers he'd taken from the clipboard and handed them to Quinn. "I want you to check these."

"Yes, sir."

"Are we going to stay here in the desert forever?" Yakov asked.

"We can't trust the government," Turcotte said, "so we're going to have to go to a place where we can trust who is in charge."

"And that place is?" Yakov pressed.

"Head for North Carolina," Turcotte ordered Quinn.

"And then?" Yakov asked. "Do you persist in searching for Ms. Duncan?"

Turcotte stared at the Russian, meeting his gaze. The silence lasted several seconds. "She's not a priority right now."

Yakov nodded. "That is a good decision, considering we don't even know who she is."

"We do what we planned on doing. The Master Guardian and Excalibur. Nothing's changed."

Yakov raised a bushy eyebrow. "How can you say that?"

"We're alive," Turcotte said. "We've got a bouncer. We've got all our data. We're still in business." He looked around at the others. "Everyone agree? I think it is what Che Lu would advise us to do."

Slowly the other four nodded.

"Good. Let's get going, then."

STRAIT OF TAIWAN

The naval battle in the Strait of Taiwan was over quickly. The Taiwanese navy fought bravely but had never expected to face the brunt of the Chinese navy without any American aid, despite the lack of a standing treaty. There had been a tacit assumption among the ranking officers of Taiwan's military that an aggressive move by the mainland would be met by a strong response from the United States and Japan simply in light of those countries protecting their own interests in the Far East. The Americans simply had no forces to deploy. The Japanese were quiet, calling up their reserves but keeping all their forces inside their borders.

The air battle was lasting longer, but the Chinese commander didn't wait to gain complete air superiority. The invasion fleet set sail across the hundred-mile-wide stretch of water, every ship packed with troops. Overhead, Chinese rockets, guided by technology stolen from the West, roared through the air. Massive explosions peppered key military targets throughout the island. Half the rockets, though, were aimed at population centers to spread fear and panic. Their warheads contained chemical and biological weapons of mass destruction.

It didn't quite work that way, though, as the Taiwanese, most having spent their entire life under the specter of potential assault from the mainland, reacted with fortitude. Every male of age on the island had served his required time in the military and was then placed in the reserves for the rest of his life. They kept their weapons at home and when the sirens had gone off indicating the beginning of the conflict, they kissed their families good-bye, directed them toward their shelters, and went to their local call-up center. The men reported to their induction centers and the women and children to bomb shelters, all donning their gas masks and protective suits. As the Chinese fleet appeared offshore, the beach defenses were manned and ready.

One of those who waited for the invaders on the beaches was General Chang Tek-Chong. The general had planned and prepared for years for this awful possibility but he had never envisioned the current scenario in his darkest nightmares. Even though there was no formal treaty with the United States, it had been tacitly assumed that an aggressive move by the mainland would be countered by American forces. But there were no American forces in the western Pacific except for those stationed in South Korea. Taiwan was on its own.

The general was typical of many of those who were defending the island in that he was actually part of an army that traced its roots to the invading KMT army, which now faced another invading force from the mainland. Tek-Chong's father, Tan, had been illegitimate, the result of a liaison between a Japanese police officer and a Taiwanese woman. Despite this poor beginning Tan had become a police officer, then a lawyer. When the KMT invaded, he'd been arrested and tried for treason. He'd been tortured, then dragged through the city streets. When a soldier ordered him to kneel, Tan had refused and met his execution standing, with a smile on his face.

Tek-Chong kept a black-and-white photograph taken by a KMT officer of his father's execution in his wallet. It showed him the moment before death, the muzzle of a pistol pressed against his right temple. The fortitude and proud stance of his father was something that Tek-Chong had always tried to emulate.

Like that earlier conflict, the only difference between the two sides fighting now was an ideological decision made before the lifetimes of almost all those who died. It was a difference being exploited by Artad to expand his new empire.

CHUNCHON, SOUTH KOREA

Camp Page was less than ten minutes' flight time from the DMZ. The camp consisted of a long runway and a cluster of hangars and barracks surrounded by a cinder-block wall topped by barbed wire. Parked along the runway were two American army units. One was an attack helicopter battalion of Cobras. The other was a lift company of Blackhawks. The mission for the Blackhawks was highly classified. They were the transportation for the tactical nuclear warheads the United States kept in South Korea. The warheads were housed eighteen minutes' flying time away in an underground bunker that was the most secure place in South Korea. They included nuclear warheads for the eight-inch howitzer battalion of the Second Infantry Division, along with nuclear mines that would be emplaced in already prepared positions along major axes of advance.

With the heightened tensions in the area, the entire unit was kept on a three-minute alert, pilots and crew chiefs living in the hangars, next to their aircraft. When the Klaxon indicating a scramble sounded, it was almost a relief for the men and women who dashed to their helicopters and started the engines. One by one, the Blackhawks rolled out of the hangars and lined up on the airstrip until all eighteen were in line. Then, on the order of their commander, they all lifted into the air and turned to the southeast toward the bunker. As the choppers cleared the edge of the compound a flurry of SAM-7 antiaircraft missiles sliced into the air, striking home. All eighteen helicopters were destroyed in less than ten seconds.

The North Korean commandos who had crossed the border the previous night and crept down to their hide positions outside the airfield were hunted down and killed by the South

Korean forces, but they had accomplished their mission. The tactical nuclear warheads remained secure inside the bunkers as North Korean and Chinese forces crossed into the DMZ.

EASTER ISLAND

Kelly Reynolds felt like a shadow trying to hide in the dark. While there was a good chance she wouldn't be seen she also could do little other than observe. She had no sense of her withered body, just a core of self, that existed next to and mostly in, the guardian computer. She had been watching the data flow for a long time, and she was getting better at discerning the component parts. It was as if she were standing next to a hundred-lane-wide superhighway with thousands of cars shooting by at very fast speeds. After a while, she was, in essence, able to start noting the colors and makes of various cars. There was much happening and she caught glimpses of a number of plans.

She knew of the nanovirus at Pearl Harbor and the failure to find the remainder of the American fleet. If she'd been able to control her body she would have smiled as she sensed Aspasia's Shadow's anger over the failure to complete the coup de grace of the American military in the Pacific. But she could also sense his overwhelming confidence that this was just a minor setback and that his ultimate victory was inevitable.

The guardian on Mars still maintained a communications link with this guardian. She was confused by this data stream, as it appeared that Aspasia's Shadow was in essence ignoring the few surviving Airlia at the Cydonia Base on Mars despite a series of entreaties from them.

The Alien Fleet approached Pearl Harbor with more submarines being built in the hold of the *Jahre Viking*. Aspasia's

Shadow was issuing new orders, directing the fleet to adjust course and search for the surviving American ships and convert them.

Guides around the planet were attempting to rally people to Aspasia's Shadow's cause and subvert their own governments. Tapping into satellite communications and then into the Internet, the guardian, as directed by Aspasia's Shadow, was issuing orders to those Guides, directing them to cause as much dissension as possible to keep the world from forming a united front and to spread propaganda regarding Artad.

The infected people on the surface of the island went about the tasks designated to them by the guardian.

The nanotechs widened the tunnel to the thermal power source underneath the island.

All were part of the information and communication flow. Kelly could also see the truncated avenues of communication that she knew had been to other guardians around the planet. And the major break, the line that had once been connected with the Master Guardian but had been severed so long ago. She also "saw" that the guardian was opening up its end of that communications link, as if preparing for the other end to open also.

And in the midst of all this she saw it. The name Johnny Simmons. Like a flashing light.

She homed in on the thin data flow with his name. It was piggybacked on a GPS signal to the Alien Fleet. Unnoticeable, unless someone was looking for that specific name. There was no reason for the guardian to notice, nor Aspasia's Shadow, but for Kelly it was a bright shining light.

She accessed the data stream.

Turcotte wanted more information. About Excalibur. The Master Guardian. The request was like a jolt of energy as it gave her a purpose. She came farther out of the shadows into the guardian's data field to search for the information.

THE COLONEL JAMES N. ROWE
SPECIAL OPERATIONS TRAINING
FACILITY, NORTH CAROLINA

The Special Operations Training Facility was located forty miles west of Fort Bragg and had been established during World War II as a training base for the Eleventh Airborne Division. A couple of decades later it served as the place where Colonel Bull Simon trained the Son Tay Raiders in preparation for their mission into North Vietnam. Years after that, Charlie Beckwith had utilized the area to prepare his Delta Force commandos for their ill-fated mission into Iran. It was now home to the field division of the Special Forces Qualification course as well as constantly being utilized by Delta Force, the Air Forces Special Operations Wing, and CIA covert forces as a training area.

In the nineties the fixed training site had been named the Colonel Rowe Training Facility, after a Special Forces officer who had escaped imprisonment in North Vietnam and was later assassinated in the Philippines. At the present moment, given the heightened state of alert for the US military, the Rowe Facility was empty, the instructors and students shipped out to the Special Forces Groups to get them up to strength. Next to the camp, there was a full-sized airstrip.

Thus, when Quinn brought the bouncer to a hover outside a large, rusting hangar, there was no one there to see. Turcotte exited, slid open the large doors, the rusted metal squealing in protest. Quinn flew the bouncer inside and landed it. They all exited and looked at Turcotte, waiting for the next step.

Turcotte checked his watch, then nodded to himself as

he heard the whop of helicopter blades approaching. He went out of the hangar onto the runway and looked to the east, in the direction of Fort Bragg. A Blackhawk helicopter painted flat black came in low over the trees, circled about, and landed forty feet away. The side door slid back and a quartet of heavily armed men in unmarked fatigues exited. While two took the flanks, two others ran up to Turcotte.

He held his hands up, empty palms forward. One of them started to pat Turcotte down, but a fifth man who had just gotten off the helicopter called out: "That's all right. Secure the perimeter."

Turcotte snapped a salute even though the fifth man wore no insignia. "Colonel."

The man returned the salute. "Major."

Turcotte turned to his fellow refugees from Area 51. "This is Colonel Mickell. Delta Force commander."

Yakov nodded, remembering the assistance Mickell had given them during the mission taking down Devil's Island. Turcotte quickly introduced the others, then they moved inside the hangar.

"What do you need from me, Mike?" Mickell asked.

"First, no word of our existence."

Mickell nodded. "That's a given."

"Second, local security. We can trust no one."

"I'll leave the four I brought with me and send you a dozen more for outer perimeter. All men I trust."

"Third," Turcotte said, "we need one of your mobile command posts." He knew that Delta had perfected a two-van setup that was mobile and could link into the secure military communications system anywhere in the world. It wouldn't be as good as Area 51, but it was the best they could do under the circumstances.

"We're stretched pretty thin," Mickell said. "There's a lot of stuff going on around the world. Communication has been lost with Hawaii. North Korea has invaded the South with Chinese support. Taiwan and the mainland are going at it. The Middle East is going nuts, especially with Saddam dead."

"Do you have a mobile command post available?" Turcotte pressed.

"Why don't you clue me in?" Mickell asked in turn.

Turcotte figured that was a fair enough request given that the colonel was putting his military career, and most likely his life, on the line. "We think we have a way of stopping Aspasia's Shadow." He quickly briefed Mickell on the Master Guardian he suspected was hidden inside a mothership on Ararat and Excalibur being on Everest.

"All right," Mickell agreed, when Turcotte was done. "I'll have a command post out here as quickly as I can."

Turcotte walked out of the hangar and stood on the runway. He'd trained here at Camp Rowe many times in his army career, often preparing for real-world missions overseas. A slight breeze blew over the pitted concrete, making him shiver. He had a feeling this next mission was going to be harder than any he had ever been on before.

He pulled the collar of his battle dress uniform tighter around his neck.

CHAPTER 11: THE PRESENT

GULF OF MEXICO

"When you partook of the Grail," Dr. Garlin asked, "did anything else happen?"

"The minute I put my hand in," Duncan said, "it took over my body."

"What about before?"

" 'Before'?"

"You were in the Hall of Records," Garlin said. "The Ark was there. You were wearing the robes and crown of a priest. The only things you didn't have were the stones. Did anything happen before Aspasia's Shadow gave you the one stone?"

Duncan frowned. "There was a connection on the top of the Ark. Leads. That went to the crown I was wearing."

"And you made the connection?"

"Yes."

"And?"

"I saw something when I was connected to the Ark," she said. "Something strange."

Garlin leaned forward slightly. "And that was?"

"I saw a mothership," Duncan said. "I was inside it. There were bouncers in cradles."

"The main hold of a mothership," Garlin said. "Similar to what was found inside the one at Area 51."

"Yes."

"What else?"

"I saw the Ark." Duncan closed her eyes, replaying the

vision. "An Airlia was putting the Grail inside of it. They put it on board a bouncer. The large bay doors opened. We were about a mile up in the air. We were over water. I saw a talon fly by. The bouncers began flying out of the hold. Going in different directions." She fell silent for a moment, her face tight as she drew up the memory.

"Perhaps that is how the Airlia arrived here," Garlin said, "and began—"

Duncan held up a hand. "No. It wasn't. It wasn't how they arrived here. Because when the talon passed by below the hold I saw its shadows."

Garlin frowned. "What?"

"Shadows," Duncan said. "Plural. There were two suns in the sky of this planet. It wasn't Earth."

"It makes sense the Airlia would have traveled to other worlds," Garlin said.

"But taking a Grail and an Ark to other worlds?" Duncan asked.

"Interesting," Garlin said. "Two suns. We're going to run a full-body MRI on you."

Duncan seemed resigned. "What do you hope to discover doing that?"

"We have Majestic's EDOM data. We want to see if you've been—" He paused, searching for the right word, but Duncan interrupted with a sharp laugh.

"Changed?"

"We know you've been changed by the Grail," Garlin said. "We want to find out what else has been done to you. Before the Grail."

PEARL HARBOR

If a nanovirus could be disappointed, the collective swarm that controlled the humans at Pearl Harbor would be expressing that emotion. The hope had been to catch the remaining American fleet in the Pacific in the harbor and absorb the ships and crews into the Alien Fleet that was still approaching. With that combined might, the next step would be a multipronged assault on the West Coast of the United States.

Instead, the harbor was empty, everything that could move having gone to sea. As per commands from Easter Island, scout planes were sent out searching while the nanovirus spread, taking over all shore personnel. Civilians were ignored for the time being as they had no useful skills and there was no present need for cannon fodder. The exception was any type of communications off the island. All radio, telephone, TV, and satellite transmitters were seized, the personnel running them absorbed via the nanovirus. Oahu was cut off from the rest of the world. The other islands in the Hawaiian chain held little interest for Aspasia's Shadow and were ignored.

In the hills above Pearl Harbor, members of a few Special Forces A-Teams and a couple of SEAL squads crouched in the jungle and observed, radioing reports back to both the fleet and the United States. The reports were intercepted by the alien forces, and squads of infected Marines began to spread out from Pearl Harbor, searching for the teams.

In the harbor itself, the nanovirus did find one ship of the line, albeit not in working order. That, however, was more of a challenge than a problem. The nanovirus began constructing nanomachines that went to work on the submerged ship.

KATHMANDU, NEPAL

McGraw and Olivetti arrived in the middle of the night, the F-14 Tomcat landing on the main runway at Tribhuvan International Airport exactly as programmed by the guardian. Their incisions were healed with the aid of the nanovirus and the adjustments that had been made to their bodies had been adapted to. As the plane came to a halt, the two SEALs saw the headlights of a vehicle approaching. They slid back the canopy and stiffly climbed out of the aircraft.

McGraw had an MP-5 submachine gun and as a pickup truck pulled up the plane, he slid back the bolt, loading a round into the chamber. A man got out of the truck, yelling something in Nepalese, obviously not pleased with the middle-of-the-night arrival. McGraw shot him through the forehead.

The two SEALs pulled their gear out of the plane and threw it in the back of the pickup. There didn't appear to be any other activity at the airfield given the late hour. McGraw slipped on a set of night-vision goggles as he got behind the wheel of the truck. He turned the headlights off and the goggles on as Olivetti got in the passenger side.

McGraw scanned the airfield, then spotted what he was looking for: a pair of helicopters parked near a hangar. He drove the truck over to the choppers. One was a vintage Russian-made MI-17, a large cargo chopper. The other was more modern, a French-made Ecureuil AS350B.

The two men paused, looking at the two for a moment, then they loaded their gear in the back of the Ecuruil. McGraw went over to the hangar and broke in. He found an office in one corner. Searching the top of the desk, he found a list of phone numbers and names. He ran his finger down until he found the Nepalese word for pilot.

He dialed the number and when a confused voice answered, he simply said the Nepalese word for airport, then hung up.

Twenty minutes later, headlights cut through the night, approaching the hangar. A door opened and an angry man stepped out, yelling in Nepalese and looking about in the darkness. Olivetti stepped up next to the man, shutting him up by the succinct method of slamming the barrel of the MP-5 across the man's mouth, smashing teeth.

The pilot dropped to his knees, hands going to his mouth, blood gushing out. Olivetti put the muzzle of the submachine gun next to the pilot's head, finger on the trigger. McGraw knelt in front of the pilot, spreading a map on the tarmac, shining a flashlight on it.

"Sagamartha," McGraw said, tapping a spot on the map.

The man looked up, confused.

"Sagamartha," McGraw repeated, then pointed at himself, Olivetti, then at the helicopter, and finally at the pilot. Then he pointed to the northeast.

The pilot shook his head, a movement that was cut short by Olivetti jabbing the muzzle sharply against the man's temple. The man said something in Nepalese. When the pilot realized they didn't understand, he thought for a moment, then pointed at the helicopter, indicating he needed to get something.

McGraw gestured and Olivetti let the man get up. They walked over to the helicopter and the pilot opened the door, then pulled out a logbook. He flipped through until he came to a certain page. He shoved it in front of McGraw, his finger on a certain part. A number and letter: 6100M.

Then the pilot put his finger on the map, at the same point that McGraw had pointed to. "Sagamartha," the pilot said, and tapped the number: 8848M. He then waved one hand horizontally and shook his head.

McGraw's expression didn't change. He ran his finger along a road that ran east out of Kathmandu, then turned to the north, crossed the border into Tibet, then looped around again to the east. His finger came to a halt north of Everest.

The pilot frowned, started to say something, then realized the situation and his mouth snapped shut. McGraw pointed toward the helicopter, then jerked his thumb up. Olivetti added emphasis by jamming the muzzle of the MP-5 into the pilot's ribs hard enough to cause him to double over. Cursing, the pilot climbed into the pilot's seat and strapped himself in, as the two SEALs climbed in and shut the doors.

The pilot started the engines.

PETHANG RINGMO, TIBET

A cold wind blew from the south across the stone veranda that faced the army barracks. It was always cold there and the air was thin at over a mile-and-a-half-high altitude. The barracks overlooked the small village of Pethang Ringmo, where less than a hundred hardy souls lived. The village was at the end of an often-washed-out track that could be negotiated in good weather by a four-wheel-drive vehicle.

Despite centuries of self-rule, Tibet was occupied in 1950 as Communist China sought to expand its sphere of influence. For nine years an uneasy peace existed in the land as the Dalai Lama tried to rule in conjunction with the invaders. That changed in 1959 when the country rose up against the interlopers. Thousands of Tibetans, including the Dalai Lama escaped, seeking asylum in India.

It's estimated that since that time, over a million Tibetans who were left behind have died as a result of the occupation and the attempts by China to make it a Chinese province. It is believed that these efforts at genocide and repopulation have succeeded to the point where there are a million more Chinese living inside Tibet than natives. Of the six thousand monasteries that existed prior to the occupation, only twelve remain, the rest destroyed, many as a result of target practice by Chinese artillery. Reports had filtered out that the Chinese were sterilizing Tibetan women and also dumping nuclear waste in the country.

All those things meant little to a Chinese major who stood on the barracks' stone balcony. He had been stationed in Tibet for another reason altogether. At the moment he was staring at the three people in front of him, then down at the orders he'd been faxed from Beijing. The fax was signed by the president himself, so there was no doubting whether he would comply. The people had arrived via helicopter less than ten minutes ago. The major, who only went by one name in the climbing community—Aksu—was a short wiry man with leathery skin. He had summited Everest twice, once from the south and once from the more difficult northern approach, blazing a new trail in from the northeast, rather than the accepted northwest route. According to these orders, he was to take these people up the northern route.

Even here, far from the capital, word of the fighting in Korea and Taiwan had reached the major's ears. He wasn't certain how these strangers fit into all of that, and the fax explained nothing. It grated on the major that the three were obviously foreigners with their pale skin, red hair, and eyes hidden by sunglasses. Even more than that, though, what truly rankled him was the fact that he could tell they weren't climbers. And their leader was a woman.

"Everest is no place for amateurs," he brusquely informed them.

Lexina nodded. "I know."

Aksu spit into the gravel that lined the runway. "One of five who go up, die."

"We only need one of us to come back," Lexina said.

"Why do you need to go?"

"We need to recover something from the mountain."

"What?"

"I cannot tell you that."

"If you tell me what it is you seek," Aksu said, "my team will get it."

"No. We must go."

Aksu turned away from the three and looked to the southwest. The horizon was lined with white peaks, but there was no mistaking Everest. Aksu had been on all sides of the great mountain and there was no doubt that the view was more spectacular from this side. The triangular shape of the peak was visible, despite being over eighty miles away. It was a clear day, which was unusual, as the peaks were normally embroiled in clouds. He also knew, though, that the weather could change in a matter of minutes.

"It will take two weeks."

"We don't have two weeks," Lexina said.

"It is impossible to go any faster. You must spend at the very least a week at base camp to acclimatize to altitude. If you go up too quickly you will suffer cerebral edema. Your brain will swell. You will die."

"We have been prepared for the altitude," Lexina said.

"The only way to prepare for altitude is to be at altitude," Aksu said simply.

"Major." Lexina's voice took on an edge. "You have your orders."

Aksu shrugged. "We leave in one hour."

DIMONA

The Blackhawk settled down inside the secure perimeter of Dimona and Sherev relaxed slightly. He'd been listening in on the secure military net as they'd flown out of the carnage in Jerusalem. There were those already claiming the suicide attack on the Ark had been the act of Arab terrorists and were clamoring for war, demanding that Israeli conduct a preemptive strike against her surrounding enemies. Sherev thought such thinking and demands premature.

He was proven right as a new report indicated the pilot was Israeli. A captain. An Orthodox fundamentalist. As several men carried the covered Ark into the bunker, Sherev shook his head. Zealots were dangerous people. He knew they were scared because of reports that the Ark of the Covenant wasn't made by man as the Bible said. And it wasn't made according to God's instructions. And it didn't carry Moses' tablets. It was alien. And that meant many things that people believed and underpinned their faith on were lies. Sherev knew that when people's faith was threatened, the core of their existence was also threatened.

For the moment he was content to put the Ark back in the vault and wait to see how the burgeoning world war was going to be played out. However, he felt a sense of anxiety deep in the pit of his stomach, knowing full well that inactivity was the worst of all options in military and covert operations.

THE GULF OF MEXICO

Garlin opened the door and gestured for Lisa Duncan to enter the room. He'd retrieved her from the examining room just a moment ago and brought her down a corridor. She saw no one else during the short trip. It was as if the two of them were the only occupants of the new Area 51. The new room held a massive machine with an opening in the center from which a human-sized metal stretcher was extended. A white sheet covered the metal.

"Have a seat." Garlin indicated the stretcher.

Duncan sat down and waited as Garlin washed his hands. He came back with an IV needle.

"What's that for?" Duncan asked.

"We're going to do several things at the same time and compare the results," Garlin said. "This machine is not only an MRI but also a CAT scanner and PET." He continued talking as he expertly slid the needle into the back of her hand. "The MRI will give us not only a cross-section view of your body, but also give us an idea of what's happening biochemically. This IV will put a solution in that targets the telomerase. The PET scan will give us an idea of what's happening with that."

The IV was in. He rolled over a hanging solution and hooked it to the tube. "Do you know how an MRI works?"

Duncan shook her head.

"Three stages. First, you are placed in there." He indicated the large machine. "It's a cylindrical magnet that will create a steady magnetic field thirty thousand times stronger than the Earth's magnetic field. Then the body is stimulated with radio waves to change the steady-state orientation of your body's protons. Then we shut off the radio wave and the machine basically, for lack of a better term, listens to your body, picking up the electromagnetic frequencies emanating from it at certain frequencies."

Garlin had his back to her now and was looking inside a black medical bag.

"It's really quite amazing," Garlin continued.

"What do you hope to discover?" Duncan asked. The table she was sitting on was cold and she didn't fancy the idea of lying inside the machine for however long the process took.

"How your body comes back to life," Garlin said.

"What—" Duncan began, but she didn't get another word out as Garlin spun about, a pistol in his hands and fired, all in one smooth movement. The round hit her in the chest, splintered through a rib, tore a path through her heart, and exited, slamming into the metal wall behind her. The impact knocked her body backwards onto the table and she was dead by the time Garlin walked up to her. He swung her legs up, orienting the body, then pressed the button that slid Duncan's lifeless body into the machine.

THE COLONEL JAMES N. ROWE
SPECIAL OPERATIONS
TRAINING FACILITY

Turcotte turned his head away from those gathered around the table and peered out of the hangar doors. He was still, as if listening.

"One of—" Larry Kincaid began to say, but Turcotte held up his hands, indicating silence.

After a minute, Turcotte shook his head. "I thought I heard something. Or"—he paused, uncertain—"I felt something." He turned to Kincaid. "What were you going to say?"

"One of Professor Nabinger's coordinates is on Mount Ararat," Kincaid said. He had Che Lu's notebook and had been examining the information inside.

The survivors of Area 51 were inside the hangar next to the runway. Besides the bouncer, two trailers also filled the inside, cables looping from them to numerous antennas set on the roof of the hangar. Colonel Mickall was also present, coordinating their support through his Delta Force channels.

The others gathered around as Kincaid made a pencil mark on a map. "Right here."

"The Ahora Gorge." Yakov read the small letters. The spot was just to the northeast of the peak of the mountain. "It is high up."

"About thirteen thousand feet lower than where I'm going," Turcotte noted.

"I have a simple question," Yakov said.

"Yes?" Turcotte waited.

"If this mothership is hidden in a cavern like the one was here, how do I get into this place, considering no one has reported finding it over the centuries?"

Turcotte turned to Quinn. "How did they get into the mothership hangar here? And how did they find it in the first place?"

"They found it," Quinn said, "when survey teams at the beginning of World War II noticed a magnetic anomaly in the area coming from inside Groom Mountain. They tunneled in and found the cavern and mothership."

"Are you sure of that?" Turcotte asked.

Quinn shrugged. "No. It's what I was told. It could be a cover story. Who knows what the truth is?"

"I'm not going to be able to do much tunneling on Ararat," Yakov said. "How do I get into the cavern?"

"Demolitions," Turcotte said. "Otherwise called tunneling in a hurry. Find a cave or a crack or something and blast your way in toward the coordinates."

Yakov frowned. "Not the best plan."

"The best we can do right now," Turcotte said, "and I think the right now is the more important aspect."

"We shall see," Yakov said.

"Also . . ." Turcotte paused.

"Yes?" Yakov prompted.

"There will most likely be others seeking the Ark. Perhaps they will know the way in."

Yakov nodded, understanding what Turcotte was telling him.

Turcotte turned to Kincaid. "Did Che Lu have any coordinates on Everest?"

"Not that I can see," he said. "Nothing close."

Mualama spoke up. "Excalibur was put on Everest by a rogue group of Watchers under the command of Myrrdin—Merlin. It is doubtful that Nabinger would have picked the coordinates up from High Rune markings."

"How do you know that?" Turcotte asked.

Mualama held up Burton's missing manuscript. "It's in here."

"Nice to let us know that now," Turcotte said.

"I translated the manuscript in the order you wanted me to," Mualama said. "Remember? Information on the Grail and the Mission was the priority."

Turcotte didn't buy that explanation. They'd been totally dependent on Mualama to translate Burton's text, written in ancient Akkadian. His information about the location of the Mission's base under Mount Sinai had been accurate but Turcotte had to wonder if there was anything else the archaeologist was holding back. In fact, they had to trust that Mualama had brought forth the entire manuscript, given that the African had traveled all over the world tracking it down.

"What does Burton say about Excalibur?" Turcotte asked.

"According to what Burton learned at Avalon," Mualama said, "Merlin came there after Arthur died and took Excalibur from the Watcher of Avalon, Brynn. The Watchers didn't know where he took it, but in the course of tracking down the scepter for the Hall of Records, Burton came across stories about a special sword and indications it had been taken by Merlin toward southern Asia—beyond the edge of the known world at that time.

"When Burton was stationed in India, he was part of a group that mapped the northern districts, in the foothills of the Himalayas. As was his wont, he disguised himself and went among the locals, listening to their legends and stories. And he heard tales that a magical sword had been brought from the West many years ago by a sorcerer and taken high into the mountains, to the roof of the world."

"That doesn't give me an exact location," Turcotte noted. "Everest is a big mountain."

"The entire point of putting it up there was that no one could get to it," Mualama said. "Or get up there, recover the sword, and make it down alive."

"People have climbed Everest," Turcotte noted.

"Only in the past fifty years," Mualama said. "And from what Burton wrote about what he heard, it's not on the very top, but close to it, on a portion of the mountain that is very difficult to get to. In a place where climbers heading for the top wouldn't go."

Something didn't sit right with Turcotte about all of this. "If Burton knew where it was hidden, what about Artad? And Aspasia's Shadow? Do they know?"

Mualama shrugged. "I would imagine so. After all Kelly Reynolds got the information out of the Easter Island guardian, right? Aspasia's Shadow certainly has access to the same resource."

"Why hasn't anyone recovered it, then?" Turcotte asked.

"It would have broken the truce," Mualama said.

Turcotte shook his head. "Hell, both sides have broken the truce numerous times over the years."

"I don't know," Mualama said, shrugging.

"Perhaps"—Yakov drew the word out—"activating the Master Guardian would have had much the same effect as activating the interstellar drive of the mothership. Perhaps it would draw in this enemy of the Airlia—the Swarm?"

"How do you know that?" Turcotte asked. That was the thing that had started all this, when Majestic had planned on test-flying the mothership and Turcotte had stopped them at the last minute.

"I don't know it," Yakov said. "But while both sides broke the truce, neither side attempted to fly a mothership until recently and that seems more an automated response by Majestic's guardian than a plan. Perhaps there are aspects of the truce both sides tried to respect."

"Too much conjecture," Turcotte muttered. "And remember, Excalibur was used during Arthur and Merlin's time. I don't like the idea of wandering around on Everest looking for a sword that could be hidden anywhere. Hopefully we'll get another message from Kelly with the exact location."

"Ah—" Colonel Mickell held up a hand.

Turcotte paused. "Yes, sir?"

"Mike, you have any idea what it's like to be on Everest?"

"It's a mountain," Turcotte said, looking down at his boots.

"No," Mickell shook his head. "It's *the* mountain. Two of my men were on an expedition there last year. They didn't make it to the top. And they were the best climbers we have. You can't just go up there," Mickell added. "You have to acclimatize over a long period of time or you will die."

"I don't have time to acclimatize," Turcotte said. "I'll be on the bouncer. It won't take but a couple of minutes."

"Mike." Mickell said the one word like a slap in the face.

Turcotte's eyes couldn't meet the colonel's. Finally, he nodded. "I know, sir. Nothing ever goes as planned, but I don't see what I can do other than just go."

"You can be prepared for the worst," Mickell said. "We did some research after our men came back. We don't expect to have to operate on Everest but we do have to plan that we might have to conduct a short-notice operation at extreme high altitude someday. That's the major reason we sent our two men up there."

"And?" Turcotte was anxious to be going. He could hear an aircraft landing on the runway and from the sound of the propellers, he knew it was a C-130—Yakov's ride to Turkey.

Mickell glanced at his watch. "As soon as I heard where you were going I alerted my people. A chopper should be here any minute with our high-altitude packet and one of my men who was part of the expedition.

"The problem is oxygen, Mike. The minute you get above twenty-five thousand feet you're in the death zone. Your body starts dying. You only have about one-third the oxygen you're used to at sea level."

"People have climbed it without oxygen, though," Turcotte noted.

"Yeah," Mickell allowed. "Sixty. And an equal number who tried it without have died. Like those odds?"

"I assume your man will have oxygen for me to use," Turcotte said.

"Even among those who use oxygen one-sixth die. And all of them take weeks to months to acclimatize at high altitude before making a summit attempt."

"So you've got oxygen in this packet, right, sir?" Turcotte repeated.

"Mike, it isn't just lack of oxygen that's a danger. There's pulmonary edema, cerebral edema, hypothermia—"

"Sir—" Turcotte looked his superior officer in the eyes. "I've got to go. Whatever you've got in this packet beyond the oxygen that can help—"

Mickell suddenly seemed to notice all the others gathered around. "Mike. We never really planned on doing this. Unless—"

Turcotte nodded and completed the statement. "Unless there was absolutely no other option."

"Right."

"So what do you have besides oxygen?" Turcotte asked, not really wanting to hear the answer.

"Blood packing. Drugs. Experimental stuff that has never been used."

"OK."

Mickell didn't argue, accepting Turcotte's decision. "The

man I'm sending with you not only made the climb, but he's also a medic. He can prep you on the way there."

"All right." Turcotte looked around. "Anyone have anything else before we split up?"

Quinn spoke up. "I'll continue to go through the archive information you got from Moscow and I'll reread what has been translated of Burton's diary."

"Whatever you get, forward to Yakov and me," Turcotte said.

"Yes, sir."

A Delta Force soldier popped his head in the hangar. "Anyone want a ride to Turkey?"

"I'll walk you out to the plane," Turcotte said to Yakov. He turned to Mualama as the two headed out. "Make sure all the gear is loaded on the bouncer."

A specially modified C-130 transport aircraft was fifty meters away as they exited the hangar, engines running, back ramp down. Turcotte stopped just short of the ramp. Twenty Delta Force commandos were already inside, geared up and ready to go. Turcotte didn't envy them the long flight to Turkey. Colonel Mickell's staff had already coordinated in-flight refueling for the trip.

"Good luck." Turcotte shook Yakov's hand.

"You also," Yakov said.

"I'll meet you in Turkey," Turcotte said as he stepped back from the ramp.

"I will see you there." Yakov stood in the shadows as the ramp slowly rose and the top came down from above. Turcotte walked away from the plane as the prop blast washed over him. The smell of burning fuel was one he always associated with C-130s and parachuting. He waited as the plane accelerated down the runway and rose into the air, banking toward the east. It was quickly out of sight, hidden by the pine trees surrounding the airfield.

Turcotte paused as a Blackhawk helicopter swooped in. The side door opened and several Delta operatives got off, carrying gear toward the hangar. Mualama directed them toward the bouncer.

Colonel Mickell waited for him with a tall soldier with graying hair. "Mike, this is Jim Morris."

The medic had a large plastic case in each hand, so Turcotte just nodded. "I got your blood types from the colonel. We should be good to go."

Turcotte had always trusted Special Forces medics. They were highly trained and often, on missions to developing nations, worked as doctors, dentists, and surgeons. "You ready to go?"

"Yes, sir."

Turcotte turned to Mualama. "You ready?"

The African nodded.

"Let's do it, then."

CHAPTER 12: THE PRESENT

TAIWAN

As the first wave of mainland forces headed toward shore in their landing craft, Tek-Chong waited in his command post bunker eight hundred meters inland. He saw the golden dragon flying to the north about four miles up the beach, but like his comrades did not know what to make of it.

The Taiwanese forces put aside their shock and opened fire as soon as the mainland craft were in range, only to receive their second, and much more devastating, shock as their projectiles hit a shield wall projected by Chi Yu that covered the Chinese forces. Their bullets were stopped and shells exploded harmlessly. The weapon superiority that Taiwanese commanders had counted on to counter the numerical edge of the mainland forces was lost. The first wave hit the beaches, the ramps dropped, and thousands of men stormed ashore under the protection of the shield wall.

Despite the fact that he could see that the artillery wasn't penetrating the invisible shield in front of the landing forces, Tek-Chong ordered his forces to keep firing. He watched as rounds smacked harmlessly into the same shield and thousands of mainland troops poured ashore untouched, establishing a beachhead.

Not certain what to expect, Tek-Chong held his post. He could see the mainland forces digging in, setting up their artillery, deploying armor, all with impunity. The most difficult and dangerous part of an invasion was being accomplished without a loss.

Reluctantly Tek-Chong ordered his forces to cease firing in order to save ammunition. He kicked the concrete wall of his bunker as he watched the mainland forces deploy.

His frustration was gone in an instant, though, when the mainland artillery suddenly opened fire. Tek-Chong screamed into his radio for his forces to fire back as the shells impacted among his forces. He realized the shield was down, but for how long?

The mainland troops fired ten volleys while his artillery managed to respond with three before the mainland ceased fire. His forces' next volley impacted on the shield and he called a halt. The pattern repeated five minutes later and Tek-Chong realized that his forces were on the losing end of this battle of attrition as long as the mainland forces knew when the shield would be active or inactive.

Tek-Chong reluctantly issued the order for his forces to pull back.

SOUTH KOREA

Nearly 1 percent of land in the Korean peninsula had been completely untouched by the intrusion of man for almost fifty years. While environmentalists in other countries would be thrilled, this was not the result of an ecological decision, but rather one of war. When the cease-fire was signed in 1953, the front line between the United Nations and Chinese troops zigged and zagged across the peninsula. Under the terms, both sides simply pulled back two kilometers, leaving a four-kilometer gap between the forces, which stretched from the Sea of Japan to the Yellow Sea.

Inside this no-man's-land rested discarded weapons,

skeletons, and minefields—and a pure ecology untouched by humans. On the south side, about five hundred meters back from the DMZ, was a barbed-wire fence, mostly electrified, with a ten-meter cleared area on either side. Patrols moved along the southern side of the fence continuously, checking the plowed earth for footprints. Overlooking the fence were observation posts manned by squads of soldiers.

With fifty years to plan, the North Korean assault into the DMZ was perfectly coordinated. And just as perfectly, the Americans and South Koreans began their defense. Within sixty seconds the perfect plans of both sides dissolved into the confusion and terror of all-out war.

Behind a large hill on the North Korean side of the border, out of direct line of sight from the south, was a large warehouse that appeared to be part of a motor pool complex. Crammed inside were two thousand soldiers comprising an infantry regiment of crack North Korean commandos under the command of Colonel Lin.

In the center of the large space that encompassed the interior of the building, was a sixty-foot-wide door, angled at forty-five degrees. Checking his watch, Lin held his wrist in front of his face as the second hand slowly made its circuit around. When it reached twelve, he chopped downward with his other hand, giving the signal to the engineers. The door slowly rumbled open, revealing a mine shaft that angled down into the ground toward the south, dimly lit by a row of naked lightbulbs strung along the roof. A platoon of engineers quickly ran into the tunnel, which was wide enough for ten men to enter abreast. Lin followed, his regiment behind him, tightly packed together.

The men were hungry, Lin knew. Literally. North Korea had slowly been starving as a nation for over a decade.

Famine was a vulture on everyone's shoulders. The army got food first, but that brought little solace to men who knew their families at home were worse off. Tens of thousands had died in the past several years.

Lin skidded to a halt as the engineers paused in front of him. He put his arms out wide and the thousands behind him also halted. He could feel his men, almost like a single living thing, a snake, slithering through the ground to attack their enemy to the south.

They moved for almost thirty minutes, moving farther and farther to the south. The chief engineer put his hand on a plunger set in the center of the tunnel. Wires led from it ahead. Lin knew they had passed under the DMZ between North Korea and South Korea and were across the border.

The charges had been in place for twenty years, ever since this particular tunnel had been dug. Every six months volunteers had sneaked into the tunnel and checked them.

The earth shuddered. Lin blinked as a cloud of dirt and dust came billowing down the tunnel toward him. He closed his eyes, feeling his skin covered, blanketed by the debris, a wind rushing down the tunnel. Then all was still.

Lin opened his eyes. There was daylight ahead. The way was open. Lin began moving forward even as the engineers set up ladders to help in the ascent. He felt that if he didn't move, the men behind would trample him, pound him into the dirt, in their desire to go up.

Lin paused for just the slightest of moments as he reached the ladder. Were they so desirous to attack or to join with their brethren in the south?

TURKEY

Five miles. The road was rising up, the land swelling toward Ararat. Two vehicles had already broken down and been left on the side of the road. General Kashir had his map out and was scanning the terrain ahead, searching for the best route toward the Ahora Gorge. It was on the northeast side of the mountain, so he directed his lead vehicle to leave the road and angle to the right.

The first indication of the incoming Turkish jets was when their ordnance obliterated the front third of Kashir's column. The blast wave from the bombs blew over Kashir like a warm wind. He craned his neck but the planes were already miles away, making a long turn to come back for another run. Glancing forward, he saw the smoking ruins of the front vehicles.

"Disperse and make for the rally point," he ordered.

The Iranian vehicles spread out and raced toward the mountain as the Turkish jets unloaded the rest of their bombs. Half of the tanks and APCs were destroyed, but the rest continued on course, heading up the slope of the mountain.

IN AIR

"We've received a message from Kelly." Quinn's voice sounded tinny and distant in the headphones, the result of being scrambled by the Delta equipment and descrambled by the receiver set next to Turcotte.

Turcotte glanced over his shoulder. Mualama was seated with his back against one of the plastic cases, his eyes closed, apparently resting. Morris had another case open and was going through the gear inside. Turcotte was seated in the depression in the center of the bouncer, his hands on the control. They had just crossed the East Coast of the United States and were headed east at over three thousand miles an hour across the Atlantic.

"And?" Turcotte asked.

"We've got a grid for Excalibur. I'm sending it hard copy via onetime pad."

Turcotte nodded slightly as the machine scrolled out a piece of paper. "So if we have it, Aspasia's Shadow has it."

"A good assumption," Quinn said.

"Anything else in the message?"

"Just the coordinates and one word."

Turcotte waited.

"Beware."

CHAPTER 13: THE PRESENT

SOUTH KOREA

The capital of South Korea, Seoul, has the disadvantage of being a relatively short distance from the demilitarized zone. As North Korean and Chinese forces poured over and under the border, General Carmody and the South Korean president had to make some quick recalculations based on the dual facts that they had neither tactical nuclear weapons nor American naval and air support from the fleet as expected.

The major advantage they did have in conducting their defense was the land itself and time. A mountainous land, the terrain of Korea lent itself to the defense by channeling attacking forces. And time played a role in that South Korea had had almost fifty years since the cease-fire that suspended the all-out war of their forebears to prepare themselves for another assault.

Unlike the war in the 1950s, both sides were more mechanized, making them more powerful, but also limiting their terrain mobility. As columns of North Korean and Chinese forces moved south, they were first struck by American and South Korean jets. Farther south, engineers placed conventional charges in preconstructed choke points along all major axes of advance.

Sides of mountains slid down onto roads, bridges crashed into rivers below, and dams were blown open, releasing torrents of water. To save their country, the South Koreans were sacrificing a good portion of it.

At the Presidential Palace in Seoul and at Eighth Army Headquarters, men and women hurriedly packed up critical equipment and paperwork as a mass evacuation began. General Carmody was with President Pak, making last-minute decisions as they walked down the steps of the palace. They paused on their way to waiting helicopters as a swarm of Chinese-made M-11 missiles thundered into downtown Seoul, exploding two thousand meters above the ground in a breathtaking exhibition of flashes and bangs.

"I don't understand," Pak said, looking up at the sky and the apparently harmless detonations.

General Carmody, dressed in battle dress, flak jacket, and the other accoutrements of his profession, understood exactly. He ripped open the case on his left hip and pulled out the contents, extending it to the South Korean president. "Put this on."

Pak stared at the gas mask, comprehension dawning. His eyes shifted to the streets of his capital city, home to millions. He slowly shook his head, pushing the mask back toward the American general. "No. This"—Pak spread his hands wide, taking in the city—"is my responsibility. You defend the rest of the country. Make them pay for what they are doing now."

Carmody, knowing he had scant seconds, slipped the mask over his head. He also pulled his hands—his only exposed skin—into his sleeves. The crews of the helicopters were better prepared, already in their protective suits. They slipped on masks and waved for Carmody and the rest of his staff who had masks to hurry. The general paused, then dashed down the stairs and into the helicopter. The door immediately slammed shut behind him.

On the stairs, President Pak could swear he felt the first drops of the deadly rain touch his skin, although when he looked at his hands, he could see no liquid. The sound of the engines powering up on the choppers mixed with the noise of the blades cutting air as the helicopters lifted off and headed to the south. He could see masked faces in the windows turned toward him.

Pak reached up and rubbed underneath his nose as it began to run. He heard screams in the distance. As he tried to draw another breath, his lungs felt as if strong rubber bands had been placed around them. He struggled to draw in air. Blinking, Pak looked for the fleeing helicopters but his sight was blurred. His field of vision was diminishing, until all he could see was a pinprick of light. He continued to struggle to get air, knowing as he did so that he was simply drawing in more of whatever was killing him.

A spasm ripped through his stomach and intestines as strongly as if he had been cut open with a sword. He dropped to his knees, doubled over in agony. He could still faintly hear the helicopters.

Pak retched at the same time he experienced involuntary urination and defecation, his body trying to expel whatever was killing it, even though the attempt was in vain. He rolled to his side, desperate for air, but his diaphragm was locking up, unable to work the lungs anymore. The president died of suffocation, as did over two million of his fellow citizens in the capital city.

AIRSPACE, AFRICA

"What do you have?" Turcotte asked into the radio that connected him with Major Quinn. He was doing two things at once, or rather he was doing one thing and having another done to him. He was piloting the bouncer over Africa, still heading east, and Morris had an IV stuck in his arm and was pumping oxygen-rich blood into Turcotte's veins. Mualama was in the same place, also with an IV in his arm. Although he hoped to be able to go directly to the coordinates that

Kelly had sent, Turcotte had long ago learned to prepare for the worst possible contingency, and in this case that was having to spend time on the mountain.

The concept of blood packing was several decades old. Some athletes had tried it in the Olympics, particularly those competing in distance events, before it was outlawed. Since their bodies wouldn't have time to adjust to less oxygen coming in from their lungs, what normal climbers of Everest spent months at altitude doing, they were going to increase the amount of blood in their systems, trying to keep the amount of oxygen relatively level for a short period of time.

"The North Koreans and Chinese have hit Seoul with a nerve agent," Quinn's voice came out of the speaker. "There're reports of hundreds of thousands, if not millions, dead."

Turcotte could see the brown sand of the Sinai Peninsula below. He wasn't far from Mount Sinai, where the Mission had hidden for so many years. "Seoul's just the beginning. Artad and Aspasia's Shadow don't care if they have to stand on the corpses of billions of humans to win their war. We mean nothing to them."

"Why are you so certain of that?" Mualama asked from across the way.

"What do you mean?" Turcotte asked.

Mualama shrugged. "If humans meant so little to them, why didn't they destroy us long ago?"

"They tried," Turcotte said.

Mualama shook his head. "No. They controlled the balance of power with things like the Black Death and various wars. At any time in history they had the power to completely wipe us off the face of the planet, as the Mission recently attempted with its plague. But they never did."

Turcotte considered that. "So we're important to them?"

"To Aspasia and Artad humans were. Not to Aspasia's Shadow."

"Why are we important to them?" Turcotte felt the hair on the back of his neck stand up. There was something about the way Mualama was talking that disturbed him.

Mualama shrugged. "That is part of the great truth yet to be discovered." He spread his long arms. "There is much more to this universe than this planet." And with that he sank back into silence.

MOUNT ARARAT, TURKEY

General Kashir had forty men left alive when he reached the rally point at the base of Ahora Gorge. According to the map and the coordinates he had been given, they were still four miles from the target. Four miles that would be gained in over three thousand meters in altitude. The terrain was now so steep, the armored vehicles could no longer negotiate it. He ordered his men to dismount.

Helicopters would have been better, Kashir knew, but he didn't have access to them. He'd used what he'd had, lost over 60 percent of his force getting there, and he'd be damned if he'd stop now. Turkish jets still circled high above, but they were refraining from further strikes. He assumed that Turkish ground forces were on their way to surround the mountain.

He set off up the gorge on foot, his men following.

KASHGAR

Efficiency was not a highlight of Chinese military operations, especially this far from the capital on a front facing neither Russia, Taiwan, nor Korea, but rather the splinter states of the former Soviet Union and surrounded by ethnic and religious majorities opposed to Beijing. Add in the two fronts being fought against Taiwan and South Korea, and the country's resources were stretched to the limit.

Long after the request was put in, the cargo aircraft to carry the waiting commando team had finally arrived at the local military field. More time was wasted as the planes were refueled.

Finally, well after the order had been transmitted from Artad to Beijing to Kashgar, the four planes were ready. The delays, however, mattered little, because the special envoys the commandos were to await had not yet arrived.

The Chinese soldiers did as most soldiers were very used to doing—they waited, lying on the side of the runway, their equipment and parachutes loaded on board the planes. The flight route was complicated, crossing several countries' airspace, going over Uzbekistan, then Turkmenistan, the Caspian Sea, and into Turkey for the drop.

The soldiers slowly got to their feet as a military transport plane swooped down and came in for a landing. The back ramp slowly lowered. A half dozen figures walked off, having the complete attention of every man present because their proportions obviously weren't human. Each was covered from head to toe in black armor, the joints articulated. The helmets had shaded visors, hiding their faces.

The six Kortad, each with a brilliant sword attached to his waist and a spear in hand, walked past the staring soldiers and onto one of the waiting planes. The contrast between the advanced armor and the apparently antique weapons was startling. Snapping out of their amazement, officers yelled orders and troops scrambled aboard the planes.

Within minutes all four aircraft roared down the runway and into the air, heading west toward Turkey and Mount Ararat.

THE GULF OF MEXICO

Buried alive. Lisa Duncan screamed, the sound echoing around her inside the enclosed space. She tried to move, but her arms and legs were strapped down. There was a pain in her chest, a burning sensation.

Garlin. A pistol. She remembered and with that came the awareness of where she was, inside an imaging machine. She forced her diaphragm to slow down, to stop from hyperventilating. She'd had a tremendous fear of enclosed spaces ever since she'd been trapped in a culvert as a child when—Duncan stopped that train of thought as she realized there was a good possibility it had never happened. But the fear was real, of that she had no doubt. And where had it really come from, she wondered, as she tried to think hard to keep the emotion at bay.

There was light. A faint glow in the direction of her feet, but she couldn't lift her head because there was a strap across her forehead locking it in place.

"Relax." Garlin's voice was low and faint. "It'll be over in just a minute."

"You—" Duncan began, but Garlin anticipated her anger.

"You would have preferred being told what was going to happen?"

"I'll remember that," Duncan promised. "Was it worth it?"

"This is simply amazing," Garlin said. "Yes, we think it was."

The metal table under her vibrated and she realized she was moving. She slid out of the machine, blinking in the room's light. Garlin was at her side, unstrapping her. She sat up as soon as she was freed, taking deep breaths.

"What did you find out?" Duncan finally asked as her

hands automatically went to her chest, rubbing the new skin where the bullet had entered.

"You have telemorase," Garlin said. "We expected that. But we didn't understand how your body could so quickly replicate new cells when it was damaged."

"So you shot me," Duncan said. "Fatally."

"We wanted to see how your brain managed to stay functional and how long it took you to come back to life."

Despite her anger Duncan was also fascinated, especially since she also had no idea what her body was doing when she "died" nor how it repaired itself. Plus there was the possibility that her immortality might have some flaws in it.

"And?" she prompted.

"You had no life signs after you were shot." Garlin had a stack of images in his hands and he was looking through them. "You were in the MRI within forty seconds and we were getting some imagery. You were dead but—*but*—" he emphasized, "there was still movement in your circulatory system. Your heart wasn't beating yet the blood still moved."

"How?"

"You've been infected with a virus."

Duncan remembered something. "Von Seeckt. That's why he survived so long."

Garlin nodded. "He had trace amounts of Airlia blood in him. According to Majestic's records there's a good chance this vampire myth of immortality sprung up from the long-lost fact that Airlia blood has this immortality virus. Maybe the priests on Atlantis knew this. It's certain that the SS searched for any trace of Airlia blood, even from the hybrid Ones Who Wait during the thirties. And they had ceremonies where blood was transfused."

"What do you know about the virus?"

"It's in your bloodstream and can actually keep your blood flowing at a very slow rate when your heart isn't beating. How it does that we're not sure yet. It also seems to be able to manufacture oxygen at a sufficient level to keep cells from dying, particularly in your brain. It's like a cancer, but a good cancer." He showed her an image of her brain. "You were technically dead when this was taken, yet your brain is still oxygenated enough to keep it from degrading."

He showed her another picture, this one of her chest. "The virus also stimulates cell growth in areas of damage." He then showed her four more of the same shot. "Look at this activity and cell growth."

"How long before my heart started beating?" Duncan asked.

"Two minutes."

She frowned as she considered the implications. "Still—there are ways I could die, aren't there? Decapitation? I don't imagine this virus could grow me a new head. And what if I were to be burned?"

"Interesting, isn't it?" Garlin said. "Those are the ways you are supposed to be able to kill a vampire. Perhaps the stake through the heart must stay to keep the heart from regenerating?" He shrugged. "We don't know. We agree—there are probably injuries you could not recover from." He held up his hand as she began to say something. "Don't worry. We don't plan on testing those theories. You were shot where you had been before. We knew you could recover from that."

Duncan put her finger in the bullet hole in her shirt. The skin was completely healed. "What now?"

"Now we try to get your memory back," Garlin said. "Your real memory."

AIRSPACE, INDIA

The mountains first appeared as a slight white bump on the horizon. Turcotte had spent time in Colorado, climbing in the

Rockies, and he'd always been impressed at being able to see Longs Peak and Pikes Peak, over two hundred miles apart, from Denver. But what was rising in the distance made the Rockies look like the sculpting of a child, while these were the work of God. Even Professor Mualama was leaning forward, staring through the front of the bouncer at the sight.

On average twice as high as the range that ran through the western United States, the Himalayas soon filled the view to the front. Turcotte slowed the bouncer as they passed over the foothills in northern India, approaching the border of Nepal. The magnitude of the mountains ahead amplified the warnings Colonel Mickell had given him.

"Everest is there." Morris was pointing to the right front.

What surprised Turcotte more than the sheer size of the mountain was the multitude of other peaks in the area almost as tall. He couldn't imagine entering the area on foot. He turned to Morris. "You were one of the two guys Delta sent to climb it?"

Morris nodded. "Last year. Made it to within two hundred meters of the top."

"And?" Turcotte asked.

"We turned back."

Mualama turned and looked at the medic. "Why?"

"We passed our window of opportunity, so we turned around."

"What do you mean?" Mualama asked.

"You've got to get down from elevation before dark. That's why climbers leave base camp at two in the morning to try to reach the top before noon, so there's time to turn around and get back down. We had rough going, bad weather, worse conditions than we expected. Besides the altitude, the wind is the great enemy on Everest. You feel as if it is always in your face, trying to keep you from going up.

When the beeper went off on our watches and we weren't at the top, we turned around."

"But you were within two hundred meters," Mualama said.

"That's how people die. Breaking the rules on the mountain. It's unforgiving. On the way back we were passed by two New Zealand climbers. They kept going. And they never came back down. When you die on the mountain, your body stays there, frozen forever. There are quite a few bodies up there."

Turcotte had the bouncer at a complete halt now. Morris's words and the sight in front of him were causing him to rethink his plan. He respected what the medic was saying about turning around no matter how close they had gotten. A plan had to be followed. But he also knew they weren't going to have the option of turning back.

Morris pointed. "That's Changtse to the left at seventy-five hundred meters high; Lho La between it and Everest at just above six thousand meters, then Everest, then to the right there, Nuptse at over seventy-eight hundred meters."

Turcotte didn't feel anxious to move forward. The mountain range intimidated him and he had a feeling it wasn't going to be as easy as flying the bouncer to the grid coordinate and picking up the sword. "Tell me about the mountain's history and climbing it," he said. He'd learned in his special operations career that knowledge was power and he had a feeling he was going to need all he could get to accomplish his mission. Also, if Excalibur had been up there so long, he wanted to know if anyone else had gone up after it and failed.

"I don't know about this stuff you've told me about Merlin and all that," Morris said. "As far as history records, the mountain was first mapped in 1590 by a Westerner. He was a Spanish missionary to the court of the Mughal Emperor

Akbar. The Brits were the first to identify Everest and make a calculation as to its height in 1856. But nobody got close to it for a while after that. It wasn't even so much the difficulty of the terrain, but rather politics. Tibet and Nepal, which bracket the mountain, didn't welcome visitors. The Brits had to get a special dispensation from the Dalai Lama in 1921 to send a team in via Tibet. Up till then Everest was just a location on a map. No one really had any idea if it could be approached, never mind climbed."

"But we think Merlin and others climbed it well over a thousand years ago," Turcotte said.

"If they did, they never made it public," Morris said.

"Most likely because they climbed it," Turcotte said, "but only went up and never back down."

"Everest has claimed many." Morris was sitting on one of the plastic cases he'd loaded on the bouncer, his eyes on the mountains, his voice low, as if in respect for what nature had laid out before them. "Most climbers approach from the south," Morris said. "The north face is more technical. What's the location you were given?" Morris asked.

Turcotte hadn't had a chance to decrypt the coordinates. Letting go of the controls and leaving the bouncer at a hover, he took the sheet. Quinn had sent it in the only format that couldn't be decrypted even if intercepted using a onetime pad. There were only two copies of the pad. Turcotte had one, Quinn the other. They had been given to him by Colonel Mickell since they had no doubt any communications they had were being intercepted.

He matched up the correct date using a trigraph, which had three-letter combinations. He aligned the letter from Quinn's message, with the letter on his onetime pad, and used the trigraph to come up with the correct letter/number. It only took a few moments, as it was just a two-letter/eight-digit grid designator. Turcotte handed the result to Morris, who had a 1:50,000 map of Everest spread out on the floor of the bouncer.

"Damn," Morris muttered as he made a small mark on the map with his pencil. Mualama was looking over his shoulder.

"What do you have?" Turcotte asked, unable to see from the pilot's seat.

"North side. At the top of the Kanshung Face. That explains why no one's stumbled across it."

"Is that spot bad?" Turcotte asked.

"The first major attempt to climb Everest in modern times was by George Mallory and Sandy Irvine in 1924," Morris said. "They approached from the north because of politics. And when they did their reconnaissance of the area during the 1921 and 1922 trips, they kept moving up the mountain in that direction. They even made it as far up as the North Col in 1923. But even Mallory said the south appeared to be the more desirable direction to approach the mountain from and subsequent mappings and climbs have confirmed this."

"What happened to Mallory and Irvine?" Mualama asked.

"No one really knew for a long time except that they never came back down." Morris shook his head sadly. "They were last seen alive disappearing into clouds just before the Second Step, which is high up on the north side. Mallory's body was found by an expedition in 1999." Morris ran his finger along the map. "Here. Far below the second step. The body was in bad shape. They buried it on the mountain. Some say he might have summited and been on his way down when he fell. Irvine's body has never been found."

"Curious," Mualama said.

"Others tried to climb the mountain over the years," Morris continued, "but the first true summit came in 1953 by Sir Edmund Hillary and a Sherpa, Tenzig Norgay. Since then about seven hundred people have summited while several hundred have lost their lives attempting it." Morris looked at the map once more. "This spot is not on any route, even the most difficult ones. I'm not surprised no one's seen Excalibur."

"What's the best route to the coordinates?"

Morris looked up. He pointed. "Let's follow the West Ridge, then go over it near the top."

SOUTH KOREA

General Carmody, Eighth Army commander, could hear his own breathing echoing inside his gas mask. He brought the panting under control, then picked up a headset off the firewall of the Blackhawk and slipped it on.

He was patched into the Eighth Army command frequency and could hear reports from his senior commanders over the secure network. The massacre in Seoul was being buried under frantic calls for reinforcements from forces in the Uijongbu Corridor, northeast of the capital city. The North Koreans and Chinese had used both nerve and chemical agents in their initial assaults, and while the American and South Korean military forces were prepared, the dual assault degraded their ability to defend.

The fact that it degraded the ability of the assaulting forces to be as effective as possible didn't seem to matter as four corps worth of PKA/Chinese troops poured across the border into the choke point where Carmody had planned to deploy his tactical nuclear weapons. Fierce fighting raged in the corridor, between the Taebak Mountain Range in the east and an estuary of the Han River. The corridor had always been a major advance route for invaders, from Mongols and Manchus to the North Koreans in 1950 to the present.

Eighteen South Korean divisions along with the American

Second Infantry Division were now engaged along the entire 151-mile-long border from coast to coast, but Carmody knew Uijongbu was the key.

And then he heard the voice of the artillery commander of the Second Infantry Division come over the net. North Korean soldiers were appearing *behind* his batteries by the hundreds, no thousands, the excited voice reported.

Carmody knew immediately what had happened. During the years since the signing of the armistice dozens of tunnels had been discovered being dug from north to south. But he knew, and his intelligence staff had briefed, that they would never find them all. Now one had obviously opened up to the rear of his frontline defenses.

"Alpha four," Carmody yelled, his voice carrying out of the mask, into the mike pressed against it.

The pilot twisted his head, appearing like a machine with his mask and helmet, not a single bit of skin exposed. "Sir?"

"Alpha four. Now."

"Yes, sir."

The Blackhawk banked, the other three carrying his staff following. Carmody knew all his forces were tied up and he had neither reserves to throw into the breach nor spare helicopters to do what needed to be done. As the helicopter flew to the destination he had ordered, Carmody accessed the computer bolted in front of him, bringing up a tactical display forwarded to him from Eighth Army's battle headquarters.

Images flashed across the screen, satellite photos from a KH-14 spy satellite in orbit overhead. He had never expected to be in this position, without the support of the Seventh Fleet. His options to stem the flow of forces he could see building up behind his artillery were limited.

MOUNT EVEREST

The blades were struggling to find purchase in the thin air, just as the engine strained for oxygen to combust the fuel. Below lay the Rongbuk Glacier, a desolate stretch of ice, snow, and rock, caught between ridges. Directly ahead, Mount Everest blocked the horizon.

Neither SEAL glanced down as the helicopter passed over the desolate site of the Rongbuk base camp where most of those who attempted Everest from the north side made their first acclimatization stop. It was empty now, just a scattering of ruined tents and abandoned gear, as it was too late in the season for any sane person to attempt Everest.

The pilot yelled something in his native tongue, the fear obvious even if the words meant nothing to either SEAL. The engines were skipping slightly, a sign the helicopter could not go much higher. They were less than fifty feet above the glacier.

Olivetti pointed ahead with one hand, while jabbing the barrel into the pilot's ribs. From the information the guardian had given them about the traditional north route, it was a three-day march from the Rongbuk base camp, up the glacier, to the Advanced Base Camp that was at the foot of the north face of Everest itself. Every meter the helicopter gained up the glacier meant that much less time they would have to spend climbing.

On the right, Khumbutse appeared, and on the left, Bei Peak. The two mountains framed the north face, which was mostly hidden by blowing snow and clouds. McGraw had a map out and was orienting it to the terrain. A thin red line was drawn on it, the route they were to take. He leaned forward between Olivetti and the pilot and pointed to the right. The pilot turned in that direction. Everest was now off to the left and a long, sloping ridgeline ascending toward it was ahead.

The engine stuttered, went out for a second, then was restarted by the desperate pilot. McGraw pointed down, at a relatively smooth stretch of ice on the glacier. Gratefully the pilot descended quickly. They touched down hard, the impact jarring all on board. The pilot flipped switches and the loud whine of the engine was suddenly gone. The only sound now was the wind, the constant companion of those who came near Everest.

McGraw slid open the cargo bay door. The wind whipped inside, icy fingers clawing at any exposed skin. He tossed out their two heavy rucksacks of equipment. McGraw exited the copilot's seat and easily lifted one of the 180-pound packs, throwing it on his shoulders. The pilot was slumped in his seat, thankful to have made it that far.

McGraw went to the engine compartment and unlatched it. The pilot heard the noise and turned. Startled, he opened his door and came up to McGraw. The SEAL put a finger to his lips, indicating for the man to shut up. McGraw reached in and removed a small piece of the engine. The pilot's eyes went wide and he shook his head, protesting.

McGraw stuffed the piece in his rucksack. He then faced the pilot and held up two fingers, then pointed at himself, toward Everest, then back at the helicopter. Then he jabbed his finger in the pilot's chest and indicated the helicopter.

The pilot looked back down the miles of torturous glacier he had just flown up, knowing there was no way he could make it down on foot. Not dressed like he was. McGraw took him to the cargo bay and pointed inside. There was a sleeping bag on the floor. Then McGraw once more held up two fingers. He then picked up his pack and put it on his back. Without a backward glance, the two SEALs set off up the last part of the glacier, heading toward the West Ridge.

• • •

"Most go that way on the northern approach." Aksu pointed through a narrow gap between Bei Peak and the ridge they were on to another ridge ten miles away. "The West Ridge, via Rongbuk Glacier. It is safer, but it is slower. It is the way Mallory and Irvine tried so many years ago."

Lexina didn't say anything, a tall figure swathed in cold-weather gear, her face hidden behind dark goggles and a face mask. Coridan and Elek flanked her like sentinels, also silent. They were standing on a knoll on the Northeast Ridge, buffeted by the howling wind. Twenty meters below, a line of fourteen of Aksu's men made their way along a narrow track just off the knife edge of the ridge.

"I was the first to complete this route," Aksu continued. "It is faster, but more dangerous, especially if the wind picks up."

Lexina broke her silence. "How long?"

"We will make it to a camp spot I know on the ridge by dark. We will rest four hours. We will then depart at 0300 for the final assault to the location you have given me. It will require some technical climbing to get across the top of the Kanshung Face."

Lexina nodded.

"I must warn you," Aksu said, "that without acclimatization you will not last long on the mountain."

"Our blood—" Lexina began, then halted. "You need not worry about us." She then left the knoll, joining the end of the column. Aksu paused, looking to the southwest toward the mountain hidden in the clouds. The weather was bad, that was obvious to his experienced eyes. He could see a twenty-mile-long plume of snow coming off the top of the peak. If it was the same in the morning, they would not be able to make the attempt, as the Northeast Ridge was too narrow to chance with a strong wind. However, he also knew that Everest was fickle. The weather could change in a flash. There was nothing to do but continue on for the moment.

The controls were getting sluggish, something Turcotte had experienced once before in a bouncer, but that had been when he had taken one as high as it would go, away from the surface of the planet, much higher than their present altitude. He saw no reason why it should be happening, so close to their goal. They were just south of the West Ridge, flying parallel to it, a route suggested by Morris.

"We've got a problem," Turcotte announced as he pushed on the controls, edging them closer to the ridge.

"What's wrong?" Morris asked.

"We're losing power." Turcotte looked to the left, searching for a level spot. "Buckle up," he advised the medic and Mualama.

With his free hand, Turcotte tightened down the straps holding him in the depression in the floor of the bouncer. "I'm open for suggestions where to put this down." All he could see was an extremely steep snow- and ice-covered slope leading up to the ridge above them. About two thousand feet below them was a wide glacier, but Turcotte didn't want to descend, knowing that however far he took the bouncer down, they'd have to make up for on foot.

"Can you put it on top of the ridge?" Morris was pointing up.

Turcotte pulled on the controls, but not only wouldn't the bouncer rise, he realized they were losing airspeed and descending. He knew he needed to do something before they completely lost power.

"Screw it," Turcotte said. He pushed over on the controls and headed for the slope. "Hold on!"

The edge of the bouncer hit hard, digging into the ice and snow, striking rock. The alien metal gouged into the side of

Mount Everest as Turcotte kept his hands on the controls. The bouncer came to a stop and he slowly let go of the controls. The bouncer was stuck into the side of the ridge, enough power in the craft to keep it in place. Turcotte looked up. The top of the ridge was out of sight above them. Looking down, he could see that there was an almost vertical drop below.

"Let's gear up."

Morris checked his watch. "It's late. We'll have to camp on the mountain."

"Let's get as high as we can before dark," Turcotte said. He had some experience of cold-weather operations from his time in Special Forces, so he carefully put on the layers of clothing Morris had brought. First they all put on skintight underwear that would wick any perspiration away from their skins. Turcotte knew one of the great dangers of operating in the cold was sweating and then stopping and having the moisture freeze next to the skin. Next were several more layers of specially designed clothing, topped by a Gore-Tex outer shell.

Morris had laid out the three packs and filled them during the flight. Each contained several oxygen cylinders, a sleeping bag with waterproof shell, and a little food. Turcotte strapped his MP-5 submachine gun to the outside of the pack. He knew he had to keep it away from his body or else the gun might "sweat" and then freeze up. A clanging clutter of climbing gear was also on the outside of each pack.

"Here." Morris held a canteen in each hand and a packet of pills. "Put the canteen in the inner front pocket of your parka. Anyplace else and the water will freeze. The pills are amphetamines. Take them only if you absolutely need a surge of power. They'll give you a couple of hours of energy, but coming down from the high will be bad."

Turcotte stowed the canteen and sealed the Velcro flap to

the pocket. Then he took the harness Morris gave him and put in on over all the clothes, making sure it was tight. He stepped into crampons and cinched them to his boots. He put a lined helmet on, then attached the oxygen mask over it. Morris adjusted the flow for both him and Mualama.

"Most people couldn't last more than a couple of minutes up here going from ground level to this altitude," Morris said, his voice muffled by his mask. "The acclimatizing that is done on a normal Everest climb is primarily to get the blood to change; after several weeks at altitude you develop twice the number of red blood cells that carry oxygen. The blood packing we did on the way here accomplished the same thing—the problem is that the doubling is artificially produced, not by your own body. So it isn't being renewed. We've got a forty-eight-hour window. Past that, your blood will start thinning and you'll be in big trouble."

"How much trouble?" Turcotte asked.

"You'll die."

MOUNT ARARAT

Yakov stumbled as the MC-130 banked hard right. The interior of the plane smelled of vomit and sweat. As experienced as the Delta men were in this type of low-level flight, this one had exceeded even the wildest they'd ever been on. The pilots had surpassed the standard safety margins in effect during training and pushed their training and equipment to the limit, rarely climbing more than one hundred feet above the ground.

Just a year previously such a flight would have been impossible, owing to the likelihood of either striking the ground, a tower, a building, or high-tension wires as they infiltrated Turkey. But a year earlier, NASA had launched an eleven-day operation called the Shuttle Radar Topography Mission.

The mission had mapped over 80 percent of the planet's landmass using C- and X-band interferometric synthetic aperture radars to produce a digital map of the planet's surface. The accuracy of the results was far beyond anything done previously. Altitude data was within sixteen meters' absolute accuracy and horizontal data was within ten meters. This led to the MC-130's crew's ability to fly at double that possible error with no fear of striking anything. The pilots had a three-dimensional display of the terrain ahead on their monitors. The aircraft's computer also had the data loaded and was constantly using a ground-positioning receiver, updated every half second, to monitor the route and warn of possible collisions.

There was the slightest of possibilities that something might have been constructed along the flight route since the shuttle mission, but it was a risk the crew would rather take to avoid being picked up on Turkish radar and having fighters scrambled to intercept.

Yakov reached inside his parka, pulled open the Velcro on an interior pocket, and pulled out a flask of vodka. He extended it to the Delta commando next to him, indicating he should partake. The man looked at him incredulously, the front of his own parka speckled with vomit. Yakov shrugged, unscrewed the cap, and took a deep swig. He extended it around to all the men close by, but all passed. Yakov put the top back on and slipped it back inside.

The man next to him slapped him on the shoulder and pointed to the rear. One of the Delta men was on his feet and yelling something, the sound lost in the roar of the engines. However, he also had both hands extended, fingers spread, so Yakov assumed they were ten minutes out from the drop. The interior of the plane was dimly lit with red lights. A violent cut to the right by the pilot slammed the jumpmaster against the side of the plane. The man regained his balance, wrapping both hands around the static line cable.

Yakov swallowed, tasting bile, but he smiled broadly as the man next to him passed the time warning. He tested the straps of his parachute once more, making sure they were snug. All he wanted was to get out of the plane. He didn't care if there was a division of Turkish soldiers on the drop zone. His stomach was pressed downward as the plane's nose went up.

The jumpmaster was holding up six fingers. He then pantomimed more jump commands and Yakov simply did what the man next to him did, getting to his feet and hooking his static line to the cable. His knees buckled as the plane once more made a violent maneuver.

The roar inside increased as a sliver of daylight appeared in the rear of the plane. The rear ramp slowly went down until it was level, the upper half ascending into the tail of the plane. The nose of the plane was angled up about forty degrees and getting steeper as they ascended the side of Mount Ararat. Looking out the rear, Yakov could see the mountainside less than three hundred feet below. Looking to the side, Yakov blinked in disbelief. They were going up a narrow gorge with the sides above the aircraft and less than ten feet from either wing. He trusted that the pilots knew what they were doing. He was slammed against the side of the aircraft as the MC-130 banked hard right, angling the wings so that they passed through a narrow spot in the gorge.

The man in front of Yakov slammed a fist into his chest to get his attention. Yakov looked to the rear. The jumpmaster had a single finger extended. One minute. Yakov realized he was hyperventilating and fought to control his breathing. Both his large hands were wrapped around the static line, using it to keep his balance. The man in front of him moved and

Yakov edged closer toward the rear of the plane. He glanced up, noting the red light above the ramp. It went out and a green light flashed on.

The jumpmaster was gone, stepping off the ramp. Yakov shuffled forward as the commandos went, and before he was ready was at the edge of the ramp. At that moment the plane banked hard and Yakov stumbled to his knees, then pitched forward off the ramp into the air. The static line unraveled on his back to its full length, then ripped the parachute out of its casing.

Yakov was knocked breathless as he went from a free fall to a controlled descent. He barely had time to take a couple of breaths before his feet hit the ground hard. He collapsed to his right, doing a parachute-landing fall as he'd been taught in the Russian army's airborne school so many years previously. The trip wasn't over, though, as he slid down a steep ice- and rock-strewn slope while scrambling with his feet to stop his descent. He came to an abrupt halt as he tumbled into a boulder, the wind getting knocked out of him for the second time.

Yakov lay still on the ground for several moments, savoring the experience of facing death and living. He tried to get his breath back, then slowly got to his feet and looked around. They had planned to drop right next to the location Che Lu had plotted. He was high up on the side of the mountain, the peak less than a half mile away to the southwest. He saw why the plane had made such an abrupt maneuver, as an almost vertical wall was less than a quarter mile away. The ground sloped steeply down in the opposite direction and he was flanked by two steep ridges. The surface nearby was a jumble of boulders, ice, snow, and rock face.

He could see parachutes scattered about the area as he unbuckled his harness. He untied the MP-5 submachine gun from above his reserve and pulled the bolt back, putting a round in the chamber. He threw his rucksack over his large shoulders and pulled out his ground-positioning receiver, checking his location and finding the assembly point. He was less than eighty meters from the spot they had designated for the team to rally.

Yakov carefully made his way to the point, at times having to use his hands to keep himself from falling. Sixteen of the eighteen Delta men were assembled when he arrived.

"Where are the other two?" he asked.

"We've got an injured man," one of the commandos replied, pointing to the right. "Broken leg. One of our medics is working on him."

Yakov nodded, but his mind was already racing ahead. This was the place, but all he could see was rock, ice, and mountain. He realized he was breathing hard, his lungs straining for oxygen, as he was at about sixteen thousand feet in altitude. The coordinates that Che Lu had come up with were toward the peak, inside the vertical wall. The sun was low and darkness would descend soon.

Yakov pointed toward the wall. "Let's go and find our keyhole."

MOUNT EVEREST

Turcotte kicked the toe of his crampons into the ice wall and edged up another ten inches. Looking up, he could barely see Morris ten feet above him. It was getting dark and visibility was rapidly decreasing. The top of the ridge was still over a hundred and fifty feet above. Glancing down and following the rope he was hooked into, he could see Mualama's form. The bouncer had faded into the darkness although Turcotte knew they were less than a hundred and fifty feet above it.

Turcotte felt as if he had entered a surreal existence. His entire world seemed to consist of this ice wall. He could hear every breath he took as the regulator added oxygen with each intake. Morris had set the flow on what he said was the minimum they needed. Figuring they would have to spend the night on the mountain and each carried only three cylinders in his pack, he estimated they would have just enough to get to the site and return to the bouncer. Despite the additional oxygen and the blood packing, Turcotte felt as if he was suffocating, his lungs straining. He had a pounding headache, worse than any he had ever experienced.

Still he kept moving, one foot up, kicking in, putting his weight on it, then the other foot. Creeping up the side of Everest.

Just on the other side of the ridge Turcotte and his companions were climbing up, "Popeye" McGraw and Olivetti had stopped for the evening in a small divot along the ridgeline. They slid into their sleeping bags and immediately fell asleep, their modified lungs allowing them to breathe relatively easily without any additional oxygen.

Their sleep, though, was not so easy, as their sleeping minds were troubled with the battle between memories of self and the part of the mind subordinated to the nanovirus and guardian programming. Both men moaned and kicked in their sleep, but the nanovirus and guide programming remained firmly in control.

On the northeast ridge, Lexina collapsed to the ground as Aksu called a halt. His men quickly set up tents and rigged stoves, brewing hot soup. She couldn't even drag up the energy to speak, gratefully accepting a steaming cup from Aksu. Despite the additional lung capacity from being part Airlia and the beneficial effect of the half-Airlia blood, the climb had been a strain.

The climbing leader pointed in the darkness. "We must

start climbing in six hours. Three o'clock. I will wake you and your companions prior to that so you will be ready. We must make your location just after dawn so we can be down before tomorrow evening. Do you understand?"

Lexina nodded. All she wanted to do was sleep. Aksu reached down and pulled up her dark goggles. Her eyes were closed. He lifted an eyelid and hissed as he saw the red within red eye.

"What are you?" he asked.

She pushed the empty cup back toward him, then turned her back. Aksu looked at her companions, Elek and Coridan. Both were already asleep—or unconscious. He had seen many strange things on the mountain and knew the dangers. He knew he should check both for signs of cerebral edema but her eyes and her attitude put him off. It was not his business.

Something lightly hit Turcotte's head and he paused in his climbing. He looked up. Morris was just slightly above him, hammering pitons into the ice. Grateful for the halt, Turcotte leaned against the mountain, breathing hard, his lungs trying to get every molecule of oxygen. He glanced to his left. Mualama was steadily coming toward him, closing the gap.

Morris slipped a nylon strap through a snap link attached to one of the pitons, then clipped the other end into Turcotte's harness. He did the same with another piton-sling combination. When Mualama arrived, Morris did the same, leaning around Turcotte, who tried to help even though he couldn't quite figure out why the medic was doing this. He realized that he was having a very difficult time focusing his mind. Morris then pulled Turcotte's pack off his back and hooked it to a third piton sling, so that it dangled right next to him.

Turcotte pulled his oxygen mask to the side. "What are you doing?"

"This is it for the night," Morris said.

"What?"

"We stay here for the night," Morris repeated. "You can sleep in your harness. Get your bag out and snap it around the safety lines. Five hours." He reached up and checked Turcotte's oxygen flow, then swung around him on his rope to check Mualama's and repeat the instructions.

Turcotte looked down in the fading light, then up and to each side. The view was the same. A sheer rock wall mostly covered with ice and snow.

"Great," Turcotte muttered into his mask.

CHAPTER 14: THE PRESENT

SOUTH KOREA

Alpha Four was built into the side of a mountain fifty miles south of Seoul, not far from Osan Air Force Base. General Carmody saw the devastation that had been wreaked on the Air Force Base by suicide squads of North Korean commandos as his helicopter flew by. Burning wreckage littered the runway and aprons and he could see that there were still pockets of resistance here and there.

Disaster. That was the only word that Carmody could think as the chopper began going around the mountain. So far his command's performance in the field in the face of the invasion had been a disaster. Seoul was practically devoid of life. North Korean forces were infiltrating behind his front lines. His Air Force power had been severely hamstrung by the unexpected ferocity of the suicide attacks from groups of North Koreans who had been in place prior to the onslaught, combined with the nerve gas rocket assaults by the Chinese, something they had not expected.

The Blackhawk landed on the concrete pad next to a vault door. Bodies were strewn about and it was obvious the North Koreans had sent several suicide squads against Alpha Four, but Carmody had confirmed over the radio that the bunker remained unbreached. The large steel vault door set into the mountainside slowly swung open. A Humvee came racing out, a large plastic case in the back. Carmody slid open the cargo bay door and helped the crew chief load the nuclear bomb on board. As soon as it was secure, the chopper lifted into the air and the second of Carmody's aircraft landed to on-load its bomb.

"Where to, sir?" the pilot asked over the intercom.

Carmody had already made his decisions on the way down. He gave his pilot coordinates and then radioed the other five helicopters with their own coordinates.

The Blackhawk banked to the north.

TAIWAN

The pattern was one that could not be allowed to continue. Tek-Chong knew that, but he didn't know how to counter the mainland forces' strategy. As soon as he pulled his men back out of range, the shield wall would be turned off, the mainland troops would advance within range, and then the shield would go back on, only coming down when the mainland forces were dug-in and prepared to fire. He'd already retreated four times, falling back over fifteen miles from the beach.

Through his binoculars, Tek-Chong watched the Chinese forces advancing under the protection of the newly forwarded shield and he noticed something. Machine-gun fire burst out from a buried bunker of his own forces, men who had apparently survived both the bombardment and the shield passing over and had not been able to follow the order to retreat. The bunker was immediately destroyed by point-blank tank fire, but it planted an idea in Tek-Chong's mind.

He immediately issued the orders.

The Taiwanese soldiers dug in, hunkering down in their foxholes and bunkers and remained still. Some were killed by the preparatory bombardment, but most survived. And when the firing ceased, Tek-Chong did not give the order to retreat. Instead, the men stayed in place underground, allowing the shield wall to pass over them as it was moved forward.

After the wall passed over them, they then sprang up and engaged the mainland forces at point-blank range. It was brutal fighting, face-to-face combat not seen since the advent of gunpowder. Small arms, bayonets, entrenching tools, fists, and teeth, it was man against man in the most elemental of combat.

And it worked for the defenders.

The mainland army was forced to slow down, its superior firepower negated by the fact that its front lines were mixed with those of the Taiwanese. The shield wall was negated by the close-in combat.

The mainland advance ground to a halt as the commanders pondered how to deal with this new development.

SOUTH KOREA

Six machine guns were set up in position overlooking the main highway running north to south that bypassed Seoul. Colonel Lin had personally positioned each gun on the hillside and now he watched the road through his binoculars. Thousands of South Korean refugees crowded the road, making it difficult for American and South Korean reinforcements to make their way north. Lin planned on making it even more difficult.

"Fire," he ordered.

The machine guns erupted, spewing out thousands of rounds per minute. The bullets chewed into the defenseless civilians, killing them by the hundreds, wounding many more. Bodies littered the road, the wounded and the dead.

After two minutes, Lin issued another order. "Cease fire."

When the guns fell silent, the screams of the wounded civilians echoed off the mountains. Lin scanned the carnage with binoculars, seeing the women and children, their bodies torn apart by the large-caliber bullets. Unbidden, an image of his family back in the north came to him and for the first time he wondered what exactly victory would bring for anyone.

MIDWAY

One thousand forty-two nautical miles northwest of the main Hawaiian Islands lies Midway Atoll just short of the International Date Line. Despite the distance, the three Midway islands were actually part of the Hawaiian Island Archipelago. A coral reef surrounded Sand, Eastern, and Spit islands, whose landmass totaled less than sixteen hundred acres. The atoll was first discovered in 1859 and since it consisted of little more than three tiny spits of sand, little attention was paid to them. They were claimed by the United States in 1876 and annexed in 1908.

The first inhabitants were employees of the Commercial Pacific Cable Company in 1903, who'd come to administer the first round-the-world communications cable. In 1935 Pan American Airways established a base for their Pan-Pacific Clipper seaplanes on the island. In 1938, as tensions rose in the Pacific, the US Navy began building a naval air station. The base was finished in August 1941 and bombed on December 7 of that year.

Midway, though, is most famous for the sea battle that took place in its vicinity in June 1942. The remnants of the United States fleet that had survived the disaster at Pearl Harbor just six months previously had sallied forth to meet another Japanese onslaught. Three American carriers—the *Enterprise, Hornet,* and *Yorktown*—waited near the island for an invasion fleet using intelligence gathered by American code breakers.

A much stronger Japanese fleet approached the atoll, led

by four aircraft carriers and numerous other ships. In a desperate series of strikes and counterstrikes the Americans delivered a stunning defeat on the Japanese, sending all four carriers to the bottom of the Pacific while losing the *Yorktown*. The Battle of Midway shifted the tide of war in the Pacific and marked the beginning of the setting of the Rising Sun of Japanese imperialism.

Perhaps it was memories of that battle that had caused Admiral Kenzie to make Midway the destination for his fleet, even though the naval base there had been abandoned in 1997 and the entire area turned into a national wildlife refuge.

Kenzie positioned his fleet to the northwest of Midway, escort ships surrounding his lone surviving carrier, the *Kennedy*. Linked back to the mainland by satellite communication, he remained up-to-date on the burgeoning world war. He'd already received contradictory orders from Washington—one set from the Pentagon directing him to sail west and support American forces in South Korea, another order from the National Security Advisor directing him to sail east to San Francisco to defend the West Coast.

He ignored both sets of orders and maintained radio silence, listening to the satellite communications but sending nothing. All of his ships were powered down, running on the minimum required energy. Kenzie was more tuned in to the mood of his sailors than to the information coming in from the satellites. Many had left family behind in Hawaii. Fear, anger, despair, confusion—all floated through the fleet like a dense fog.

PEARL HARBOR

Captain Lockhart was to receive her first command. Despite being corrupted by the nanovirus and even knowing deep inside that she was aiding and abetting the enemy, a small part of her was thrilled. Especially this command.

She was on Ford Island, in the center of Pearl Harbor, sur-rounded by a cluster of similarly infected sailors. Waiting. Behind them were two dozen Tomahawk cruise missiles, for-gotten in a storage area in the rush of the fleet departing. Several dozen compressors were pumping air into hoses that ran from the island into the water.

Just offshore, the white memorial building was gone, the material stripped and used by the nanotechs. The dark water was boiling as if some great beast were stirring below. Lockhart took an involuntary step backward as a metal mast appeared, poking up through the surface and rising.

Slowly, as air filled sealed chambers, the reconstructed USS *Arizona* saw the light of day for the first time in well over half a century. As the ship's main deck became awash, Lockhart supervised the sailors in transferring over the cruise missiles as the nanovirus began construction of launchers for them in place of the guns that had once graced the ship's decks.

Where oil-burning conventional engines had once been, the nanotechs were changing rusted metal into a modified version of the engines that had been developed on the *Springfield* and its clones. Lockhart had her orders via the nanovirus from the guardian—as soon as the *Arizona* was seaworthy she was to put to sea and join the Alien Fleet that was now off to the south of Oahu. The mission: search for and assimilate the remains of the American fleet.

THE GULF OF MEXICO

"What the hell is that?" Lisa Duncan asked as Garlin opened a door to a room she hadn't been in before. A long, coffinlike object was in the center, next to a control console with what appeared to be numerous computers stacked around it.

"That's how we're going to try to break through this programming in your brain," Garlin said.

"And I'm supposed to trust you?"

"We don't care if you trust us or not," Garlin said as he walked over to the control console and hit a button. The lid of the tube slowly swung open, revealing a contoured interior, roughly the size of a person, but someone much taller than Duncan.

Duncan didn't move from the door. "That looks very similar to what Mike Turcotte told me was being used in the lab in Dulce."

"Very good," Garlin said. "It is."

"Where did it come from?"

"We recovered it from the ruins at Dulce. Where else?"

"That thing caused people to go crazy."

"It can be used for that," Garlin acknowledged. He turned from the machine toward Duncan, who still had not moved. "You have good reason to be afraid of it. We think it's what was used to give you your false memories."

"That makes no sense," Duncan said. "Why would Majestic have done that to me? I ended up investigating them."

Garlin shrugged. "Remember that Von Seeckt was a renegade from Majestic. We think it might be possible he used you as the key to get the government to prevent the mothership from flying. Or there may be a similar but different machine like the one at Dulce that was used on you."

"You don't know much, do you?"

Garlin took a step closer to her and shook his head, a strange smile on his lips. "For someone who has false memories, you're very sure of yourself. You don't know who you are. And let me tell you something else you don't know. You don't know who Turcotte is either."

"What do you mean?"

"After we discovered you weren't who you appeared to be, we checked everyone else. Turcotte's past—it's all fake too. He was never in a classified antiterrorist unit in Germany. That charming story he tells about trying to save the pregnant woman . . . never happened. He's as false as you are."

Duncan didn't believe him. Why that thought came to her with absolute certainty, she wasn't sure. Turcotte was who he appeared to be. But accompanying the thought was an almost overwhelming sense of guilt, which confused her. What about Turcotte did she have to feel guilty about? That she had involved him in this? But the feeling was much stronger than that.

As Garlin came forward, his hands up to grab her, Duncan stepped back and felt a pinprick of a needle in the back of her neck. She didn't even manage to turn her head to see whoever had done it before she passed out.

TAIWAN

Brutality was being met with brutality. The mainland forces, realizing they were going to be slowed anyway by the defense tactics of the Taiwanese, now resorted to lining up artillery hub to hub along their main axis of advance. They fired a barrage just inside the forward edge of the shield wall, devastating the terrain and killing many of the dug-in Taiwanese soldiers and destroying everything in their path.

But as armies had learned ever since the invention of gunpowder, despite this tremendous effort, many of the defenders still survived. The mainland infantry still had to follow behind the artillery and dig out the survivors. As their commanders pressed them forward so relentlessly, they lost significant numbers to friendly fire, but if there was one thing the mainland didn't lack it was bodies.

So the slaughter went on. But to Chang Tek-Chong and the others in the Taiwanese high command, the result began to appear inevitable. They could only trade so much terrain before they were pushed into the ocean.

QIAN-LING

Artad cared little how many humans were dying in Taiwan or South Korea. The two assaults were just the beginning. From intercepted satellite traffic he knew the United Nations, the closest thing these humans had to a planetary government, was considering Aspasia's Shadow's ultimatum.

It was time for a counteroffer.

MOUNT ARARAT

Yakov had not been impressed by the plan he had been given and events were proving him correct. His team had scoured the cliff face and while there were several crevasses, there had been nothing significant enough for him to order the Delta Force demolitions men to do their job. If the mothership was behind the cliff, he had yet to see the way in.

Night had fallen and the men had gathered together in a small depression. No fires, just a cluster of men huddled in the dark. They'd heard gunfire from farther down the mountain just before dark and noted several overflights by Turkish jets. Thus Yakov wasn't surprised when one of the Delta men reported movement nearby.

Yakov slipped off into the dark to investigate, leaving instructions with the commandos to remain in place. He passed between two boulders, his weapon at the ready, then froze when he heard the sound of an AK-47's slide being worked. The sound was echoed by several more assault rifles.

He took a step backward toward the hide site when he felt

the muzzle of a weapon poke him in the back. Letting his MP-5 hang on its sling, Yakov slowly brought his hands up.

"Who are you?" a harsh voice asked in accented English.

"From America," Yakov said.

"You don't sound like an American."

"I am Russian, but I am working with the Americans."

The muzzle was pulled away as figures appeared in the darkness, surrounding Yakov. The man who had been behind him came around in front. He was wearing a sheepskin coat and a black watch cap. Definitely not Turkish military, Yakov realized.

"What are you and the others up there"—the man jabbed the muzzle of the gun in the direction of the Delta hide site— "doing here? We saw you parachute in."

"Who are you?" Yakov asked instead, not certain how to proceed.

The man spit, narrowly missing Yakov's boots. "This is our land. Our mountain. You do the answering."

"We search for the ark."

The man's head snapped up and he said something in a different language. From the excitement among the men, Yakov knew he had broached a sensitive subject. He realized they were Kurdish guerrillas.

"Freeze!" The voice came out of the darkness and Yakov knew the Delta commandos had the group covered.

The man cursed, shoving his gun into Yakov's face. "You die first."

"Easy," Yakov said, keeping his hands up. "They're friendly," he called out to the unseen commandos.

Several Delta commandos with night-vision goggles on appeared out of the dark, weapons at the ready. Yakov could see the guerrillas relax as they saw the American flag patch on the commandos' shoulders.

"Come." The leader of the guerrillas gestured. "There are others on the mountain."

"Let's go," Yakov said to the Delta men as he followed the guerrillas. They clambered toward the cliff face, then turned right. Yakov was surprised when the man in front of him seemed simply to disappear into the cliff. Edging around a boulder, Yakov saw there was a narrow crack that they hadn't spotted during their search. He could barely force his way in, then he was in darkness, stumbling forward. The Delta commandos followed, two of them carrying the man with the broken leg.

Yakov went about twenty feet before the tunnel turned to the right and he saw a dim light ahead, the forms of the guerrillas silhouetted against it. The tunnel widened into a cave, about sixty feet wide by thirty deep. The ceiling was low, forcing Yakov to remain slightly bent over. Two oil-burning lanterns illuminated the cave and the interior smelled of their burning as well as unwashed bodies. There were several women and children inside and they greeted the men with smiles and hugs while casting suspicious glances at the strangers.

"Sit." The man who had first met Yakov indicated a spot near one of the lanterns. Yakov squatted and he was joined by the commander of the Delta commandos.

"I am Kakel," the man said.

"Yakov. And this is Major Briggs," he added, introducing the senior Delta man.

Kakel shook their hands but his words were less than pleasant. "Americans. You promised us much and you delivered little. You asked my people to rebel in Iraq and then abandoned us. You side with the Turks and let them hunt us down like dogs." He sat down with a sigh. "This is our land. It was called Kurdistan long before there was a Turkey or an

Iraq. Do you know it is illegal for us to speak our own language here?" Kakel didn't wait for an answer. "Why do you seek the ark?"

"We think it is an Airlia spacecraft."

"Airlia?"

"The aliens."

"The gods of old." Kakel glanced around to see if any of the others were listening. "There is much history on Agri Dagi—that is what we call this mountain. There is the legend of the Ark of Noah coming to rest here after the Great Flood. My people believe we are the direct descendants of Noah. And now you say it might be a craft of these aliens." Kakel shook his head. "Did you know that Lawrence of Arabia hid in this very cave?"

"No, I did not," Yakov said.

"There are those who have a different"—Kakel searched for the right word, then shrugged—"sight. Some come here."

Yakov wanted more information on that, but he knew he had to stay with his priority, so he remained silent.

"We call this the back door." Kakel pulled the magazine out of his weapon, checked the bullets, then slammed it back in. "Outsiders are not supposed to see this."

"I thank you for taking us in," Yakov said.

"There are others on the mountain," Kakel repeated himself. "Iranians have crossed the border. Many were killed by the Turkish planes, but some still climb up the mountain. They are not far off. Of course that means the Turkish army is close." He smiled fiercely. "But they have learned not to come into our land. They wait around to catch the Iranians when they try to leave. I assume the Iranians seek what you seek."

"It is most likely," Yakov agreed. He saw a twitch on the side of Kakel's face. Yakov had been around men like this before—

men who spent their entire lives hiding and fighting. The stress wore them down, making them old before their time.

"It has been here for many centuries," Kakel said. "Beyond the time of remembering. Why do you need to find it now?"

"There is war all over the world," Yakov said. "We think—"

"We have been at war here for a long time. No one was ever interested."

"It is worldwide. In many places people are dying—" Yakov began, but Kakel again interrupted him.

"There have been world wars before."

"Not—" Yakov halted, realizing he had been about to say not with aliens involved, but who knew how much the two sides had been involved in previous wars. "The aliens have shown their true natures and come out of the shadows," he finally said. "The ark holds the thing we need to defeat the aliens."

"And my people? What good will it do us?"

"I do not know," Yakov answered.

Surprisingly, Kakel smiled, revealing several broken teeth. "I like you, Russian. At least you are honest. We have had too many promises and every one was broken." He put the AK-47 down. "The legend is that my people, the Kurds, are the descendants of Noah and the survivors of the Great Flood. That we came here in the ancient time, brought by the gods on the ark, which landed on this mountain when the waters receded.

"My father, and my father's father, and through my family beyond what can be remembered, have lived here on the mountain. He told me, as he was told, that there would be a day when the ark would be needed again. Others have come seeking the ark."

"And have you shown it to any?"

"Those who had the correct symbol. Yes."

Yakov reached into a pocket and pulled out a Watcher ring. "This symbol?"

Kakel pulled a chain from around his neck. On it was attached a Watcher medallion. "Yes."

"Who were these who came? Was Sir Richard Burton one of them?"

Kakel nodded. "Yes."

"Who else?"

"Tesla."

" 'Tesla'?" The name sounded familiar to Yakov, but he couldn't place it.

"A man named Nikola Tesla came here many years ago."

"Why?"

"To go into the ark."

"For what?"

"I do not know that. But he had the proper symbol, so he was allowed in."

"Anyone else?"

"As I said, there have been those who had a different sight."

Yakov returned to his mission. "I seek something inside the ark."

Kakel considered that. "You have the proper symbol. Tomorrow I will show you what you seek. But only after you help me."

"Help you do what?" Yakov asked.

"Does it matter? You want to see the ark, do you not?"

UNITED NATIONS

"Aspasia's Shadow lies." The sound of Artad's voice echoed through the General Assembly.

"First let me tell you the truths among his lies. Aspasia was indeed the first Airlia to come to your planet. And he did establish a base at Atlantis. And his mission was to protect your planet from the Swarm.

"That is the extent of his truths. Long after he had been sent here, communication ceased with our home world. I was sent to investigate when we didn't hear from him. It was feared that this planet might have been overrun by the Swarm.

"I arrived to find that Aspasia had become corrupt. He had begun acting like a God and treating your people as slaves who should worship him. He had become fearful he would be recalled and have to rejoin the fight against the Swarm.

"We battled. There was much death and destruction, which I regret. When neither side could completely gain the upper hand and we feared an escalation of the combat would send out signatures into space that would be picked up by the Swarm we came to terms on a truce.

"His base at Atlantis was to be destroyed and he was banished to our base on Mars. Before I destroyed Atlantis, I rescued as many of your people as I could. I came here to Qian-Ling and went into a long sleep.

"The atrocities committed against humanity by both sides throughout that long sleep cannot be laid at my feet. They were reactions by my guardian computer and my Shadow against actions by Aspasia's Shadow.

"But I am awake now. You have killed Aspasia for which I give you great credit. But you will not be able to destroy his Shadow without my help, which I offer freely. And after we have destroyed him, I will assist you in moving forward in technology in order to join the rest of the peace-loving sentient species in the universe. You have seen the mothership and know we are far more advanced than you. There is much I can give you that will make life on your planet many times better.

"The Chinese government has already joined me. Do not let old enmities stand in your way. You must come together as a species if you wish to join the other sentient beings of the universe.

"And there are greater dangers beyond this planet. You will need my help to face those threats. The Swarm is still out there destroying planets like yours. You cannot face them alone.

"Aspasia's Shadow threatens all of you. He has corrupted many humans with his nanovirus. He wants all of you back under his thrall. To worship him. I want you to join me as equals.

"The choice is yours, but make it quickly. Events are moving and there is not time for you to waver."

The transmission ended. An explosion of debate roared in the Assembly Hall. Given what was already happening in Taiwan and South Korea, Artad's words weren't exactly greeted with applause. Still, though, there were those countries that saw Artad's offer as a chance to ally with the enemy of Aspasia's Shadow. Perhaps it would be the lesser of two evils?

The debate went on.

SOUTH KOREA

General Carmody slipped the gas mask over his head as the helicopter slowly descended. The nerve agent that had been spread over Seoul would most likely have already dispersed, but he was taking no chances. The Blackhawk landed on the Tongjak Bridge over the Han River. There were bodies everywhere and no sign of life. Carmody slid open the cargo bay door and, with the aid of the crew chief, off-loaded the nuclear weapon.

There were sixteen bridges over the Han. Four within

view of this one. Carmody opened the plastic case and punched in the arming code for the bomb. He set the delay at fifteen minutes. The other Blackhawks were doing the same thing in a pattern designed to destroy all sixteen bridges. It was a desperate act, but one that Carmody felt had been forced on him by the use of nerve agents.

He got back on board the helicopter and the pilot began to take off. It was then that he noticed the squad of men moving through a street a quarter mile to the north. The men wore protective suits and gas masks—North Korean versions. They carried AK-47s and were headed toward the bridge, drawn by the sound of the helicopter.

"Land again," Carmody ordered.

The Blackhawk touched down. Carmody opened the door and went over to the bomb. He heard shots, then the door gunner on the Blackhawk returning fire. He entered his code on the keypad. Then he accessed the timer code. 14:21 and going down. Carmody hit the scroll key and the number rapidly went down until he reached :10.

Then he waited as the last seconds ticked off.

CHAPTER 15: THE PRESENT

MOUNT EVEREST

It was most definitely not dawn. That was Turcotte's first thought as Morris nudged his shoulder again. He felt like he'd tied one on the previous evening and then spent the night in a snowbank while being suffocated. His head was pounding and his body was stiff and chilled to the bone. Turcotte opened his eyes. Ice-covered rock was less than six inches in front of him. The sound of his breathing echoed loudly inside the oxygen mask. He couldn't remember ever feeling so bad, but then again his brain wasn't working very well so he couldn't really trust his memories. He did know from his various training and combat experiences that misery tended to fade in the memory and never seemed as bad looking back as it really had been.

A shaft of light penetrated the dark as Morris put a headlamp over his forehead and turned it on. The medic was doing something and his action stirred Turcotte to move. He unzipped his sleeping bag, careful not to drop it, shoving it into the pack dangling next to him. He pulled out his own headlamp and put it on. He was amazed as Morris handed him a hot cup of coffee. The medic has chipped out a small ice ledge in the side of the ridge and set up his stove. Turcotte knew how difficult it was to operate under these conditions and he was deeply grateful for Morris's extra efforts. He took a sip, then twisted, handing the cup to Mualama.

He noted that Morris was looking up in the darkness, trying to see the route he would lead them on, the headlamp penetrating about forty feet up. There was no wind, for which Turcotte was grateful. The cold was so extreme it was sheer pain on any exposed skin and he knew a minute of exposure would cause instant frostbite.

Mualama passed the cup back and began packing his gear. Turcotte had spent a good portion of his life in the field in all sorts of conditions, but he'd never spent a few hours sleeping at twenty-five thousand feet clipped to the side of a mountain.

"Grab hold of the mountain," Morris advised as he reached down for the safety lines he'd attached.

Turcotte looked down. His legs were dangling and he was supported only by the lines. He kicked and dug the toe of his crampons into the ice. Morris had put his pack on him while he slept and Turcotte felt a moment's embarrassment to be taken care of like that. The medic had done the same with Mualama. Looking at the African in the darkness, the older man's face, what little Turcotte could see, was haggard.

"Let's move," Morris called out. He began to lead the way up the ridge, Turcotte and Mualama following.

McGraw and Olivetti were pushing through waist-high snow. Each man would take ten steps, moving up the ridge, then step to the side and let the other take his place blazing the trail. They'd been doing this routine for over an hour and the muscles in their legs burned in agony, yet that didn't slow them in the slightest. Both men wore night-vision goggles and the clear night sky gave enough illumination that they could see the way clearly.

McGraw had just taken lead and was on step number five when his crampon hit something buried in the snow. He paused and leaned forward, brushing snow away from the object. Two bodies. Frozen solid. Wearing modern climbing gear. Casualties from some climbing expedition. McGraw stepped over them and continued. Olivetti did the same.

Lexina was awakened by Aksu switching out her oxygen cylinder.

"Your companion is dead."

Lexina slowly sat up. "Which one?"

Aksu shrugged. "You did not tell me their names."

"Cause?" Lexina slid out of her sleeping bag, feeling the bite of the cold. It was a clear night and thousands of stars glittered overhead.

"His oxygen tube was slightly crimped. He didn't get enough air. As near as I can tell, this brought on cerebral edema."

Lexina stiffly got to her feet and walked over to Coridan's body. He was curled up in a fetal position. Aksu stripped off the mask, then unscrewed the oxygen tube, sliding it into his own pack. She lifted one eyelid. There was no doubt he was dead. Unzipping his bag and parka, she went through the layers of clothes until she uncovered a small medallion in the shape of two outstretched arms. She removed it from the body.

Elek had joined her and the two hybrid human/Airlia clones stood silently over the body of their companion for a few moments.

"The spirit of Coridan must pass on," Lexina finally said.

"The spirit must pass on," Elek echoed.

Lexina held up the medallion. "We take his spirit, the spirit of Coridan. We take his *ka* so that he might be reborn."

Aksu was watching carefully, surprised at the ceremony.

Lexina handed the *ka* to Elek. Then she took a small black case out. Opening it, she sprinkled a little bit of black powder on the body. Aksu took a step back as the black powder began eating the body as if it were some powerful acid. Soon nothing remained except the clothes.

Lexina turned to Aksu. "We are ready to proceed."

Olivetti tapped McGraw on the arm and pointed down. Three cones of light pierced the darkness several hundred feet below them and to the west. The lights showed up like searchlights in the SEALs' night-vision goggles. The two SEALs paused in their climb and watched the lights for almost a minute. It was clear that whoever was wearing them were moving slowly and straight up, which meant they would cut across the SEALs trail. McGraw knelt, pulling off his pack. He removed a claymore mine from the pack and placed it next to their trail, hiding it with a facing of snow. He then ran the trip wire across the trail, knocking snow off the side of the furrow to cover it.

McGraw faced back up the ridgeline and began climbing. The two were moving at an incredible pace, their legs churning through the waist-high snow, cutting a path straight along the knife-edge top of the West Ridge.

THE GULF OF MEXICO

Being immortal had turned into a curse, Duncan realized as she regained consciousness via a severe jolt of pain as if a red-hot poker had been shoved into her forehead. As the pain from the jolt receded, her head pounded from an almost blinding headache. She opened her eyes, but it made no difference. She was in absolute darkness and her body couldn't move, no matter how hard she struggled. She tried to scream and realized that something was shoved down her throat.

A slash of pain, slightly to the left of the previous one, above her eye, caused her to choke on whatever was in her throat as she tried to scream. Then even as that subsided, another spike. Her body slammed against the restraints, muscles twitching. And another spike. She felt as if she were losing her sanity, overwhelmed by waves of pain that were increasing in intensity.

Then she realized she could see something very faintly. Shadowy gray images moving against a black background, but she couldn't make out details. Then with another bolt of pain they were gone and the darkness returned. She realized there was a copper taste in her mouth, but she couldn't move her tongue around whatever had been shoved down her throat.

She also became aware that she was submerged, her entire body enveloped in a fluid, which was at body temperature. The tube in the throat must be giving her oxygen, she thought, but it was wiped away by more pain, this time in her left temple.

Then blessed nothingness for a moment. Her body was rigid, waiting for the onslaught to be renewed, but instead she was blinded by light as the top of the tube opened. The light was diffused through the liquid, which had a dark tint to it and the clear plastic of a mask which was molded to her face. There was someone standing over the tube. She began struggling again, but the figure held up his hand indicating for her to wait.

She realized the liquid was slowly draining as the level dropped below the top of her body and she felt the chill of cool air on wet, exposed skin. Garlin remained still, waiting, and Duncan mentally cursed him.

Garlin reached in and in one smooth move pulled the tube out of her mouth. She coughed and gasped for air. He quickly unstrapped her, then tossed a towel into the tube. She wrapped it around her body as she sat up.

"I am done with you and your tests."

"We don't care what you're done with," Garlin said, "because we're not done with you."

"You keep saying we, but I haven't seen anyone but you," Duncan said.

"That's because we don't trust you," Garlin said.

"Screw you."

"Do you want to know what we've learned?"

"Since I still have the same memories," Duncan said, "I don't think you learned much."

Garlin shook his head. "On the contrary. The fact that we weren't able to break through your conditioning with this machine indicates that this type of machine wasn't used to implant your false memories. Something more sophisticated and more powerful was used."

Duncan remained silent, her arms across her chest, holding the towel tight against her body.

"And"—Garlin drew the word out—"we think we know what that was."

Duncan finally spoke. "And that is?"

"The Ark of the Covenant."

Duncan remembered the crown, and the leads from the Ark that she had attached. And the vision she'd had while hooked to it inside the Black Sphinx.

As if reading her mind, Garlin nodded. "The vision you had when you were hooked up to it probably didn't come from the Ark of the Covenant. We think it came from your repressed memory."

"That doesn't make sense," Duncan said. "I was on board a mothership. How can I have a memory of that?"

"Good question," Garlin said. "And one we hope to answer shortly."

"How do you plan on doing that?"

"We're going to bring the Ark of the Covenant here."

THE COLONEL JAMES N. ROWE
SPECIAL OPERATIONS
TRAINING FACILITY

Larry Kincaid was tapped into the military's secure Internet, using Delta's access to get him the imagery he needed. The line of mechs moving between Cydonia and Mons Olympus was larger than ever. And the first of those carrying the black material had reached the site high up on the extinct volcano's side, less than a kilometer from the summit.

While the material was being laid out in the beginnings of a grid pattern, Kincaid noted that a cluster of mechs were in the very center of the location and still digging into the side of the mountain. Excavation and a grid—something tugged at Kincaid's mind, but he couldn't quite put his finger on it. He had a strange feeling he'd seen something like this before, but where? And how could he have, given that this was being constructed by aliens on another planet?

QIAN-LING, CHINA

Artad stared at the same imagery of Mars, which the Chinese had intercepted via their tap into the American military's supposedly secure web server. He also had seen the same thing before, except he knew exactly what he was looking at. Startled, Artad put the pictures down and accessed the guardian. He had it run a program to determine how long it would take for the thing being built on Mars to be completed. The answer was somewhat reassuring—more than enough time for his forces to complete their conquest and/or destruction of the humans and Aspasia's Shadow.

Still—Artad picked up the photo and stared at it. Why would the Airlia on Mars be building this? he wondered.

They were Aspasia's people. But, then again, Aspasia was dead. Were they allied with his enemy's shadow? Or were they on their own now?

Possibilities.

Artad composed a message to the Airlia at Cydonia and transmitted it via the guardian.

DIMONA

"We need the Ark of the Covenant along with the priestly robes and crown in order to find out who exactly Dr. Duncan is."

Sherev stared at the speakerphone, considering the request he had just received. This Garlin fellow claimed to be from the new Area 51 and he had quickly updated Sherev on Duncan's status. Sherev had seen her body taken aboard the bouncer after he had led Israeli commandos in storming the Mission's base inside Mount Sinai. He also remembered Turcotte and Yakov and their bravery attacking the Mission.

"So the Grail works?" he asked.

"Yes."

"It brought her back to life?"

"Yes."

"Where is Major Turcotte?" Sherev asked.

"Currently climbing Mount Everest," Garlin replied.

"And Yakov?"

"Mount Ararat."

Sherev frowned. "Why is he at Ararat?"

"That is not important right now. Our priority is to figure out exactly who Lisa Duncan is."

"Why?"

"Because she caused the demise of the original Majestic committee and in essence started all of this."

Sherev leaned back in his chair and steepled his fingers.

The intelligence reports of recent events were as often confusing as enlightening. "I thought the original Majestic started all of this, as you say, when it became corrupted by the guardian they found in Temiltepec?"

"Are you going to help us or not?" Garlin snapped. "I'm relaying this request directly from Major Turcotte. He's afraid to go through diplomatic channels because he doesn't want this compromised."

Sherev knew he was in an untenable situation. What had happened in Jerusalem was a clear indicator that the Ark of the Covenant was a dangerous icon. While it was again safe in his vault, how long would that last? The threat to Israel from the countries ringing it was also growing. There were reports of fighting along the Iranian-Turkish border and also between Iran and Iraq. Egypt was claiming sovereignty over the Sinai Peninsula again and asserting that any artifacts removed from Mount Sinai were Egyptian, as they must have originated from that country.

"You know Aspasia's Shadow has the Grail," Garlin pressed. "We need to unlock whatever secrets are inside Duncan's head before he grows too powerful."

Sherev wasn't quite following what was so important about Duncan, but he also knew that just sitting there with the Ark of the Covenant locked in a vault wasn't doing anybody any good. "I will be heading toward your location with the Ark of the Covenant immediately."

PEARL HARBOR

Over sixty years late, the *Arizona* exited the channel at Pearl Harbor into open ocean to link up with the rest of the fleet. Unfortunately the fleet it was going to join was controlled by an alien force.

The ship glided through the water, increasing speed as it

cleared the channel. The acceleration continued, water being sucked into vents built into the sides of the bow by the nanovirus, channeled through large pipes, put under pressure, and expelled at the stern where the ship's mighty propellers had been replaced, the metal used to help construct the new propulsion system. Soon the ship was moving at over sixty knots.

In place of the turrets where mighty guns had once been, there were cruise missile launchers. The nanovirus had done such an efficient job resurrecting the *Arizona* that it was more modern than any ship in the Alien Fleet it was going to join.

Captain Lockhart stood on the bridge of the ship, a set of binoculars to her eyes, trained to the right, watching the southwestern corner of Oahu slip by. She put the binoculars down and turned as a crewman handed her a message—the location of the Alien Fleet. She issued the appropriate order to the helmsman and the *Arizona* sliced through the ocean en route to the rendezvous point.

MOUNT ARARAT

General Kashir had only twenty-five men left from the three hundred he had crossed the border with. At least the Turkish jets weren't flying in the darkness. His men had made a miserable camp on the side of the mountain, among the rocks, snow, and ice. He forbade them making fires for fear of being seen by Turkish patrols, which they had spotted below them just before dark. They could see vehicle lights far below as the Turkish army surrounded the mountain, but it didn't appear that the troops were moving upslope yet.

He pulled a sealed envelope from his jacket pocket and pulled a poncho over his head so that his flashlight wouldn't be seen. He turned on the light and opened the envelope. A piece of paper was inside, folded in half. He extracted the paper and unfolded it. A set of directions handwritten in Arabic directed him on the final stages of finding his way into the cavern that held the mothership. And then further instructions on how to get inside the mothership and what to do once he was inside. He found it all overwhelming.

He had met Al-Iblis just once and the "man" had chilled Kashir to the bone with his aura. But Al-Iblis had been a valuable ally over the years, the ultimate reason why Kashir held the rank he did and had wealth that far exceeded that which was equal with his rank. At that one meeting Al-Iblis had given him this envelope and told him he must be prepared upon receipt of a certain code word to execute this operation. Kashir had always hoped that day would not come. He imagined the man who had assassinated Hussein had felt the same way, as there was little doubt in Kashir's mind that Al-Iblis's long reach had been involved in that.

Satisfied that the entrance to the cavern wasn't far off, Kashir turned off the flashlight and removed the poncho. The first thing he saw as his eyes adjusted to the dark was the small red dot trained on his chest. Kashir slowly got to his feet, peering about in the dark. Men were moving—men with something on their faces. Night-vision goggles, very advanced, something that Kashir knew his army did not possess. The red dot was still on his chest. Then, as his eyes adjusted further, Kashir noted that his men lay still, too still.

One of the figures came up to him. Kashir now saw that the muzzles of their weapons were bulky—silencers. His men had all been killed while he had read the instructions underneath the poncho. He felt his stomach quake and bile rise in his throat.

The man held out his hand. Kashir handed over the envelope and letter.

"Please," he whispered in Arabic.

He never saw the Kurd who was behind him. He did feel the steel as it slid across his throat and the explosion of warm liquid on his chest.

Kakel wiped the blade on the dead general's coat, then sheathed it. "What is that?" he asked Yakov, indicating the letter with the point of his knife.

"Was that necessary?" Yakov asked.

"You killed the rest while they slept," Kakel noted. "Was what I did any worse than that? They are Iranians. They kill my people without a second thought. I feel nothing killing them."

Yakov dropped the matter, flipping up the night-vision goggles. He put a red-lens flashlight between his teeth and turned it on. Then he opened the letter. "It is directions into the chamber."

"Let me see." Kakel looked over his shoulder. The Kurd cursed. "Someone knows the back door."

"There's more," Yakov said as he read. He nodded. "The way into the mothership. I was concerned about that. Good. Now it is your turn to live up to your end of our bargain," he said to Kakel. He signaled to the Delta commandos. "Let's go." They headed back toward the cave.

VICINITY MIDWAY

Radar was an active electromagnetic activity, so Admiral Kenzie had ordered his ships to turn off their chief means of detecting an enemy's approach in order to keep his ships from being detected. To give early warning, he kept one E-2 Hawkeye constantly on station two hundred miles to the southeast, the direction from which he assumed the Alien Fleet would approach. The Hawkeye had three means of detecting objects— radar, IRR (infrared radar), and a passive system.

He hoped keeping the Hawkeye over two hundred miles

away would give him both early warning and some distance in case it was detected by the Alien Fleet. He also had two F-14 Tomcats with the Hawkeye to give it some protection.

The craft were currently flying a figure eight, two hundred miles southeast of the fleet. The Hawkeye was at thirty thousand feet while the Tomcats were ten thousand feet higher than that. The dome receptor on the top of the Hawkeye gave the crew coverage out to just short of Hawaii.

They picked up incoming aircraft just about the same time several surface targets appeared at the edge of their detection to the southeast. The aircraft originated in the same location, so the crew had to assume they were carrier-launched. The Hawkeye tracked the aircraft as they spread out in a search pattern, a dozen planes on tracks ranging from southwest through almost due north of Hawaii.

And one of those craft was on a track for Midway, and if it went beyond the atoll, it would definitely discover the American fleet. Under radio listening silence, the commander on board the Hawkeye had to make a command decision. Using low-power radio he contacted the two F-14 pilots.

For a long moment there was silence from both planes in response to the plan he proposed. Then both pilots WILCO'd— will comply.

EASTER ISLAND

Aspasia's Shadow held the thummim in his hand, feeling the warmth that came out of the stone. The Grail was on a table in front of him, top end open. The end he had not yet partaken of.

He knew much of what Aspasia had known, but not everything. There were a few things his progenitor had withheld from the first incarnation of his Shadow via the *ka*. The knowledge of the ability of the Grail to grant immortality had not only been given him through the *ka*, but it was a well-known legend among the human priests on Atlantis. It had been part of the carrot Aspasia had dangled in front of humans to keep them in line.

But the other end of the artifact. There was nothing from the *ka* although the legend said the other end of the Grail granted knowledge. But knowledge of what? Aspasia's Shadow wondered. He supposed Artad knew, but it wasn't likely his ancient enemy would give him the answer.

Plus, the legends said that knowledge was also linked with the Ark, which he had left behind when he fled Mount Sinai. Aspasia's Shadow held the thummim over the end of the Grail, tempted ever so much to place it inside and let the alien machine do whatever it had been designed to.

AIRSPACE, PACIFIC

The F-14 pilot spotted the target aircraft visually, his radar turned off. He'd been flying on dead reckoning to the northeast. The Hawkeye had given him the speed and track of the bogey and the F-14's navigator had plotted both, picking the interception point. They were almost due north of Hawaii and the bogey was the one farthest right on the search fan the Alien Fleet had deployed.

"Ready?" the pilot asked his navigator over the intercom. "Yes."

Both men had families back in Hawaii and had no clue as to their fates. But they had known their own fates from the minute the senior officer on the Hawkeye had radioed his plan.

"Going in," the pilot said. He kicked in afterburners and roared toward the bogey. He could tell it was also an F-14 with extra fuel tanks slung under the wings. The bogey must have picked them up, because it began to turn in their direction.

The F-14 pilot fired his 20mm nose cannon, deliberately aiming wide and to the right. He banked slightly left, racing past the alien plane. He recognized the insignia painted on the tail. He knew men who had been in that squadron.

Keeping his afterburners firing, the pilot raced to the north. The alien plane followed. The F-14's navigator could hear the alien plane reporting their presence back to the fleet. As expected. The Alien Fleet would most likely assume he was heading back to his carrier and would report his location and direction, sending them in the wrong direction.

"We're good," the navigator reported.

"Roger that." The pilot pulled back hard on his stick and the F-14 did a loop and they were behind the alien plane. This time he didn't miss as he riddled the slow-reacting craft. It broke apart, pieces tumbling to the ocean.

"Well?" the navigator asked as they leveled off.

"We don't have enough fuel to get back to the fleet," the pilot said, something he knew the navigator was aware of.

"And they're probably tracking us now," the navigator added.

"Yeah." They continued to fly north for several moments in silence.

"Ah, hell," the pilot finally said. "Let's see what this sucker can do."

The second F-14 was above and behind the scout plane heading directly toward Midway and the fleet. It didn't miss as it made its first gun run, coming in out of the early-morning sun. The scout plane was blown to bits before it could radio a message.

EASTER ISLAND

Aspasia's Shadow slowly lowered the thummim toward the Grail, his hand trembling slightly. He paused as he noted one of the Marines monitoring the satellite radio coming toward him.

"What?"

"One scout plane has reported making contact with an enemy plane that was fleeing to the north. It has since ceased transmitting. We have lost contact with another scout."

Aspasia's Shadow cursed as he put the thummim back in its wooden box. He went to the guardian to make direct access to the information. The northernmost scout plane had reported an intercept, then went off the air. Another had simply disappeared. It would be most logical to assume the American fleet was to the north. His fleet was already turning to the north in pursuit.

Aspasia's Shadow had fought many battles and matched wits with the brightest mankind had to offer. He ordered his fleet to the northwest in the direction of Midway. He also noted that Artad had sent a message to Mars. There was no time to experiment with the Grail—he needed to ensure he won first.

MOUNT EVEREST

Turcotte was happy simply to have his feet underneath him, even though the top of the ridge was extremely narrow, less than a foot wide in places. He was bent over, breathing hard, trying to catch his breath, knowing from his experience climbing the side of the ridge that it was a futile effort. He reached down and extended a hand, helping Mualama up over the edge.

"Someone's ahead of us," Morris said.

Turcotte finally noticed the path dug into the snow.

"It's very recent," Morris said. "The wind yesterday would have wiped this out, so it happened during the night."

Turcotte looked up. There was a slight hint of dawn in the

air and he could barely make out the silhouette of the bulk of the mountain above them. There were no lights to indicate another party in sight. Morris checked the rope that connected all of them, making sure it was secure to each man's harness.

"I don't suppose it could be a party of civilian climbers," Turcotte said.

"No." Morris was checking Mualama's oxygen mask. "They'd have to be insane to be climbing this time of year."

"That makes me feel better," Turcotte muttered. He knelt and checked the snow. A couple of people, not many. He stood and slipped the MP-5 around so that it hung across his chest. He'd removed the trigger guard so he could fire it with his gloves, but as a precaution against accidents while climbing, there was no round in the chamber. He corrected that by pulling the bolt back.

He held the MP-5 in one hand, his climbing ax in the other. "Let's go."

Morris moved past him and took the lead. He began climbing up the ridgeline. The incline was slightly over forty-five degrees and Turcotte found it was all he could do to concentrate on putting one foot in front of the other and trying to breathe. He didn't even bother to look over his shoulder and check on Mualama—he assumed that if the line around his waist didn't pull him back, then the African archaeologist was keeping pace.

He bumped into Morris's back. "What's the matter?"

Morris simply pointed at the spot his headlamp illuminated. Two men lay dead, their faces frozen in silent agony. Both had packs on their backs with climbing gear and ropes attached.

"Who are they?" Turcotte asked, simply glad to halt and try to catch his breath.

"There are a lot of bodies on the mountain," Morris said.

"Over a hundred. I don't know who these two are." He knelt and scraped some more snow away. "They've been here a couple of years." Morris stood and stepped over them. "Let's go."

Turcotte looked down at the faces as he went over them. He couldn't imagine why anyone would come here unless they absolutely had to. These two men had died simply for the glory of climbing Everest. Glory was something that had lost its luster for Turcotte early in his army career. Without realizing it, Turcotte was lost in his thoughts, going slower and slower, more rope paying out between him and Morris in the lead until the medic was thirty feet ahead and twenty feet above.

The crack of the claymore going off shocked Turcotte out of his reverie, as did Morris's body slamming into him and knocking him backward into Mualama. The three men ended up in a pile on the ridgeline. Turcotte felt the body on top of him, not moving, even as Mualama was pushing to get free.

"Morris?" Turcotte slowly rolled the body to the side. The medic had been peppered by the steel balls the claymore sprayed out and Turcotte knew he was dead even before he checked for a pulse. "Son of a bitch," Turcotte muttered as he pulled his glove off and slipped it under Morris's mask. Nothing. No pulse, no breathing. Just blood, that was already freezing solid.

"What happened?" Mualama asked.

Turcotte had recognized the sound as soon as he heard it, but failed to react. "Booby trap," Turcotte said. "Claymore mine." He leaned his head down until his chin was just above Morris's face. His heart was racing, whether from the constant attempt to pump blood to his oxygen-starved body or from the brush with death.

"We need to keep moving," Mualama said.

With great effort, Turcotte lifted his head and looked at

the African, whose face was hidden by the goggles and oxygen mask. Slowly Turcotte unclipped Morris from the rope.
"Whoever's ahead of us doesn't want us following." He
knew if he'd been closer he'd be dead too. Morris's taking
the bulk of the blast and his being below were the only things
that had saved him.

Turcotte stood up, trying to focus his mind. Without
Morris—could they make it? He looked up. The first rays of
dawn were cutting across the mountain. He had a ground-
positioning receiver. And a map with the location. He knew
he could find the spot, but could he get to it? Morris had
said—what had he said? The last part would be technical
climbing. Across the top of the Kanshung Face.

Could he and Mualama do it? Turcotte took several deep
breaths, but he still felt light-headed. There was no choice.
He stepped over the medic's body. "Come on," he said to
Mualama.

MOUNT ARARAT

One of the Chinese transport planes had been shot down by a
Turkish jet after crossing the border. The other three had
pressed on, flying low, trying to stay under the Turkish radar.
Unfortunately, the Chinese did not have anything approaching the mapping and navigational tools the American MC-
130 had. As the three approached Mount Ararat and the
commandos inside prepared to jump, one of the craft clipped
the side of the mountain and exploded in a fireball. The other
two made it into the Ahara Gorge and men began jumping
out the doors in the rear of both craft, parachutes blossoming.

"More visitors," Kakel said, watching the paratroopers descending. They were standing in the mouth of the cave,
drawn out by the sound of the low-flying aircraft.

"Chinese," Yakov noted, seeing the insignia on the tail of one of the planes as it roared up the gorge, jumpers tumbling from the doors. "Mainland forces." He had no doubt why they were here. "Sent by Artad. This is his mothership and I suppose he wants it back."

Kakel cursed. "Things have changed, haven't they?"

"You can't keep the mothership hidden away anymore," Yakov said. "The world is at war and this is one of the pieces that is being fought over." He had a set of binoculars out and was watching the descending troops.

"Ah!" Yakov exclaimed. He extended the glasses to Kakel. "Look," he said, pointing.

Kakel peered up at the figure Yakov had indicated. "Who—or what—is that?"

"An Airlia. From Qian-Ling. It must be one of Artad's people." Even with just his eyes he spotted another dangling below a parachute, the long black, helmeted form easy to spot among the shorter Chinese commandos. "There are several of them."

"Come." Kakel slipped into the chamber, Yakov and the rest of the Delta commandos following. They went past the other Kurds who made their home there, toward the rear.

"We call this the back door," Kakel said. "I don't know why. It is the name that has been passed down. I have never seen a front door, if there is one."

Yakov assumed that if the mothership lay ahead, there had to be another entrance, a large one capable of allowing the vessel to exit. Kakel went into a narrow tunnel and Yakov and the others followed. The floor of the tunnel sloped down and Yakov noted that the stone was cut smoothly, as he had seen at other Airlia sites. He had seen photos of the mothership at Area 51, so he knew what to expect, but still, his heart was beating rapidly as they descended into Ararat.

"Why have your people kept this secret?" he asked Kakel.

"The legend is that this is the path through which those saved on the ark came out into the world," Kakel said over his shoulder. "We believe we would be the chosen ones to go back down this path and be saved if the ark ever were needed again. Why would we tell others about it?"

Yakov had traveled much of the world while working for Section IV, the Russian version of Area 51. He'd seen how many ancient societies had built much of their religion and their belief system around Airlia artifacts or legends. He could understand how the Kurds had kept the secret of the mothership for generations.

The tunnel came to an end, a solid rock wall blocking the way. Kakel didn't hesitate, walking up to it while reaching inside his shirt. He brought out a medallion with an eye inscribed on it and placed it in the center. An outline of a door appeared and it slid up, revealing an opening.

Kakel went through. Yakov ducked his head and passed through the opening. He came to an abrupt stop as he took in his new surroundings. He was in a massive cavern, over a mile long and a half mile wide, barely enough to contain the huge black ship resting in a metal cradle in front of him.

CHAPTER 16: THE PRESENT

MOUNT EVEREST

McGraw and Olivetti had heard the claymore go off, the sound echoing up the mountain. They felt no sense of elation or relief that whoever was following them was dead. They simply kept climbing according to the demands of their programming and the nanovirus. Even with the augmentation they had been given by the guardian, their bodies were beginning to break down as they climbed through the "death zone."

A hundred-foot-high, almost sheer wall appeared in front of them. The Second Step. McGraw pulled a piton off his rack, reached up, and hammered it in. Then he attached the rope and climbed up. He continued up the step, putting in protection all the way to the top. He secured himself and turned to belay Olivetti. The second SEAL came up the step quickly, simply unsnapping from the protection, not bothering to pull it out.

He reached the top of the step and they both looked up. They could see the top of Everest now, about five hundred feet above them. The Kanshung Face was off to their left. McGraw squinted, peering in the distance, then pulled a set of binoculars out of his pack. A small series of dots along the northeast ridge zoomed into focus. Climbers. A large party. They were at about the same altitude.

McGraw shifted the binoculars, taking in what he could see of the Face. The ridge he and Olivetti were on would take them within a hundred meters of the spot they were headed toward, then they would have to climb out onto the Face. He checked the other party once more. It was moving at a good pace. He calculated it would reach the Face about the same time as he and Olivetti, but they had the longer traverse. He put the binoculars back in his pack and resumed the climb.

UNITED NATIONS

The Chinese delegate stormed out.

That was expected. What wasn't expected was the number of delegates who indicated their country wanted to assume a neutral stance with regard to both Artad's and Aspasia's Shadow's ultimatums.

The Secretary General sat at the front of the General Assembly listening to the bedlam of arguments, while shuffling the various intelligence reports, some of which, frankly, he didn't believe. The UN had always suffered from reliance on member countries reporting to it and now many of those countries were either withholding information or deliberately lying. He picked up a piece of paper, which the header indicated had originated from Israel. It reported that Arab extremists had attempted to destroy the Ark of the Covenant. That was in direct conflict with an American intelligence report, which said the attack had been the act of a Jewish extremist.

The Secretary General knew the clock was ticking. Reports of biological and chemical warfare in South Korea were being overshadowed by reports American forces had detonated nuclear weapons. The American delegate was not only not commenting on these reports, he also would not say anything about the rumors that Hawaii had been overrun by alien forces and all American sea power in the Pacific had been assimilated, leaving the West Coast of the United States open to attack.

The isolationists in many countries were very powerful and there were indications that Guides working under orders from Aspasia's Shadow were behind many of the groups as well as some of the progressives who were urging their governments to join forces with Aspasia's Shadow.

Shoving the reports aside, the Secretary General stood and began pounding on the podium with a gavel. He continued for over a minute until the noise in the General Assembly gradually subsided.

"Enough." The single word echoed though the hall. He held up a single finger. "We will vote in one hour."

PACIFIC OCEAN, SOUTHEAST OF MIDWAY

The USS *Seawolf* was Admiral Kenzie's second trip wire and the only one remaining as he pulled in his air cover, hoping that he had diverted the Alien Fleet to the north. Located eighty-seven nautical miles southeast of Midway, the *Seawolf* was the most advanced submarine in the world, designed from the first concept with only one mission in mind: kill other submarines.

There were several key elements designed into the submarine to allow it to do that task efficiently and with minimum risk. The first was the emphasis on quiet. From the specially shaped propellers, to the rubber coating covering the entire ship that minimized water disturbance when moving, to the shape of the craft itself, everything about *Seawolf* was focused on making as little noise as possible.

It was also capable of diving deep. The exact depth was classified, and even the crew didn't know how far down they could go. On trials the captain had taken the sub down below three thousand feet with no problems. Beyond that, safety constraints limited their testing but it was felt the modular hull might even be able to go down to five thousand feet, far beyond any other submarine's range.

For weaponry, the *Seawolf* boasted Tomahawk cruise missiles with which it could target 75 percent of the Earth's land surface, and MK-48 torpedoes with both conventional and nuclear warheads with which to destroy other vessels.

Surprisingly, the *Seawolf* was relatively small. Just 353 feet long, it wasn't much longer than the first submarine of the same name that went to battle during World War II. Considering that the rear two-thirds of the sub were taken up by the nuclear power plant, engine room, and environmental control systems, the crew of 134 men was crowded into the front one-third. However, with a beam of over forty feet, it was twice as wide as those earlier subs.

Speed was another factor. Its nuclear power plant could propel it at over thirty-five knots, faster than any other submarine it expected to encounter. However, as those who had faced the alien threat had already found out, expectations were useless.

"We've got two bogeys," the targeting officer called out, relaying a report from the sailors monitoring the submarine's passive listening devices. "Range seventy miles."

"Direction?" the captain demanded.

"Tracking—tracking—straight at us, sir."

"Speed?"

The targeting officer relayed the question. When he got the answer from the sonarman he was disconcerted and repeated the question while the captain waited impatiently.

"Eighty-seven knots, sir. They're loud—some sort of water-pressure propulsion as near as we can determine."

"Bring us up to missile launch and surface scan depth,"

the captain ordered. His primary weapon against other submarines, the MK-48 torpedo, was an impressive combat system. Over nineteen feet long and weighing almost four thousand pounds, the MK-48 had a range of five miles. However, the torpedo's speed was thirty-five knots, more than sufficient to track down any other normal submarine but almost useless against those which were approaching.

"Plot interception angles on both targets," the captain ordered as he pondered the situation. If the bogeys picked up his shots, they could easily outrun the torpedoes. If he didn't fire, they would be at Midway in an hour and most likely attack the fleet shortly thereafter.

They certainly hadn't ever presented this tactical problem at the Naval Academy or the various schools the captain had attended over the course of his career. He was reasonably confident his ship hadn't been detected, as neither bogey had changed direction, and he was running silent and in place.

"At launch depth," the targeting officer informed him. "Underwater bogeys, fifty-two miles."

"Give me a surface scan," the captain ordered.

"Multiple surface targets bearing one hundred degrees at eighty-seven miles. Two carriers at least. Course same as bogeys."

The Alien Fleet. They hadn't been fooled, the captain realized. Two problems. At least the advance subs were probably ahead of the shield.

"Forty-three miles," his targeting officer announced. "I've plotted intercept vectors for the MK-48s but once they detect our launch—" He left the rest unsaid.

"We need to launch now," the captain said.

"Sir, they're out of range."

"Here's the plan," the captain began. As he rapidly issued his orders, his crew sprang to life, implementing them.

"Thirty-five miles," the targeting officer announced, sliding

his arming key into the slot at his position. "We're green on torpedoes and missiles and at launch depth."

The captain reached under his shirt and pulled out his own
key and inserted it. "Arm," he ordered. Both men turned at
the same time. The other two launch safeguards had already
been initiated when they went to combat alert and a red light
flashed as all four were now set.

"Launch," the captain ordered.

The submarine vibrated as torpedoes roared out of their
tubes and a half dozen Tomahawk cruise missiles fired upward, one after another.

"Dive," the captain ordered as the last missile left its
launcher.

"Twenty-two miles," the targeting officer reported.

"Let's see how smart these alien machines are," the captain muttered to himself as the floor of the control room
sloped forward as the *Seawolf* headed into the depths. The
sound of the Tomahawks should have covered up the noise
the torpedoes made leaving the tube. The torpedoes were set
for their slowest and quietest speed. As the Tomahawks
arced upward into the sky, the torpedoes were headed out at
right angles, not on a direct intercept course with the bogeys
but in a direction to get to their projected paths before they
arrived.

"Underwater, seventeen miles. Time to target on Tomahawks, two minutes."

Just less than eighty-seven miles to the southeast of *Seawolf,*
the Alien Fleet was steaming at flank speed. The two supercarriers flanked the *Jahre Viking,* which was in the process of
spitting out two more Springfield clones. In the front was the
resurrected *Arizona,* with Captain Lockhart on the bridge.
She'd received the report from the two submarines running

point for the fleet of the cruise missile launch and her crew
was tracking the incoming missiles.

"Launch decoy," the *Seawolf*'s captain ordered.

From the top deck, a small submersible was fired out of a
tube. It went up to fifteen hundred feet and slowly began circling as it emitted the same signal a Los Angeles class submarine would.

"Level out," the captain ordered as they reached three
thousand feet depth.

"Eight-point-seven miles," the targeting officer reported.
"They've adjusted course, homing on decoy."

"Our torpedoes?"

"In place, halted." Despite all the sophisticated computers
crammed into the operations center, the targeting officer was
looking at an old-fashioned stopwatch, checking it against
his computer display.

"Tomahawks, five seconds."

Lockhart saw the explosions, one right after another as the six
cruise missiles hit the shield and detonated, a half mile in front
of her. The shield absorbed the blasts and then all was still.

Two modified Los Angeles class submarines slipped out
of the *Jahre Viking* and the Alien Fleet continued toward
Midway.

"Sonar reports torpedo doors opening," the targeting officer
reported. He checked his watch. "Five seconds."

The captain nodded. He had assumed that the alien submarines would attack "by the book." Now he would find out
if he was correct.

"Three. Two. One."

"Detonate!" the captain ordered.

• • •

Unshielded, both alien submarines took the full brunt of torpedoes detonating less than two hundred meters from each. The *Seawolf*'s guess as to their paths once they detected the Tomahawk launch had been correct.

Metal crumpled, seawater flooded in.

"We've got two breaking up," the targeting officer excitedly relayed from the sonarman. "Two bogeys down!"

A cheer rose in the operations center, to be immediately squelched by the captain's shout. "At ease!" When the yelling subsided, he spoke. "Remember there were probably sailors on those subs. Men who used to be like us." Sure that had sunk in, he ordered the submarine to surface-scan depth.

"Report."

The targeting officers face was grim. "Surface contacts, seventy-eight miles. No change."

The captain nodded. As expected. "Plot us a course back to Midway and the fleet. We've done what we can."

AIRSPACE, GULF OF MEXICO

Sherev looked out the window of the Osprey and saw the apparently abandoned oil rig to their left. The engine nacelles on the end of the wings slowly began rotating from forward into the upright position. He'd flown in an Israeli Air Force Learjet across the Mediterranean, refueling in the Azores and then across the Atlantic, before landing at the airfield Garlin had indicated for him to go to. A half dozen men clad in black fatigues and swaddled in body armor were seated along both sides of the craft. They were members of Unit 269, the most secret and elite unit in the Israeli army.

Five of the commandos carried Heckler & Koch MP-5 submachine guns. While the venerable Uzi was homegrown, these men were more concerned with functionality and accuracy. The sixth man also had an H & K gun—the PSG-1 sniper rifle.

In the center of the cargo area, the Ark of the Covenant was packed inside a large plastic case. A second, smaller case held the priest's garments that had been recovered from beneath the Great Sphinx in Egypt.

Sherev had not bothered to inform his government of his decision to bring the Ark to America. There was so much going on around the world, he had a strong feeling he wouldn't be missed for a while. He'd defended Israel for decades against enemies in all directions, but recent events had caused him to reevaluate his focus, and he had been forced to admit that the threat to the planet was greater than the threat to Israel.

With a slight bounce, the Osprey landed. The door to the pilot's compartment had been locked when it landed at the airfield and the cargo compartment empty when the back ramp came down. Sherev was irritated with this arrangement. If the Ark of the Covenant was so important, someone should have greeted them.

The back ramp slowly lowered and Sherev stood. Four of the commandos raced off the plane, taking up defensive positions around the landing pad. The other two picked up the case holding the Ark, while Sherev got the smaller case. He nodded and they walked off the plane. As soon as they were clear the ramp closed and the aircraft roared off into the sky.

A door slid open in an elevator housing directly in front of them. Sherev hesitated. He could smell the salt water of the Gulf. And as the Osprey dwindled into a small dot in the distance, silence reigned. There was no one about.

Reluctantly Sherev nodded toward the open door. He pointed at the sniper and gave him a thumbs-up. The sniper went over to the abandoned tower and began climbing up to get an overwatch position. With the other five commandos and the two cases, Sherev entered the elevator. The door slid shut and the elevator began descending.

Sherev stepped back as the five commandos aligned themselves in front of him, weapons at the ready, facing the door.

The elevator came to a halt.

Sherev cursed as he heard a noise behind him and what he had thought was a wall was obviously a door. He spun about, pistol at the ready. The silhouette of a man stood there, strangely bisected by what appeared to be a waist-high table the width of the elevator in front of him.

Behind the man—Sherev's finger was on the trigger, but what he saw behind the man froze him in shock and horror. And that was all it took as what he had thought was a table shot forward, the front edge composed of razor-sharp black metal.

The front edge hit Sherev in the stomach, slicing through his body with little regard for flesh and bone, continuing through the elevator. The top half of Sherev's body tumbled onto the case holding the Ark of the Covenant. The five commandos were also cut in half as they turned around, trying to get a shot off. It was over in less than a second.

Through the physical shock Sherev knew he was dying, blood pumping out of his torso. Despite that, his mind kept replaying what he had seen behind the man. As his last breath left his lungs he experienced a fear far beyond anything his worst nightmares had ever produced. His last thought was that he was glad that he would be dead and never have to see or face that vision again.

MOUNT EVEREST

Turcotte halted at the base of the Second Step and looked up. One hundred feet. Impossible. He squinted, trying to see through his partially frozen goggles. There were pitons set in the ice wall, each about four feet apart. He reached up, not quite believing what he was seeing, his gloved hand touching the closest one. He automatically reached down, pulled up the rope, and attached it to a snap link and onto the piton. He kicked his right foot into the ice wall and, pulling on the rope, levered himself up two feet.

He glanced over his shoulder. Mualama was waiting for him to get high enough before following. The African had been extremely quiet since they'd left the United States. Since getting on the mountain Turcotte had been so focused simply on surviving he had paid scant attention to the former Watcher. And there was no time to worry about him now. Turcotte took another snap link and piece of sling, reached above his head, and clipped in.

QIAN-LING

Artad placed his hands on the side of the guardian and was encompassed in its golden glow. His forces had landed in Turkey and were heading for the cavern holding the second mothership and, more importantly, the Master Guardian.

South Korea was a morass. The surprise use of nuclear weapons by the Americans had shut the western corridor. Troops were making progress on the eastern side of the peninsula, but slowly. Artad cared little. The entire campaign was a distraction. The same with Taiwan, where his forces were advancing slowly against the shrewd defenders. He realized now that he should have sent Chi Yu with his Kortad to Ararat, not to aid in the invasion of Taiwan. He considered the mistake a result of not having fully recovered from his long hibernation and acting too quickly. He issued an order for the shield generator to be off-loaded onto a ground transport and for Chi Yu to return to Qian-Ling for his personal use. And for more of the "flying dragons" to be uncrated by his Kortad.

The humans fought brutally among themselves, Artad noted. The history of the planet since he had gone to sleep indicated that mankind had spent its existence in constant warfare. A species warring against itself was a rare thing in the cosmos. Very rare, but Artad was not surprised.

He continued to review the situation.

Mars.

There was a reply from the Airlia trapped at Cydonia.

They would consider his proposal of an alliance if he promised amnesty, giving his word as an officer of the Kortad as his bond.

Only consider if he gave his word? What choice did they have? Artad reined in his anger and sent a reply.

MOUNT ARARAT

Yakov felt like an ant, an odd emotion considering that he had always towered over most men. But walking underneath the mothership he realized how truly puny man and his achievements were compared to the Airlia. The mothership could swallow a dozen supercarriers with no problem. And it flew, not just in the atmosphere, but through interstellar space. He could not imagine such a massive thing actually lifting out of the cradle of black metal it rested on. It was just too large. He noted that smaller Talon spacecraft were attached to the nose of the mothership, their large size dwarfed by the ship they clung to.

"Where's the Master Guardian?" Major Briggs asked.

Yakov was startled out of his awe. He pulled out the papers he'd retrieved from the Iranian general. "This way."

• • •

The Chinese entered the cave firing, not caring if their bullets struck men, women, or children. The Kurds fought bravely, but were overwhelmed by superior firepower. Once the last Kurd was struck down, the Kortad entered, swords in hand. They decapitated all the bodies, even though they were obviously dead.

Then they headed for the back of the cave and the tunnel that led to the mothership.

Yakov arrived at one of the massive braces that held the ship up. It consisted of a single arc of *b'ja,* the black metal used by the Airlia, and was over ten feet in width and depth. According to the paper, an entrance to the ship was in the metal at ground level, but Yakov saw nothing. He hadn't expected to, given that the American scientists had spent decades searching for a way into the mothership hidden at Area 51.

He checked the paper, then held it up while he looked at the brace. He pressed the Watcher ring against the spot indicated. The outline of a door appeared, over eight feet high by four wide. It slid up to reveal a room six feet in diameter.

"Going up?" Yakov looked at Briggs and Kakel.

CHAPTER 17: THE PRESENT

SOUTH KOREA

Colonel Lin fell to his knees and vomited. He was at the objective, Seoul, but it was a Pyrrhic victory. He staggered to his feet and looked about the empty downtown street. There were few dead on the streets, which was strange given that the nerve gas assault must have killed millions. He assumed most had crawled inside to die. He continued to move forward, even though he led no men. Most had been killed fighting north of the city and then when the mushroom clouds had appeared in the south, even the rigid discipline of the PKA had fallen apart and the rest had slunk away into the darkness of the previous evening.

But Lin had pushed on, his mind focused on the objective, even though he knew he was going farther into the radioactive zone. He assumed he had already received a fatal dose, as sickness was wracking his body. He reached down to his combat vest and pushed the send button for the mike attached there.

"Headquarters. Colonel Lin. I am in the objective. Over."

"Roger. Proceed to river and find crossing sites. Over."

He came around a corner and saw the Han River. And the destroyed bridges. He knew he was a dead man and now he also knew the offensive was doomed. The western route was shut and would be shut as long as the radioactivity blocked the way, which would be beyond his lifetime and that of all his countrymen. And even if they won, what would they win? A devastated country full of dead?

Lin paused, something catching his eyes. A sign on a small store. He staggered over and shoved the door open. The front of the store was empty. He slung his weapon over his shoulder as he walked around a counter and pushed open the door to the rear. There were two bodies huddled together on a mattress on the floor. An old man, his arms around an old woman.

Lin knelt next to them. He realized he had taken the streets and woven his way through the southern capital to this destination subconsciously. He'd learned the address when he'd been doing intelligence preparation for his mission.

Lin noted how tightly the old man held the woman. He reached down and pulled a wallet out of the man's pants. He flipped it open and recognized the name: his father's brother. Separated over half a century ago.

Lin keyed the radio. "Headquarters. Colonel Lin. It is over. This was wrong. It is wrong." He let go of the key.

The small earpiece squawked, as his superiors demanded an explanation of his strange message. Lin pulled the earpiece out and left it dangling. He threw his pack with the radio in it on the ground. He reached in, ignoring the radio and pulling out a thin blanket. He carefully placed it over the bodies.

Then he sat down on the floor. He put an arm up over the blanket, feeling the cold bodies underneath, and closed his eyes.

TAIWAN

Chang Tek-Chong leaned against the front of the hastily dug foxhole, watching the advancing Chinese forces. They were less than a half mile away. The tactics he had come up with had worked to an extent, but there was no stopping the wave of humanity the Chinese kept pouring ashore behind the shield. His position was located in the foothills of the mountains that ran along the east coast of the island. The entire west coast had been overrun. The most fertile and productive part of the country was in enemy hands.

Tek-Chong reached up and pulled a heavy piece of plywood over the top of the foxhole, covering it. He heard the rumble of heavy equipment and then the thud as a backhoe dumped a load of dirt on the top of the plywood, burying him and the other occupant of the hole.

Tek-Chong leaned back against the freshly cut earth. He noticed that he was breathing more shallowly, which brought a wry smile to his face. It wasn't as if his partner in the hole was taking any of it. He reached out and felt the cold steel. No comfort.

He looked at his wrist and the small glowing face told him he'd been buried for ten minutes. He thought of his father, who had died fighting the refugees from the mainland who had taken over Formosa. And now he was fighting for that same regime, against another invasion from the same mainland. He laughed out loud at the insanity, and then cut it short, realizing that mainland forces were probably walking right over his site.

He checked his watch again. Given the rate at which the mainland forces had been advancing, he was now inside the shield wall. He reached out like a lover in the dark toward his companion. His fingers lightly reached over the metal to the small keyboard. He blindly tapped in the command.

Tek-Chong died instantly as the nuclear weapon went off. The explosion roared out of the foxhole, incinerating the mainland forces nearby, then rebounding off the interior of the shield wall like a captured tsunami of fire. The effect of the single bomb was multiplied by being captured inside the shield wall and within less than thirty seconds the entire contingent of mainland forces and all surviving Taiwanese inside were dead.

THE GULF OF MEXICO

Garlin placed the priest's crown on top of Duncan's head. She was strapped to an upright table, her arms and legs bound tightly. He left the room briefly, then returned, wheeling in a cart with a large plastic case on top of it. Duncan's eyes watched his movements, but she didn't say anything. Her previous meal had been drugged, she knew that now, because her last memory was of eating the food Garlin had brought. Then she had awoken, strapped down to the table. She blinked as she noted the massive amount of blood that blanketed the top of the plastic case. Fresh blood, glistening under the bright overhead lights.

"What happened?" she demanded.

Garlin ignored her. He flipped latches and took the top off the case. Duncan recognized the Ark of the Covenant. He reached inside and opened the Ark's lid and pulled out the leads. He carefully attached them to the crown. He seemed to know exactly what he was doing, which Duncan found strange. It was as if he had handled the Ark and crown before.

Whose blood? she wondered.

What the hell was going on?

Her thoughts were cut short by a spike of pain and then a vision of a beautiful white city with a magnificent palace in the center.

Garlin reached up and gripped her chin in his hand, squeezing tight, drawing her attention from the vision inside her head to him. "We want to know where you came from."

It was a struggle to talk, to hold back the vision flooding in through the crown. "What do you mean?"

"We know you're not from Earth," Garlin said. "We want the location of your home world."

CHAPTER 18: THE PRESENT

MOUNT EVEREST

Mike Turcotte sat down in the snow. All he wanted to do was sleep. The snow felt very comforting, like a nice blanket. He leaned back, enveloped in it. So nice. He remembered Sunday mornings in Maine, his only day off from cutting, when he could sleep in, his body completely worn-out from a week on the saw. This was so much better.

A bolt of pain spiked through his brain.

Duncan.

He sat up, snow falling off his parka. Turcotte opened his eyes, but all he could see was formless white. The pain, though, was still there.

His goggles were frozen over, he realized. He wasn't in Maine. Goggles, why was he wearing goggles? He reached up and fumbled, pulling them down. He was in a depression in the snow. The sky above was clear blue, the clearest he had ever seen. Beautiful. It reminded him of someplace in his past, someplace very safe, very home.

Duncan.

What was happening?

A form intruded on the bluest sky. A figure swaddled in Gore-Tex. It stepped over him and disappeared up the mountain.

Turcotte rolled his head back. Ice. Snow. Rock.

Duncan. The pain was worse than the cold. It brought him out of his desire to sleep, to fade away, to become part of the nothingness that the mountain was part of.

The mountain.

Everest. He knew where he was. Sitting up again was the hardest thing he ever did.

He got to his feet. Mualama was about ten meters away, moving upslope. The last twenty-four hours with the archaeologist flooded over Turcotte. Mualama reminded him of a sphinx. Silent. Brooding. Waiting. Waiting for what, he wondered.

Lisa Duncan.

Turcotte turned toward the peak. He took a step. He saw that about two hundred feet above them the ridgeline steepened. Turcotte felt a shiver run up his back, not from the cold, but from the man ahead of him.

MOUNT ARARAT

The "elevator" in the strut had started slowly up the massive leg and then begun moving in a horizontal direction as near as Yakov could tell. The pace was incredibly slow, something he found strange for a piece of machinery associated with such a spectacle as the mothership. He had expected to be swiftly transported into the front of the mothership, but instead they seemed to be traversing the entire length of the ship at a snail's pace.

"Do you think there's a control panel that we don't see?" Major Briggs asked.

The walls of the room were smooth black with no visible markings, but Yakov remembered that the door to the room had been invisible on the strut.

"There might be," he acknowledged, "but I do not know how to access it, if there is one."

"We seem to be taking the—" Briggs began, but he shut up as the room came to a halt.

The three faced the door and were startled when the wall

behind them opened. They spun about, weapons at the ready. An empty corridor beckoned, the walls made of the same black metal.

"Come," Yakov said as he stepped into the corridor. The American and Kurd followed. The corridor curved slightly to the left so he could only see about fifty feet ahead. The sound of his boots hitting the floor bounced off the walls. Yakov came to an abrupt halt as the corridor straightened out.

"Oh, man," Major Briggs muttered as he came up next to Yakov.

The corridor extended straight ahead, for what appeared to the length of the mothership. Close by they could see cross corridors.

"Where to now?" Briggs asked.

Yakov studied the sheet of paper. He couldn't read the rune markings, but he did find the corridor. "That way." He pointed down the corridor. "Thirty-eighth hall to the right."

VICINITY MIDWAY ISLAND

"According to the reports we have," Admiral Kenzie said, "they are going to have to turn off the shield when they launch their aircraft."

His senior air officer, the CAG, or Commander Air Group, considered that. "We'd have to be close by and act quickly."

Kenzie nodded. "It's our only shot to get at those ships."

They had the Alien Fleet positioned eight hundred air miles to the southeast according to the intelligence report radioed back by *Seawolf*. The news of the destruction of two alien submarines by the attack sub had raised morale a little, but everyone was also aware that the subs hadn't been shielded.

"I want half your planes in this initial assault. Launch in

five minutes. We hold half back just in case—" He didn't finish the sentence. No word had been heard from the Area 51
survivors and the messages coming out of Washington were
garbled at best. "Get to it."

MOUNT EVEREST

The Kanshung Face extended to the SEALs' left and down
over a mile. It had never been climbed for the simple reason
it made absolutely no sense to climb it, as pretty much any
other approach to Everest was less difficult. McGraw and
Olivetti had taken the easiest route they could to get to the
same height as their goal, and now they had about fifty meters of lateral traverse across a ledge near the top of the face
to their objective.

McGraw put in the first piece of protection, hooked a rope
through it, attached a sling from his harness to the rope, and
set out onto the Face. When he put the second piece of protection in, Olivetti clipped into the rope and began following.

Lexina looked dispassionately at a body clad in ancient clothing lying in the snow. That humans, rogue Watchers, had
climbed this high so long ago in their attempt to hide
Excalibur, she found quite remarkable, but foolish. That no
one had removed Excalibur in the millennia since it was hidden wasn't due to the efforts of these humans but rather the
fact that the sword was so critical that any attempt by either
side to recover it would have resulted in what was happening
now: all-out war. And that had been avoided for one major reason—they had no idea what the status of the *other* war was.

Lexina could hear the Chinese climbers talking excitedly
among themselves about the body, but she simply stepped
over it. Aksu snapped out orders and the men fell silent,

continuing along the ridge until they came to the edge of the
Kanshung Face.

Lexina pointed out along the Face. "It is out there."

Aksu nodded and edged out onto the Face, putting in protection.

Left. Right. Left. Right. Stop. Breathe. Breathe. Breathe.
Left. Right. Left. Right. Breathe. Breathe. Breathe.

The rhythm was like a drumbeat in Turcotte's head, propelling him up the ridgeline. A distant part of his mind knew
he should be alert for ambush or another trip wire across the
path cut in the snow that he was following, but a larger part
almost wished a mine would explode in front of him and put
him out of this miserable state of affairs.

He could barely see five feet in front of him because his
head was bowed, his eyes focused on a spot just ahead of
where his next step would be. Beyond that he dared not look
or else he feared he would lose what little energy he had left.

Left. Right. Left—Turcotte paused, right foot lifted
barely six inches, all he could manage. The trail disappeared,
because the mountain disappeared. Ridgeline gave way to
vertical face. Turcotte slowly lifted his head. A rope was
clipped into the mountainside. Looking farther, he could see
two figures edging their way along the rock face, attached to
the other end of the rope. They were about fifty meters away
and, even as he watched, the first one disappeared around a
cornice of rock and ice.

Turcotte fumbled for his MP-5, bringing it up to his
shoulder. The oxygen mask was in the way as he tried to
sight the weapon. As he tried to unhook the mask, the second
figure also went out of sight. He became aware that Mualama
was just in front of him. Turcotte shifted the aim of the
weapon toward the archaeologist's back and his gloved finger touched the trigger.

Turcotte let the gun drop on its sling. Then he hooked into the rope and moved out onto the Kanshung Face following Mualama.

MOUNT ARARAT

The first Chinese commandos into the cavern were cut down by well-disciplined bursts of fire from the Delta Force men. It was a massacre and over a dozen Chinese lay dead in the entrance.

Then the first Kórtad entered, spear leveled under its arm. Bullets hit the black armor, ricocheting off. As each Delta man shot at it, the Kortad would shift the point of the spear and fire a golden pulse. The flash of gold would hit the American soldier, briefly envelop him, and then he would drop, unconscious.

It was over in less than twenty seconds.

The rest of the Kortad entered and the rock floor flowed with blood as they decapitated the unconscious men. The surviving Chinese forces took up defensive positions.

"Thirty-seven," Yakov said.

"Thirty-seven," Major Briggs confirmed.

They had come about a half mile down the middle of the mothership. Yakov slowed as he came to the next opening. "Thirty-eight." He turned the corner.

A twenty-foot-high dull red pyramid was in the center of a huge spherical room, a forty-foot walkway leading out to it.

VICINITY MIDWAY ISLAND

Captain Lockhart received the report of inbound aircraft with no concern. The entire Alien Fleet was under the guard of the shield. She was more involved with preparing the strike wings on the two carriers. Planes were being readied, bombs full of nanovirus were being loaded, and infected pilots were receiving their orders via the nanovirus inside them.

The Alien Fleet wasn't hard to spot. CAG (Commander Air Group) had his planes at forty thousand feet and the ships, huge as the two carriers and tanker were, appeared to be tiny toys on the surface of the ocean far below.

He'd assigned each plane a number and broken them into three groups, one for each of the capital ships. As they approached the strike point, they began to circle, waiting.

"CAG, this is Alpha-One. Over."

"This is CAG. Over."

"Do you see what I see in the lead of that fleet? Over."

CAG reached for a set of binoculars and trained them on the fleet far below and ahead of them. The silhouette of the lead ship was strangely familiar but at the same time not anything he had ever studied in his ship recognition classes. The superstructure was, well, the only word he could come up with was archaic. But the Tomahawk missile launchers where large turrets should have been were as modern as his plane.

Then he realized what he was seeing. "That's the *Arizona*." Strangely, the sight of the long-sunken warship didn't surprise CAG. It made him angry that the aliens would scavenge even that to use against them. "Alpha, Bravo, and Charlie flights. Stick with your primary targets. Our concern right now are the two carriers and the tanker. We go when they launch. Over."

He received acknowledgments from all three flight leaders. Three lines of planes were spreading out below him, each circling just outside the shield near their target. Each line consisted of twelve planes, a five-thousand-pound bomb under each wing. Twenty-four bombs per ship.

• • •

Lockhart gave the order to launch. The two carriers turned into the wind and the first planes were catapulted into the air. At that moment, the shield was shut down.

"Go, go, go!" CAG screamed into his mike.

All the planes headed for their targets.

Lockhart saw the planes coming in for the attack. She smiled, but the smile disappeared as the nanovirus took over, forcing her to put the shield back up.

CAG saw the second plane launched smash into the invisible barrier just ahead and cursed. His squadrons didn't have enough fuel to hang around here much longer and still be able to make it back.

CAG launched his bombs and then cursed as he saw the impotent explosion when the ordnance hit the shield wall.

CAG looked once more at the *Arizona*. "Flight leaders, take your planes home. Over." He turned his plane and started to circle, just outside the shield.

"This is Alpha flight leader. CAG, what are you doing? Over."

"I'm going to hang around."

Lockhart saw the planes fly away. All except one. But it had dropped its bombs already so it was no longer a threat. She ordered the shield down and the launch to resume.

She looked over at the *Washington,* seeing a third plane brought onto the parallel catapult.

CAG saw the plane rocket down the runway and into the air. At the same time, he turned the nose of his plane toward the large carrier. He could see sailors on the deck of the ship.

Infected sailors, he reminded himself. He took a look to his right as he passed by the *Arizona*. He could swear he saw someone on the bridge looking straight at him. He flicked a half salute, then turned his attention back to the deck of the carrier. He saw the two planes in launch position and aimed directly for them.

As the deck rapidly approached, CAG suddenly remembered a prayer he'd been taught by his mother so many years ago. He began reciting it as he lost altitude and continued to accelerate.

Lockhart watched the F-14 and it was only when it was less than a quarter mile from the carrier that she realized what the pilot was planning on doing. As the part of her controlled by the nanovirus yelled commands, the smaller part that was her free self mentally saluted the pilot.

The commands were far too late. The crews manning one of the 20mm Phalanxes on the carrier got off a short burst that missed badly and the escort ships were too slow to react. The F-14 traversed the last quarter mile in just a couple of seconds before slamming into the *Washington* just forward of the two planes loaded on the catapults. The aircraft exploded, ripping open the flight deck and blasting down through the hangar deck into the bowels of the ship. Secondary explosions from fuel on board waiting planes rocked the ship.

The forward speed of the carrier fanned the flames, which enveloped planes farther back on the flight deck. One by one they also exploded, adding to the carnage and destruction. The captain of the *Washington* immediately ordered the engine room to reverse thrust to bring the massive ship to a halt before the flames engulfed the entire ship. He gave the order with tears in his eyes, forced to by the nanovirus, while his core wanted to keep the ship moving, to burn it all up. He could look down on the deck and watch his sailors fighting the fire, getting too close, forced by the nanovirus, and being burned alive. More sailors would move forward to take their place.

Lockhart immediately issued orders for the entire Alien Fleet to halt. The shield generator was on board the *Jahre Viking* and the options were either keep moving and leave the *Washington* practically undefended, or halt the entire fleet until the fire was brought under control.

She checked status of repairs on the *Stennis*. The nanovirus was very efficient. It would have one catapult ready for launch in eighteen minutes.

MOUNT ARARAT

Leaving Briggs and Kakel at the entrance, Yakov had made his way along the walkway to the Master Guardian. He was standing on a three-foot-wide, black metal ledge, which went all around the pyramid. He placed his hands on the Master Guardian. Nothing. The surface lacked the glow he had seen on the golden guardians. He looked around. The pyramid was in the exact center of a perfect sphere and the walls were featureless. He could see no visible means of support for the guardian unless it was the ledge and the walkway.

"Trouble," Major Briggs called out in a low yell.

Yakov ran back to join them. Briggs was lying on his stomach, peering down the center corridor, showing as little of his body as possible. Kakel was against the far wall, also slightly leaning out and looking. Yakov peeked around the corner and saw what had alerted Briggs. Several tall figures were slowly walking their way. They were so far away that

Yakov couldn't see much detail, but he did note the red hair, the spears in their hands, and the disproportionate bodies.

"Airlia," he whispered.

"We don't have much time," Briggs said.

"We do not control our fate," Yakov said. "That is up to Major Turcotte. He must free Excalibur so I can access the Master Guardian."

CHAPTER 19: THE PRESENT

MOUNT EVEREST

Major Turcotte had stopped. Both hands were wrapped around the sling attached to his harness and he was leaning against the side of Mount Everest, hunched, lungs screaming for oxygen. He felt far removed from the world and the troubles that had precipitated his coming here and climbing the mountain.

Morris had said that the blood packing would last for forty-eight hours. Turcotte wondered how the medic knew that; had they tested it? Or was it a typical military SWAG— stupid wild-ass guess? The pounding in his head was worse; he couldn't even come close to feeling like he had caught his breath, and his extremities felt like lead pipes.

He dully felt something vibrate the rope. Again. Reluctantly, Turcotte turned his head. Mualama was still moving along the ledge, heading for the cornice, jerking the rope with each step. Turcotte saw frozen blood around the edges of the archaeologist's oxygen mask. He was amazed the older man was still moving.

Leaning back on the rope Turcotte reached inside his parka. He pulled out a small metal thermos. He carefully unscrewed the cap. Steam rose out of the small opening. He pulled his oxygen mask away, distantly feeling skin rip where it had frozen to his face. He didn't care at all about that as he slowly tipped the thermos and felt the scalding hot coffee pour into his mouth. In reality, he figured the coffee was lukewarm at best, but it burned into his core as it went down his throat.

He tucked the thermos under one arm and reached with his free hand once more inside his parka. Two pills lay in his gloved hand. The amphetamines that Morris had given him with his dire warning about their use. Turcotte took one, popped it in his mouth and washed it down with another mouthful of coffee, then did the same with the second.

The rope vibrated again and Turcotte almost lost his grip. He was reminded of the Darby Queen obstacle course at Ranger School at Fort Benning so many years earlier. There was a rope climb where there were so many students making it across at the same time that when one fell the entire thing whipsawed, often tossing off others.

Turcotte grabbed hold of the rope with both hands, pulled his left foot free of the mountain, swung it a foot to the side, and slammed it in. He was moving again.

McGraw hammered in two pieces of protection before checking out the three bodies lying on the thin ledge. Two were dressed in ancient clothing. And in the center sat someone with more recent, but still old clothing. And behind them, encased in a wall of ice, the scabbard with Excalibur inside of it.

McGraw reached over his shoulder and pulled an ice ax off his pack. As he pulled it back to strike the ice, Olivetti tapped him on the shoulder and pointed to the northeast. A line of dots extended across a ledge about five hundred meters away. Olivetti pointed to himself, then once more at the climbers. McGraw nodded and turned his attention to the ice.

Olivetti put in two pieces of protection, then leaned back in his harness. He pulled his pack off, attaching it to one of the slings, then opened it, pulling out a hard plastic case about three feet long. Wedging the case between himself and the mountain, Olivetti opened it, removing a barrel and stock/receiver. He slid the barrel into the receiver and twisted, locking it in place. A scope was already in place on top and he pulled a ten-round magazine out, slamming it home. He tucked two more magazines into his parka.

He pulled the bolt back, putting a round in the chamber. Leaning back, he ignored the case, which tumbled away down the mountain. He put the rifle against his shoulder and sighted on the last in line. In between breaths, he smoothly pulled the trigger. He was already shifting to the next figure in line before the bullet reached its first target.

For a few moments, everyone thought the trail climber had slipped as the Chinese soldier slid down the mountain, then came to an abrupt halt as the safety line cinched tight. The other eleven climbers all gripped the mountain, holding on against the weight of the fallen man. But then they all heard the echo of the shot. Just then the next-to-last man was hit and tumbled off.

Lexina, second from the front, found she was struggling even harder for air as the harness around her waist tightened from the pressure on the safety rope. It was Aksu, climbing lead, who realized the danger as his third man was hit.

"Cut the line!" he screamed toward the rear.

A bullet hit the third from rear in the head, splattering the snow and ice with blood and brains. The fourth from rear had heard Aksu and had been reaching for a knife, but abandoned the effort in order to be able to avoid getting pulled off the face of the mountain by the deadweight of three bodies dangling below.

Lexina didn't waste any time as she pulled a knife from her belt and turned around. Coridan was the climber behind her and he had both hands on the safety rope, holding tight. Another shot rang out as Lexina slashed down with the knife, cutting the rope between herself and her fellow One Who Waits.

Without the support of Lexina and Aksu, the surviving climbers behind her didn't have the strength to hold up the weight of the four dead. They were peeled off the mountain one by one, Coridan the last to go. He was reaching out toward Lexina as the rope pulled him away, tumbling down the side of Everest.

Lexina turned back to the front and looked. She could see someone leaning out from the side of the mountain ahead, a rifle in his hands, and she realized she had only gained a moment's respite with her instinctive action.

Aksu had pulled his weapon from his pack and was trying to aim, while at the same time maintaining a grip on the mountain. He was bringing it up one-handed to his shoulder when a round from the sniper hit him in the chest. His body bounced back and he dropped the gun, but still he managed to hold on to the protection he had just put in.

Lexina desperately searched for someplace to hide, but they were in the middle of a flat space. She scrambled forward toward Aksu, trying to put his body between her and the sniper.

Turcotte heard the shots and could tell they were emanating not far from his location, just around the cornice where the two climbers had disappeared. It was less than ten meters away and from the first shot he had increased his climb, trading safety for speed, closing on Mualama.

Through the telescopic site, Olivetti could see the last members of the Chinese expedition. Next to him, McGraw was working steadily at the ice, chipping away. With one hand, Olivetti ejected the empty magazine and grabbed for another in his parka. As he brought it to the magazine well, it slipped out of his fingers, falling down the mountain.

Olivetti reached for the third magazine.

Aksu turned to Lexina, blood bubbling up through his oxygen mask. He was trying to say something, but he couldn't make a noise. She reached around his body for the automatic weapon dangling by its sling.

She rested the barrel on Aksu's shoulder and took aim at the sniper. She pulled the trigger just as she saw the blossom of flame from his rifle, indicating he'd fired. She kept the trigger pulled, as the thirty-round magazine emptied on full automatic. About a third of the way through the magazine she felt Aksu's body jerk from the impact of the sniper's round.

The fire was wild, bullets spraying the rock face well above Olivetti's location. That changed the moment Olivetti's round struck the body concealing the rifle, jerking its muzzle down. A string of bullets chipped away from ten feet above his head, moving down, two rounds slamming into his body and the rest below his feet.

Olivetti blinked, feeling the wounds, not quite believing he'd been hit. The nanovirus went into overdrive, forcing him to keep moving. He reaimed the sniper rifle, shifting the reticules to the head that could be seen behind the body he'd already shot twice. Olivetti pulled the trigger.

The bullet hit Lexina directly between her red cat eyes, plowing through her skull.

Olivetti slumped in his harness, life draining from his body. Faintly he heard McGraw's surprised yell. Twisting in the opposite direction, he saw someone coming around the cornice, hooked into the protection they had put in.

McGraw was standing on the ledge, his ice ax up in a defensive position. With a dying effort, Olivetti brought up the rifle and pulled the trigger repeatedly. As the magazine ran empty, he slumped away from the mountain, held in place by his harness.

The bullets slammed into the figure, blood spraying out the exit wounds onto the cornice, a mélange of red on white. The body slid off the ledge and dangled five feet below, held up by the safety line.

McGraw turned back to the shallow cave and returned to chipping away at the ice with his ax.

Turcotte was nearly pulled from the mountain as the rope abruptly jerked downward. His harness, instead of going up, was being pulled down. With one hand on the mountain, Turcotte reached down and with great difficulty unsnapped from the line. He shoved the MP-5 around so that it was against his chest. Then he continued. He'd heard the firing and didn't know what to expect.

He reached the cornice. There was no ledge around it. He had to assume there was a continuation of the ledge on the other side. Turcotte realized his heart was racing, pounding in his chest frantically, trying to push blood that simply didn't have the oxygen anymore.

If he missed his hold on the other side—if there was no hold on the other side—Turcotte shook off that thinking. The safety line went around, even though it was down near his knees. He leaned his mask-covered forehead against the side of the mountain for a few seconds. Then he pulled away and reached as far to his left as he could with his hand, then his foot. He pushed off from the mountain, scrambling for a hold. His left foot touched the ledge and he continued to swing around until he was on the other side.

Turcotte was presented with Mualama dangling limply on the safety line; a man hanging dead in his harness; another man with his back to him, swinging an ice ax at the small cave; three bodies seated on a shelf in front of the cave; and in the cave, protected by only a few remaining inches of ice, Excalibur.

Turcotte was using both hands to edge his way closer and the man with the ax seemed oblivious to everything except the task at hand. As Turcotte stepped around Mualama's body, the man suddenly wheeled, ax held high. Unable to defend himself, Turcotte waited for the blow to fall, staring into the man's deranged eyes.

The man's eyes seemed to focus for a moment and shifted down to Turcotte's parka, fixing on the Special Forces insignia pinned there. Turcotte saw the insignia on the man's coat—the trident, anchor, pistol, and eagle symbol of the Navy SEALs. They locked eyes, the ax wavering in the air. The conditioning of the guardian tried to suppress the decades of SEAL training.

The ax came flashing down, cutting through the nylon straps attached to the man's protection. Turcotte could have sworn he saw the faintest smile on the man's lips as he fell out and away from the mountain, taking his dead partner with him. Turcotte put both feet on the ledge, ignoring the three frozen bodies, his attention completely captured by the sword. The pommel glittered as it caught the rays of the setting sun and he could see the carvings on the scabbard. Only a scant inch of ice remained.

Turcotte hooked his nylon loop into one of the pieces of protection, then lifted his ice ax.

CHAPTER 20: THE PRESENT

MOUNT ARARAT

Major Briggs fired a controlled three-round burst, the rounds hitting the lead Kortad and bouncing off. Briggs cursed and ducked back behind the protection of the wall as several bolts of gold shot by.

"This is not good," he understated to Yakov and Kakel.

"Maybe whatever they're shooting would damage the Master Guardian," Yakov said.

"And?" Briggs extended his weapon into the corridor and fired without aiming.

"If we go in the chamber," Yakov said, "they might not use it."

"That is—" Kakel began, when a golden bolt bounced off the wall behind him and struck him in the back. He tumbled to the ground unconscious.

"Damn it," Briggs cursed as he stuck his firing hand out and pulled the trigger. A golden bolt struck the weapon and his hand. A golden field enveloped his body and he slumped to the floor.

Yakov didn't waste any more time. He ran across the bridge to the Master Guardian, then around the narrow ledge to the far side, away from the entrance.

VICINITY MIDWAY ISLAND

"We've got forty bogeys inbound," the operations officer announced.

Admiral Kenzie had just finished listening to the strike report from his air wing. CAG's sacrifice was noble, but given the bogeys flying toward his fleet he had to assume the other alien carriers had gotten aircraft in the air.

He'd been dreading this moment ever since leaving Pearl Harbor, but he'd also been preparing for it. He'd maneuvered his ships over deep water and had each ship's captain initiate the preparations for what he was about to order.

For the first time since leaving Pearl, Kenzie made a transmission, making sure each ship played it over their intercom so every sailor in the fleet could hear.

"This is Admiral Kenzie. I am ordering strike wing two to launch immediately. As soon as the last plane is in the air, we will"—he paused, almost unable to say it, then forcing himself to go on—"we will scuttle every ship in the task force.

"We have no choice. If we are still here when those planes arrive, they will absorb both the ships and us into the Alien Fleet. I would rather be dead, and have our ships sunk in deep water, than allow that to happen and for us to be used against our own homeland.

"Strike wing two, begin launching and do your best to avenge us. Attack when their strike planes try to land."

MOUNT EVEREST

The last piece of ice fell away. Turcotte reached in, his hand closing around the hilt of Excalibur.

Stars flashed in his head and he fell to his knees. He tried reaching for the hilt again and once more he was struck from behind. Turcotte crumbled to the rock in front of the sheath as Mualama leaned over him. In the archaeologist's hands was a blue stone, pulsing with light.

The stone could not touch the sword. Turcotte knew that as surely as if it had been shouted out from the top of the mountain. The ax was still in his other hand. He struck out from his prone position, the point puncturing the African's leg and buckling the knee. Mualama scrambled, trying to place the stone on the hilt. Desperately, Turcotte looped one arm around Mualama's throat, pulling him back, but the African was stronger, getting to his knees with inhuman strength.

Out of options, Turcotte kept his grip on Mualama and shoved away from the mountain with his feet, sliding off the ledge. He free-fell two feet to the end of the nylon strap, pulling Mualama with him. The archaeologist tumbled backward, the stone flying out of his hand as he grasped for a hold to keep from falling, which he found by grabbing the arm around his neck.

Turcotte grunted in pain as Mualama came to a halt, dangling below him with a death grip on his forearm. Turcotte glanced up—the piton was strained, moving very, very slightly. He knew it wouldn't hold very long. He slashed with the ax he still held in his free hand. The point struck Mualama's arm, piercing skin and lodging between the bones in the forearm. Turcotte levered the handle of the ax, pressing outward on both bones, then they snapped. And still Mualama kept his grip.

Turcotte gasped as Mualama's mouth opened wide, wider than humanly possible and something gray appeared, slithering out. Three "fingers" on the end were grasping as it continued to exit the African's body, reaching toward Turcotte's arm, still in Mualama's grip. Only when they grasped Turcotte's arm did the African let go. As the body fell, the entire length of the gray creature ripped out of the body, over six feet long, pieces of Mualama's spine still attached.

Turcotte shuddered, scrambling back, shaking his arm to get the thing off, but it was slowly inching its way up his arm. Blindly he reached back, his hand finding Excalibur's hilt. He pulled it out of the sheath and slashed down, slicing the Swarm tentacle in half. The two pieces fell to the ground next to him. Turcotte staggered to his knees, completely exhausted, and watched as both ends shriveled up.

Turcotte slumped back among the three frozen bodies, the naked blade of Excalibur across his knees.

EPILOGUE: THE PRESENT

MOUNT ARARAT

Yakov peeked around the edge of the Master Guardian as he heard footsteps. Three Kortad stood in the passageway by the bodies of Briggs and Kakel. They were encased in black armor, swords strapped to their sides, and the strange spears were grasped in their hands.

One of them spotted Yakov and raised the spear. Yakov ducked back behind the red pyramid.

And at the moment it came alive, a fierce red glow pulsing out of its surface. At the same time a thick metal door slid shut in the passageway, locking the Kortad out of the room. The walkway smoothly slid back into the wall, isolating the Master Guardian—and Yakov—in the center of the empty sphere.

Swallowing nervously, Yakov raised both hands, stepped forward, and pressed them against the side of the pyramid. He was immediately enveloped in the red glow. His hands felt the warmth of the machine. He gasped as the walls of the sphere came alive with images and his mind made contact with the alien machine and was overwhelmed with data.

Yakov ignored the input and focused on the priorities of commands he knew were needed to win the world war raging on the planet.

VICINITY MIDWAY ISLAND

The last plane left the deck of the *Kennedy*. Admiral Kenzie watched its afterburners spit flame as it rocketed into the sky. He picked up the mike to give the order for all ships to be scuttled. He hesitated, holding it in his hand, all his training fighting against what he knew he had to do.

EASTER ISLAND

Aspasia's Shadow spun about as the golden haze around his guardian computer suddenly flared brighter. He stared at it, then screamed in dismay as the glow slowly faded out. He ran to the guardian and placed his hands on the side. Nothing.

He glanced over at the Marines as they collapsed to the floor, the nanovirus receiving no input from the guardian. The bodies twitched and he could see a black flow from the mouths, noses, and ears—millions of nanoviruses exiting the bodies.

Aspasia's Shadow stood still for several moments as he registered this sudden development. Artad or the humans. One of the two had beaten his men to the Master Guardian *and* freed Excalibur. He wasted no time on self-recrimination or trying to hold on to a plan that had failed.

Aspasia's Shadow went to the control console and tapped in a complex code on the hexagonal displays. Then he grabbed the Grail and wrapped it in a white cloth. He ran from the chamber into the tunnel leading to the bouncer.

On the side of the guardian, the probes that had been inserted into Kelly Reynolds's body began to retract until she was completely free of the machinery. She slid down the side of the now quiescent alien device to the floor of the cavern.

Her eyes were crusted shut, her limbs atrophied. Her chest barely rose as she took a labored breath. Her mouth was open, parched, the tongue shriveled.

And in her mind she rejoiced, as she was completely free of the guardian.

VICINITY MIDWAY ISLAND

Captain Lockhart staggered, fell to her knees, and screamed in agony as millions of microscopic metal creatures exited her body via every orifice. She threw up, her eyes teared. It was excruciating but mercifully quick. Within a minute she shook her head, slowly got to her feet, and looked about.

She was on the bridge of the *Arizona* and free of the alien control. Her hand snaked forward and she picked up the radio mike, recalling the strike force.

MOUNT ARARAT

The Kortad sprinted down the main center corridor of the mothership toward the front. Three turned at a corridor, heading to the right, the other continuing forward. They entered the main control room for the ship. One of them unfastened a panel, slid the point of a spear inside, and severed a line, effectively disconnecting the Talons that were docked around the front end of the craft from the Master Guardian's control.

Another was at the master communications console, tapping on the various hexagons, powering up the short-range transmitter. The Kortad sent a message to Artad, informing him of the failure to seize the Master Guardian and requesting further instructions.

QIAN-LING

Artad watched the glow fade from his guardian. Either Aspasia's Shadow had gotten to the Master Guardian or someone else—either way, whoever it was, they had shut him down. He paused as a message from the Kortad he had sent to Ararat played across the console in front of him and gave him the answer: The humans had succeeded where both he and Aspasia's Shadow had failed. They were in the Master Guardian chamber aboard the mothership. Artad knew he had lost the race, the Master Guardian, and the mothership. And the alliances he had made, the power he wielded on Earth, were gone with the loss of his guardian.

Commendable on the part of the humans but short-sighted, he mused.

He entered commands on the console, then turned away from it and the guardian for the last time.

"Come," he indicated to his chief Kortad. "We have only one option now."

The Kortad had not been idle. Chi Yu awaited on the floor of the main chamber along with three exact copies, built from parts that had been stored in several of the many containers in the main cavern. Artad pointed and his troops boarded the craft. He was the last to enter one of the craft, moving forward to the cockpit.

CYDONIA

The Mars guardian had been shut down, which brought the massive mech-robot army to a screeching halt.

So close. So close. The dish was completed. Two of the three massive towers equidistant around the dish were done, the third just about done.

Inside the alien base the surviving Airlia looked at the displays showing the work that had been accomplished. They knew how much was left to be done. And they knew

there was only one way it would be accomplished without
the guardian. By hand.

VICINITY MIDWAY ISLAND

"Sailors, you have done a commendable job." Admiral
Kenzie's voice echoed over the ocean. "It is better that these
ships—and us along with them—go to the bottom, rather
than become part of the Alien Fleet. I therefore now order
all captains to—"

"Sir!"

Kenzie paused and turned toward his communications
officer. He released the key for the mike. "What?"

"We're receiving an incoming message from the Alien
Fleet."

"What ship?"

"The *Arizona,* sir."

"The *Arizona*? Put it on the box."

A woman's voice came out of the speaker. "Admiral
Kenzie. This is Captain Lockhart. We're free, sir. Free of the
virus. We control the fleet."

Kenzie slumped back in his command chair. Then he
keyed the mike. "Captain Lockhart. Change your heading.
Straight for Easter Island. We will rendezvous with you off
the coast. Flank speed."

GULF OF MEXICO

Under Garlin's command, the Ark of the Covenant was penetrating further and further into Lisa Duncan's suppressed
and hidden memories. It would just be a matter of time before the information was uncovered.

Lying on the table, Duncan twisted and moaned as her

mind was invaded. Her conditioning and her subconscious fought to keep the barrier in place, but there was a small part of her mind that also wanted to know her own truth, because it knew that revealing that truth would reveal all.

MOUNT EVEREST

Mike Turcotte was seated with his back against the mountain, surrounded by bodies, frozen blood, and the sheath for the sword still held in ice at the bottom. In his hands— Excalibur. He stared at the alien blade, the setting sun glinting off the metal.

He was completely drained of energy. It took so much effort simply to breathe that he couldn't conceive of getting to his feet. He knew the cylinder in his pack had to be low on oxygen. And the effect of the pills and blood packing was declining. There was only one thing he wanted to know before the cold and altitude took him.

He reached into his parka and pulled open a Velcro pocket. The buttons on his SATPhone looked incredibly small and far away as he cradled it in his gloved hands. He was aware enough to know that if he took off his gloves his fingers would freeze almost instantly. He lightly pressed the tip of the sword on one button, accessing his call list, then again to pick who he wanted. He slid the phone inside his hood, against his ear, pulling his mask away so he could speak.

It was answered immediately. "Major Quinn."

"Did we do it?" Turcotte asked.

"Mike! Are you all right?"

"Did we do it?"

"Yes. We did it. Yakov shut down the guardians. He had control of the Master Guardian. The shields are down. The nanovirus is dying off. Artad and Aspasia's Shadow are powerless."

Quinn's voice sounded very far away. Turcotte frowned as he tried to understand through the fog of exhaustion. "We won?"

"We won, Mike."

"Good," Turcotte muttered. "That's good."

"Mike?" Quinn's voice took on an edge. "Where are you? Are you all right? Are you on your way back?"

"Duncan?" Turcotte whispered.

"No sign, but I'm still checking."

"But we won?" Turcotte asked once more as if not believing what he was hearing.

"Yes, sir."

"Finally." The phone slid from Turcotte's hand onto his lap next to Excalibur.

Quinn's voice was very far away now, fading out. "Mike? Are you all right? Can you make it back?"

"I don't think so," Turcotte whispered as he closed his eyes and slid sideways, resting partly on Merlin's frozen body. "But at least we won."

Coming this summer:
The final book in the AREA 51 series:

AREA 51
THE TRUTH

And after The Truth is revealed, a new series of
books based on this series will be forthcoming.